SO BETTER

HOME

DISCARDED

LEONA BEASLEY

eleven
light
city
press

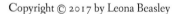

*For those who have found their homes,
and for those who are still longing for them.*

*And for Kaff*

*The fact that I was a girl never damaged my ambitions to be a pope or an emperor.*

*—Willa Cather*


*It matters less to a person where they are born than where they can live.*

*—Turkish Proverb*

## PROLOGUE

When I lived in San Francisco I walked to work. Up Mission Street I passed boarded-up flats and dodgy bodegas. On past groups of old-school winos and new-school crackheads. Past the old lady everyone said stay clear of, she's dangerous, she talks to herself. I imagined her as a girl, perhaps a gay girl, who'd lost the love of her life and now wandered the Mission like a ghost attempting to talk that love up from the grave. I turned onto Market and found my way to Flax art & design. Inside I was in charge of the paper department. When I graduated college I wanted to be a designer but it was five years later, 1989, and Reagonomics still ruled the day so design was a commodity most people did without.

It was something about papers, the smell of pulp, and the textures it created—linen, honeycomb, even lace—the wonderful assortment of pastel and richly hued colors that reminded me of the discarded dresses from my childhood, a childhood where the hope of southern Mamas for their daughters was gentility, and to marry well and to get an education. Of those standards I had only accomplished one.

But I knew I had attained something not listed, something harder to accomplish—independence, which wasn't valued where I came from, at least not for girls. Each morning as I placed newly arrived papers in flat files, the story of my life flashed like film clips from a homemade reel. In my mind the images played themselves out, starting from my earliest memory of the backyard and flickering fast forward until I walked on a train headed west to California.

## 1/ KING OF THE BACKYARD

While most girls wanted to be princesses or queens, I wanted to be a king. Kings lived in big castles, rode horses, and traveled to foreign lands. Nobody made them wear frilly Southern dresses or pick up their toys. Nobody tied ribbons in their hair or made them wear shoes. Being a king was better than being Jesus, and blood didn't seem to be involved, so in 1967 at age five I declared myself "King Onnie of the Backyard." As king I wore an old white sheet tied around my neck, on my head I placed a crown made of construction paper and Scotch tape. On days Mama had time to supervise I re-glued gold glitter around the edges. Bricks stacked up against a pine tree stump served as stairs to take me to the top of my throne. From there I surveyed my kingdom. It measured 50 by 70 feet.

I stood looking west where a group of plum, peach, and apple trees sat. The plums were small but sweet enough to pop in your mouth like candy. The Georgia peaches were uneatable because they grew hard like rocks. The apples were sizable but bitter yet Mama managed to make apple jelly. Always crafty, Mama stored the homemade jelly in store-bought jam jars and she presented it to me as if she'd bought it at the grocery store. None the wiser I ate it on toast thinking how delicious.

To the south of me lived my Sears and Roebuck swing set. It was painted with stripes and reminded me of a blue peppermint stick. Daddy secured it in the ground with cement and for a long while it stayed pristine, one of the benefits of being an only child.

To the north of me sat our tiny white-and-green-trimmed, box-shaped house. Stairs led to the backyard but also linked to the back porch, which stretched long enough to contain a rocking chair and a porch swing. A large walnut tree covered the backside of the house. It did not give us walnuts to eat, but it gave great shade on hot summer days. It also allowed the winds to tunnel through the back door and windows. It acted as a natural air conditioner, which was nice because our house didn't have one.

To the east of me Daddy's two vegetable gardens took up the entire side save the space occupied by his beloved tool shed that sat sandwiched in between the two gardens. Daddy grew turnips, collards, tomatoes, cucumbers, green beans, and yellow squash. In the shed he kept the tools he used to work his gardens: a wheelbarrow, rakes, hoes, trowels, buckets, seeds, fertilizers, and a bag or two of dry cement. He didn't use the cement for the garden, but it came in handy to keep things stationary, like my swing set, his shed, and the fences that surrounded our property and all the things Daddy needed to keep separated from me. Just outside the fenced-in garden lived Mama's clothesline. It stretched from the back door to the end of Daddy's first garden.

From my throne I could hear Mama singing an old church hymn:

> *I sing because I'm happy,*
> *I sing because I'm free,*
> *His eye is on the sparrow*
> *and I know He watches me.*

Mama's gospel permeated the yard and as long as she sang I knew I could continue to play. Sometimes Mama finished dinner late and I got to play until dusk. On those evenings, just before dark, the backyard stood in a quiet calm that only saints and bandits preferred. But I liked the sights and the sounds that rose up just as darkness hit, the cheep-cheep that crickets made while calling mates, or the stagnant movements and inaudible buzz of lightning bugs. They moved fearlessly slow as they lit their pathways. They never seemed concerned about capture. Their new home would be a mason jar that Daddy gave me with holes punched into the tin lid by a Phillips-head screwdriver and hammer. But I never got to keep the lightning bugs because Mama insisted that I set them free so they could fly wherever they wanted.

For a while Mama continued to sing her hymn and it was background music that accompanied me while I worked in my kingdom. With dirt and water from a nearby hose I made mud pies, which looked just like hamburgers. And though it was summer, these hamburgers would be the meat I needed for my winter's rations. I stacked several rows of mud pies and then went to get more water. Suddenly, Mama stopped singing and the smell of fried chicken and sweet rolls took over the backyard. I heard her bumping plates and cabinet doors in the kitchen.

"Onnie, it's time for dinner," Mama called from the screen door. "Stop playing and come inside."

I took a quick look in Mama's direction and ignored her then continued to get water for my mud pies. I felt secure in my recent discovery that Mama couldn't run. Back then it hadn't occurred to me that Mama and Daddy were too old to run, that is not until Charleston Wainwright III introduced the idea. Charleston lived on Dahlia Avenue, a street that ran directly off our street, Carver Drive. Mama said Mrs. Wainwright was a good Christian woman but she had the delusion that Charleston was made from the crumbs of Christ. I didn't know what that meant but I knew I didn't see a resemblance. Jesus had a full head of hair while Charleston's globe head was almost bald. Still, Mrs. Wainwright allowed him to play in my yard because Mama had accepted the Lord as her personal friend and savior.

Charleston stood frozen while he watched Mama move slowly down the stairs with a basket of wet clothes. There she stood at the clothesline in her house duster, her cat-eye eyeglasses, her artificial leg with a real shoe, and her real leg with Daddy's old house shoe. All my life I'd seen Mama put on her fake leg in the morning but I'd never thought about it in any terms other than that's how she walked. Charleston continued to watch Mama hang my shirt, pants, and panties so I threw the football, aiming at his noggin. He ducked. "Heeeeey," he said and stood up tall to frown at me.

Not knowing what Charleston was looking at I'd thrown the ball since in my mind I didn't want him to look at my panties, not even my wet clothes, because they felt private things, something a boy shouldn't see. Charleston ran off with the ball and I chased him as if nothing had happened.

The next day, Charleston and I played soldiers. We equipped ourselves with mud pies and ran unbridled, tossing them like they were ammo at an imaginary enemy. Then all of a sudden Charleston came to a halt, and with mesmerized eyes he watched Daddy till the soil in his garden. He locked his eyes on Daddy as he moved slowly from the garden to his tool shed to get a bag of fertilizer, and examined him from head to toe, his head full of white hair, his rounded back, his old-man overalls. Then he turned toward me with a question, "That's yo' daddy or granddaddy?"

The way Charleston sounded made Daddy seem foreign, ancient, an object of ridicule and something stirred in me that I had no awareness existed—pride. Some ole big-head boy didn't have the right to come in my yard and talk about my Daddy like he was old as Methuselah. So I threw a mud pie not at an imaginary enemy but at Charleston and it landed on his new white Keds.

"Got you," I said and I laughed "Hah, ha, ha," and turned to get more mud pies.

Charleston ran out of the backyard, headed home to tell his mama on me.

Later the same week, it was Charleston's final analysis that made me the maddest. While we were playing Cops & Robbers shouting, "Bang, bang, bang!" and pointing stick-guns at each other, Charleston suddenly stopped. "Yo' mama's leg is funny," he said nonchalantly. "Bang, bang, bang!"

Inside my head I heard, yo' Mama walks like a peg-leg pirate. I stopped and dropped my stick-gun to my side. My chest filled up fast. I couldn't control my breaths. I stood and stared at Charleston. The air released itself from my lungs and I pointed my stick-gun at him once again. "Don't say nothing 'bout my Mama," I said.

Though I'd never seen Mama run I felt certain she could. And for good measure, once Charleston and I were playing Cops & Robbers again I stomped hard on one of his pigeon-toed feet. Nobody had permission to talk about my Mama and get away with it.

One afternoon I decided to find out if Mama could run. While she stood hanging clothes in the backyard, I left the swing set and approached her from behind and simply asked, "Mama, can you run?" The sun blinded my eyes until I used my hands to shade them. Mama froze for a long second and then reached to get one of Daddy's work shirts from the clothes basket. She let out a big sigh and turned to face me.

"Not anymore, Onnie baby. When I was girl I played softball and I was as fast as you are now," she said. "And when yo' Daddy played in the Negro Baseball League, he was fast too." The sunlight haloed around her head. Mama's words were good enough for me and the next afternoon I spent my time outracing and outrunning Charleston the globe-head, pigeon-toed boy.

"Onnie Marie Armstrong!" Mama called me again, but this time with a little bass in her voice, from the screen door. "I said it's time for you to come in here for dinner. I know you hear me, now get in this house. Get in here right now."

I stood with my hair loose and wild on top of my head— a messy crown. The ribbons and barrettes had fallen short of their duties and my clothes were soiled from my rolling in the green grass and making mud pies from brown dirt and water.

"I'm not ready. I'ma come in a few minutes, 'kay," I said dismissively and continued to stockpile my rations near the walnut tree. Out the corner of my eye I saw that Mama had left the screen door. The knowledge of her prosthetic leg electrically empowered my entire body. I stood proud with an old white sheet wrapped around my neck and my hands on my hips. I was Captain America, Superman, Wonder Woman, and a king, but I was most powerful because Mama couldn't run and get me.

The screen door slammed open and the force shook the house. The buttery and sweet smells from the kitchen drifted out, and I jumped up, dropping the rocks I'd gathered to build a castle-hut. Mama stepped onto the porch with about a dozen weapons, minus or plus a few, gathered from the kitchen. Canned goods. She positioned her ammunition in her turned-up apron, cradled by her left arm. With her right hand she snapped a can back and released it like a slingshot. The first can of sweet peas bounced and ricocheted off two pine trees. I stood in place for a few seconds, and then twirled in a circle like a spinning top.

Mama the champion shot-putter threw a can of corn that landed near my feet at the base of the walnut tree. Sweating now, I hid behind a pine tree at the edge of Mama's clothesline. All I could hear was the sound of my heartbeat, thumping and echoing through my chest and eardrums. Cans of black-eyed peas, spinach, and chickpeas flew past the side of the pine tree where I hid. I ran toward open ground and dodged, ducked, and rolled like a soldier at war. Though the sun had set the backyard remained hot and the sweat that rolled down my face and into my mouth reminded me I was thirsty. As I paused Mama threw a can of green beans that landed near my feet like a grenade. I ran back toward the walnut tree and this time Mama carefully threw a can that narrowly missed my head, the wind from it brushing the tips of my messy hair. The smell of wet dirt, grass, and sweat filled my nose as I rested against the tree to take in some fresh air. I could hear Mama breathing, not hard or out of breath, but steady ready for me to make a move. Nervous, I tried to think up some story to tell her when I saw a stick and an oily rag that I'd confiscated earlier near Daddy's tool shed. I tied them together and waved a flag in defeat like I'd seen on *Bugs Bunny*.

Before Mama let me come inside, she made me collect all the cans she'd thrown. They looked like inoperative shells shot from an old Confederate canon. I'd given in to rest, to not be hit by canned goods, and to sit and eat dinner at the kitchen table. But Mama's dinners didn't come from a can, those were for rainy days or emergency rations. Mama cooked the vegetables Daddy picked from his garden. In preparation for the winter months, Mama spent endless weekend hours in the late summer canning vegetables and preserves. She'd say, "We might not be rich, but I'm gonna make sure we always have food on the table."

When Mama was a small child, there were two times in her life when food was scarce. The first was when she was living on a dirt farm with her family in Monroe, Georgia, and the boll weevil came and ate up the cotton crops. With small profit came little food. The second time was when Mama was nine years old, living in Eleven Light City, and the Depression hit. They lived off biscuits, honey, and potato soup. Each hard time reinforced the other in her mind, and each occasion made her more determined to feed her family and herself.

THAT EVENING Mama made collard greens cooked in fatback, baked sweet potatoes, fried chicken, and buttered rolls. The kitchen was tiny. It measured 7 by 11 and was made even smaller with all the appliances Mama packed in it. Though the refrigerator, washing machine, and stove were necessities, along with the sink, it didn't leave room for me to run around and I was always shooed away from playing. The kitchen table was round with four chairs. Mama placed a stack of phone books in a chair and helped me up. Daddy worked at night so it was only Mama and I sitting down to eat.

It was the dark oak cabinets that completed the claustrophobic feel in the kitchen. They covered most of the available wall space. But Mama, who'd come from meager beginnings, saw her kitchen as an extension of her tiny castle. It was in front of the sink's window where Mama sang most of her hymns. Just outside that window, safely tucked away on the side of the house, lived Mama's rose garden—a fence prevented entry from the backyard. On Sundays Mama cut fresh roses and placed them in a vase. And on Mother's Day she'd wear a white rose to signify her mother was dead, but I wore a red rose because Mama was alive.

At dinner Mama usually talked, but now, after the canned-goods attack, she acted as if I weren't there. As she ate her fried chicken and collards she didn't say a word. I babbled on about my games with Charleston in the backyard and how I was going to build a fort with the stones and bricks that Daddy had near his tool shed. Mama still remained silent. It wasn't until I asked to watch my favorite television show, *Julia*, staring Diahann Carroll that Mama give me a piece of her mind.

"No TV for you tonight and you better be glad that's all you'll miss after I called you and you didn't come," Mama said.

Mama had her rules on how to act at home and in public.

Mama's home rules: "After your dinner settles, you'll take a bath. No television except special programs. When it's bedtime you'll go without a fuss."

Mama's public rules: "When we're away from home, there'll be no outbursts, no crying, and no loud talking. When we walk, you hold my hand. When I talk, you listen and obey. There'll be no running in the streets or on the sidewalk."

Mr. Bubble was great for bathing, the concoction from his box made the best and biggest bubbles. I loved the bathroom because it gave me an escape from Mama and Daddy. It was quiet and I could play in the water without having to sneak to do it. The bathroom was small but it was the coziest room in the house. It was painted light blue, which reminded me of a spring sky without clouds. It was crowded like the kitchen, with a mirrored medicine cabinet above the sink and a toilet that sat between the sink and the tub, but somehow this crowded space didn't bother me. What I liked most about the bathroom was that it smelled of lavender flowers, except for the times when Daddy's overused face towel reeked of a musky stench.

After my bath I lay down, glad that I had made it through dinner and to bed without being punished. Sure Mama didn't allow me to watch TV but I knew she'd get past that and would let me see my program again. And yes, Mama had thrown the cans, but because she couldn't run and get me, I was the winner. After all, I came in when I wanted to, even though I eventually had to surrender. A king had to take chances. My little wooden bed with the Ace of Spades posts felt as big as what I imagined any king's would have. I laid my head on my pillow full of valor, a victorious victor.

Deep in my sleep the sting of a strop woke me up. Wasn't Daddy at work? I bolted straight up. My eyes couldn't focus right away but I could feel the remaining covers being pulled off. Now I could see—it was Mama with Daddy's belt. "I won't do it anymore, I won't do it anymore!" I yelled. Though that's what I always said to Daddy and Mama to stop them from beating me. The baby powder on my body puffed up from under my nightgown when Mama hit my legs. The powder created a hazy film, while its sweet smell perfumed my bedroom. Now fully awake I turned on my knees and desperately tried to crawl off the bed. Mama pulled me back by my legs. Whatever speed Mama lost having one leg she gained in arm strength. I cried loud hiccup tears and wriggled hard, but finally submitted to Mama's licks.

After Mama had exhausted herself beating my butt, she sat on the edge of the bed and issued an addendum to her rules: "When I call you, you better come. If you don't, there'll be more where this came from. You hear, Onnie Marie Armstrong? There'll be more where this came from."

I'd heard enough of Mama's speeches to know if she took the time to repeat herself then I'd better take note and do what she said.

AFTER I WAS BORN, Mama gave up cooking and cleaning for a Jewish family that lived downtown so she could take care of me. But Mama liked to make her own money, so around this time she started a daycare center at our house. Before the daycare children had arrived, I controlled who played in my yard. I played mostly with Charleston and he only came over if I let him come. I didn't play in Charleston's yard—he never had the rich variety of stuff that Daddy left in ours. Daddy's collection of old bricks, rags, plastic egg crates, tin buckets, and two garden hoses were the tools I used for my backyard adventures. Daddy's junk collection symbolized wealth to him. He'd learned it from his daddy, Buddy, who was a junkyard man by trade. In our Dixie Hills neighborhood, wherever there was an old man there was an old, inoperative car. These old men were young during the Depression when an old, broken-down car was still a car. Somehow Mama convinced Daddy that we didn't have enough space for some old car that belonged in the dump, but he was welcome to keep other broken things in his tool shed and in the spaces that surrounded it.

Mama's new daycare brought in money, so Daddy couldn't object to it. And she could still take care of me without leaving the house. Our teeny two-bedroom house became even more overcrowded with nearly two dozen children. During the weekdays the dining room table and chairs were moved to the side and two fold-up playpens were opened and placed on adjacent walls. A third pen was placed in front of the freezer—also in the dining room—where Mama stored frozen meat, orange juice, ice cream, and any extra items she wanted to have in reserve.

The babies and toddlers came in the morning, and the schoolchildren came after school. The fresh lavender and rosemary scents of the house were often overwhelmed by the stink of baby diapers and vomit. Of course Mama cleaned it up, but the house never smelled sweet again.

I watched Mama change diapers and feed babies. I didn't mind the babies and toddlers—they were cute like little baby dolls—but those schoolchildren filled up our den and took over the backyard. Those brats ran in and out, slamming the screen door each time. They were the primary reason the linoleum floors in the den and kitchen looked discolored and worn. The kitchen was their favorite hangout—they wanted water, juice, potato chips, corn chips, and popcorn. The hardwood floors in the dining room and living room lost their spotless shine and the backyard lost most of its grass because of the heavy foot traffic. Now Charleston's mama wouldn't let him come over because there were too many children in the backyard.

What I hated most about those schoolchildren was that they pushed and pulled for Mama's attention. They acted like she was their mama. I started to push back, kick, and fight any child who didn't understand that Mama was my mama.

Now the only place that was all mine was my small bedroom and the toys in it, like my marble collection, jacks, dolls, and stuffed animals. A small bedroom wasn't enough for the explorer that lived inside me. I preferred to be outside, free to roam without an audience.

When the rambunctious kids first arrived they also took over the family den—Daddy's sacred space—he didn't hesitate to yell, scream, or use his trusty strop to give anyone running around or jumping on his La-Z-Boy a lick or two. But Mama being Mama, methodical in her actions, put Daddy on notice.

"Amos, I'll handle these children. You'll have to make

room for them, and the den is where they'll be unless they're outside," Mama said.

"Susie, that's well, fine, and good, but those children won't be sitting in my chair," Daddy said. "And that's final."

A compromise was made. The kids could play and sit in the den, Daddy would have his beloved La-Z-Boy chair reserved, and if he needed to rest or be alone, he could either go to their bedroom or work in his fenced-off garden. So Daddy and I lost the things we loved most, my backyard and his den, to a pack of wild children. For a moment my young self saw Daddy and me in the same predicament. But weeks after the kids arrived I overheard Mama and Daddy talking, and they not only agreed it was time for me to start kindergarten but because I fought the daycare kids over Mama being my mama it was best for me to be in the extended day program. That way I wouldn't be able run around fussing with children and keeping control of the backyard.

MAMA ALWAYS FOUND it difficult to make my coarse hair presentable for public viewing. Miss Lucendy Walker, our neighbor two doors down, agreed to do my hair each morning before school. Miss Lucendy owned and operated a beauty shop out of the back of her house, which she aptly called Lucendy's House of Beauty.

"Why do I have to go to school? Why do I have to get my hair fixed? Why do I have to wear a dress?" I asked Mama over and over while she continued to dress me for school, but she never bothered to answer.

I hated it all—the idea of school, my hair being pressed and curled, and being forced to wear pastel-colored dresses with big white bows in the back or richly hued dresses with big, colorful bows. These dresses were useless, they showed my panties if I ran or bent over. Daddy polished my white high-top baby shoes to a porcelain gleam, completing my school outfit.

After Mama dressed me she handed me over to Daddy. Though Daddy was only five feet nine inches tall, he loomed over me like a hollowed-out pine tree and looked down at me like a vulture. Unless it was the hot summer, Daddy wore long-sleeved blue coveralls, which completed his bird-of-prey look. He always smelled like part aftershave and part dirt. As big as his nose was, he constantly had to push his glasses up on it. Daddy's hands were hard and calloused from the manual jobs he'd worked over the years. His nimble fingers and robust hands were why he had only acquired a first-grade education back in La Grange, Georgia. Once it was discovered just how fast Daddy picked cotton, he never again saw the inside of a classroom. Although Daddy was functionally illiterate, he learned and observed the streets of Eleven Light City like an astronomer studied and knew the stars and constellations. At a moment's notice he could direct someone anywhere in the city.

Daddy held my hand firm on the short walk to Miss Lucendy's house. He moved with purpose and I skipped to keep up. Daddy didn't say much—he seemed indifferent to my life change. But then again Daddy never said much to me, so getting my hair done or starting school didn't provoke a remark. Daddy's work schedule was perfect for delivering me to school and for pickup. He could bring me back home in time to get to work by three o'clock.

Daddy knocked on the door and Miss Lucendy answered.

"Hey there, Amos, I see the schoolgirl's ready to get pretty," she said, looking down at me.

Daddy nodded his head to answer yes.

"No I'm not," I said under my breath.

"Tell Susie I'll talk to her later," Miss Lucendy said.

I pulled away from Daddy, but he lifted me up and pushed me inside. Miss Lucendy quickly latched her burglar-barred door, then rushed me to the shampoo chair, placing a cloth robe and a funny plastic bib on me. She put it on backward to keep me dry. She washed my hair and sat me under the dryer. Her hot comb pressed my nappy hair straight. She held my locks down with multiple bows and barrettes. She greased up my hair with oil and said, "Most black folks need oil on their scalp or their hair will break off."

After Miss Lucendy finished her greasy, straightening wonders, she walked me back to the sidewalk and watched until I got to the front porch and was retrieved by Mama.

Mama looked my way and said, "Now ain't you pretty for school."

The thought of school made me want to run, but running from Mama wasn't an option, I knew what would happen once I was asleep. To run from Daddy was just as scary because he'd use the strop as soon as I came back.

Mama believed children should be punished at home, no strops or loud voices in public. Mama gave Daddy careful instructions while they talked in their bedroom. "Please don't hit her at school if she acts up. She doesn't want to go but she'll get used to it. Just don't you show yo' butt at that school," Mama said.

"Susie, I'll take that girl to school and she won't be no trouble."

"Well if she is, you better not hit her there," Mama said.

On the first day of school Daddy and I drove in his dull gray Chevy pickup truck. Usually I liked to ride in the back cab to feel the air on my head, but now I was a schoolgirl and I had to ride up front with Daddy. On the way to Haugabrooks Academy, butterflies somersaulted and loop-de-looped inside my stomach. I felt seasick, though we were on dry land. From the truck, the Haugabrooks main offices sat angular and high on a hill, hanging over my head like a sinister, indigo cloud. Daddy helped me out of the truck. A few other children had also arrived but most of them had come in shiny cars. Daddy was dressed in a white shirt, black slacks, and black loafers—he looked dressed for a weekday church service, not for delivering me to school. Like me, maybe he had to make a good impression. Daddy gathered up my hand and my new red lunchbox and walked me to my new classroom behind door number seven.

Ms. Camilla Crowe, my new kindergarten teacher, was inside with children and other parents who had dropped them off. Daddy's strong hand trembled while he held mine. We stood with our backs to the pale yellow wall near the bulletin board and the cubbies, which held the children's jackets and lunchboxes. The room smelled of construction paper, coffee, and fresh-cut oranges. Ms. Crowe approached with a hand extended out to Daddy and a big smile.

"Hi, pleased to meet you, Mr....?" Ms. Crowe asked.

"Armstrong—Amos Armstrong."

"Oh, so you're Onnie's daddy."

How did she know my name?

Ms. Crowe looked directly at me. "You're going to like it here, Onnie. Take a seat over at that table." She pointed.

Daddy gave my lunchbox to Ms. Crowe, who turned to put it in a cubby. Daddy released my hand and I grabbed his leg and wrapped my body around it like a pretzel, holding the tightest grip I could. Daddy struggled to get me off and with Ms. Crowe's help, he did. Once he was free, he ran out of the classroom like a wild dog was chasing him. Some of the children laughed at Daddy's quick departure. I fell to the floor in the middle of the classroom, rolling around and generally cleaning the floor with my new blue dress.

Ms. Crowe watched my antics. A few children looked at me with their mouths gaping, but others began to move away from the big rectangular tables and chairs. Ms. Crowe called them all back to her, and like sheep they listened.

"Onnie is new at Haugabrooks, boys and girls, and we'll have to help her get adjusted," Ms. Crowe said.

Then Ms. Crowe directed her comments to me. "Onnie, when you're finished, your chair will be waiting for you. Until then, class, we are going to start this day's lesson: sounding out the letter F." Ms. Crowe pulled out flash cards. "Frog, farm, friends, and fruit. Repeat after me."

I lay down on the floor and looked up at the white ceiling. Call me a fool or a failure, but I wanted my freedom.

The next day Daddy and Ms. Crowe peeled me off him again with great difficulty, beads of sweat popping off Daddy's forehead. And Daddy again made a mad dash while Ms. Crowe held on to me and I struggled. After Daddy escaped, I lay on the floor until I got cold and bored. Then I went to my chair and listened to the day's lesson like nothing had happened. Today we were on the letter G.

"Repeat after me: goats, girls, glass, and giant." Ms. Crowe showed her flash card pictures to back up the words.

On Friday Daddy tried to push me into the classroom without actually going inside, but I managed to wrap myself around his leg in the hallway. After he escaped and I sat down for the day's lessons, Ms. Crowe wrote the letter J on the blackboard.

"Boys and girls repeat after me: juggler, jump rope, jelly, and jailhouse," Ms. Crowe said.

A kid next to me asked, "Hey, are you gonna go to jail if you keep fighting yo' Daddy?"

Mama was forced to find an alternative to Daddy driving me to school because without his strop, he couldn't handle me. Mama wouldn't dare leave the daycare children with Daddy while she drove me to school, so she found other means of transportation.

Mrs. Heart earned her living driving children to and from Haugabrooks in her burgundy van. Several children traveled from my working-class Dixie Hills community to the more affluent Collier Heights to attend Haugabrooks. Mrs. Heart assured Mama that I wouldn't be any trouble.

After my hair was done, Daddy escorted me from the house to Mrs. Heart's burgundy van. Just as Daddy let go of my arm, I took off down the street at a gallop away from the voices in the wind urging me to return and get in the van. Daddy came after me as I ducked and dodged between shrubbery and yards, landing finally in a small indentation that I'd discovered in Miss Lucendy's yard.

The area was a good hiding place for me. Once in there, Daddy's arm couldn't stretch far enough to reach me. Mama was furious, Daddy beyond his wits, and I sat in the momentary splendor of not being bussed off to what I knew would be the end of my reign as king. Mrs. Heart was forced to leave without me so Daddy again delivered me to school, where I performed my usual leg-wrapping dance. Ms. Crowe held me once again against my will, while Daddy escaped, and the children in the classroom kept their eyes glued to me.

The next day I was prepared to do it all over again. This time Daddy carried me out and lifted me into the van. I went into one door and jumped out of the other. The jump was to prolong my liberation, to get away—at minimum Mrs. Heart wouldn't deliver me to Haugabrooks.

I exited and was headed toward the hiding place in Miss Lucendy's yard, when she suddenly appeared from behind a tree. I put on the brakes, turned, and ran to find another place to hide. I ran back in the direction of my house and Mrs. Heart's van. I managed to get past Daddy to run toward Miss Jane Lee's house, only to find her waiting on the sidewalk to assist in my capture. I looked across the street and I saw that Miss Hazel Washington had positioned herself like a blocking linebacker and was waiting for me to make a move. Miss Hazel's next-door neighbor and best friend, Ms. Inez Du Bois, stood at the edge of her driveway with a long rope that she held like a cowboy. Miss Lucendy approached from her house and Daddy gained ground as Mama orchestrated from the porch and Mrs. Heart waited at the van with the door open and the seat belt ready to hold me down.

All the grown folks approached, moving like possessed saints in search of Christ. Southern old folks stuck together like cold grits, organizing themselves to common goals for their greater good. Once a member of the family, always a member of the family. When I think back on them, they seem a lot like a mafia.

Sweaty, with my hair turned back into an Afro, and the white bow on my blue dress untied, I gave in to Daddy's hand and got into the van. Mrs. Heart strapped me in and started up the engine. I leaned into the seat and thought that maybe in school I'd learn how to outwit meddlesome old folks with extra time on their hands. I turned to look back at them when Karla and Needa Lyons, a pair of sisters who acted like twins, caught my eye. They smiled big from the seat behind me. I smiled back, and then looked beyond the sisters out the back window. There I saw the Old Folks Mafia gathered in a picture-perfect pose as they waved good-bye. Mama had joined them on the sidewalk, her smile beaming as the sun struck gold on the shiny tooth in her mouth. The distance between us grew, and at the end of the street we turned south, heading toward Haugabrooks Academy.

## 2/ WAS ONCE A CHILD

From the car I could see the go-go dancers on Simpson Road. They shook and jiggled their full brown bottoms to psychedelic lights that flashed from the tops of their birdcages, and to the Motown sounds played by a Southern DJ. The DJ spun his vinyl magic from a glass booth across from the girls' cages. The flashing lights reflected off the girls' silver-grass miniskirts and their sequined halter tops. As the music grew up-tempo the girls gyrated their hips rhythmically to the soul beat. Side to side, back and forth their hips rotated to become one with the drumbeat, one with the sounds. In white, patent-leather boots they churned their legs slowly, but jerked their arms rapidly as they pretended to swim in their cages.

Saturday nights hopped at the Tasty Dog 1 drive-in. Daddy sat in the driver's seat while Mama rode shotgun. In the backseat my best friend Lorraine and I fidgeted while we waited for the traffic light to turn green. Our eyes involuntarily opened a slit while we pretended they were closed. We opened them wider with each rotating hip the girls wiggled. It was 1969 and we were seven years old. Mama surprised me because she didn't look to see if we'd followed her instructions to keep our heads down and our eyes closed until we drove past the bird-caged women. But perhaps Mama too got caught up in the girls' gyrations.

Simpson Road was a special street—it had two Tasty Dog drive-ins. The smell of chili and Vidalia onions saturated the air three blocks before, three blocks after, and all of the blocks in between. For black folks, the two Tasty Dogs outshined the much larger Varsity drive-in that was near Georgia Tech, most notably because the Varsity only welcomed black folks as busboys and maids, not customers.

For us to get to the second Tasty Dog, we'd have to pass the first. If we went any other route it meant we'd travel unnecessary miles. For the purposes of time, gas, and innocence we traveled Simpson Road past the go-go dancers with our eyes closed.

"Welcome to the Tasty Dog 2. May I take your order, sir?" the pimply, red-faced boy asked he stood expressionless outside Daddy's car window. Without moving his head the boy got a long look at Lorraine and me. Once he realized Lorraine was also a girl he released a smile that we didn't return.

"We two grown folks will have two chili dogs each with onions and two ice-cold Coca-Colas. Okay, gurls, tell this boy what you want," Daddy said without looking back.

"We both want a chili hot dog and a Coca-Cola," I said.

"You want 'em with onions?" the pimple boy asked with a smirk as he wrote on his pad. Maybe he didn't like that we hadn't smiled back.

"No sir, we don't want onions," I said. Lorraine agreed with a nod of her head.

"No onion! Why not? Folks come to the Tasty Dogs for the sweet onions from Vidalia, Georgia," he sneered, then grinned and rocked his head in disapproval. It took me a moment to realize that what irritated me about the boy was he reminded me of Daddy with that know-it-all attitude even though he was still a kid.

Daddy lifted his head out of the window and rested his elbow on the seal of the car to stare the boy in his eyes and then piped in.

"Boy—get to getting our orders. No onions for those gurls' hot dogs, you hear me! Here's a ten and you bett' not mess up those orders," Daddy said with a growl. He reset his body in the car, but turned to yell back, "Make sure you bring me my change!"

The boy had already left the car and didn't look back to acknowledge he'd heard Daddy. It was the first time I'd witnessed a kid ignore Daddy's order. Even the older kids that came to Mama's daycare after school stood at attention when Daddy came into the den or walked in the backyard. I sat amazed the boy got away without Daddy doing something to him. This was the first time it occurred to me that Daddy's powers didn't go beyond our house. He wasn't the boss of the world like he wanted me to believe.

I looked over at Lorraine but she didn't seem to have registered what just happened. It was one of the things I liked about her—she either missed stuff or she was fearless, it was hard to tell. Either way made her appear cool. Her daddy Cab Handsom was cool. He didn't seem to care what Southern decorum dictated and he allowed Lorraine to wear boys clothes he purchased for her from the boys' shop at Sears. She wore button-up shirts with vests, jeans, and penny loafers. They'd moved here from Harlem and Lorraine didn't talk much about her mama except to say she'd run off to Chicago to live with some lounge singer. Lorraine also wore an Afro like the Jackson Five's, which inspired me to ask Mama if I could wear my hair natural. Reluctantly Mama agreed, while Daddy thought I would look wild in the head. But I didn't dare ask Mama if I could dress in boy's clothes though they looked comfortable and sporty on Lorraine. I wasn't really sure if I wanted to wear boys' clothes but a pair of jeans would have been nice.

Some days Mama let me escape the house full of kids and I went to Lorraine's. Lorraine's daddy was a jazzman—a trumpet player and a bandleader—but for a while I didn't know he had a job because he was home so often. While Mr. Handsom practiced the trumpet playing the music of someone named John Coltrane, Lorraine and I played her forty-five records. Our favorite song back then was the Jackson Five's "I Want You Back." We played it over and over until it was scratched. Lorraine sometimes accompanied the music we listened to on her drums while I tapped my hands on a wooden desktop. We talked about how one day we'd have a two-girl band with two drummers.

THE PARKING LOT of the Tasty Dog 2 was filled with cars from Chevrolet to Cadillac, all American made. The cars told the story of class. Chevrolets and Fords were more working-class cars, but a Cadillac or a Cadillac-looking Buick showed upward mobility, hence middle class. Daddy drove Mama's four-door dark blue Chevy Bel Air—it was roomy and comfortable even in the backseat. All of us at the Tasty Dog 2 were missing the marvelous way that the girls shook their hips at the Tasty Dog 1. Most of the church-going black folks thought the girls' dancing was a disgrace or, at minimum, it was a disgrace to have their children in the backseats gawking at the sights. But church doctrine hadn't caught my imagination, so I didn't understand all the shame about dancing girls. I wondered out loud, "Mama—what's wrong with us watching those girls dance?" Daddy didn't give Mama time to answer.

"Don't question us," Daddy turned and lifted the rim of his cap. "Be seen and not heard. Dancing's grown folks' stuff. When I was ah child I ne'er asked nobody nothin', I just did what I was told."

From the backseat I tried to gauge Daddy's anger. Mama touched his shoulder to pacify him, and then spoke. "Onnie, that first Tasty Dog isn't a place for children. We'll drive the long way next time."

"If it looks nasty she wants to know," Daddy said.

"Let it go," Mama said. "All children ask questions."

This time Daddy looked at Mama, then me, but said nothing. Pimple Boy's return momentarily changed Daddy's focus. The boy set the tray on Daddy's window, and intensely watched Daddy out the sides of his eyes while he dealt out the orders. The piercing smell of the Vidalia onions wrestled with the beefy smell of hot dogs and the spicy smells of the chili. From the other cars I could hear talk and the unwrapping of hot dogs, which made my mouth water.

"Will that be all—SIR?" Pimple Boy asked and handed Daddy his change.

Daddy nodded yes, and threw the boy fifty cents for his trouble.

Pimple Boy looked at the coins in his hand, then stared at Daddy, raising the corner of his lip toward his left nostril as if he smelled a rotten wiener. Daddy gave the boy no attention—he ate with Mama like they were the only people in the world, the only ones in the car. The boy looked on for a few seconds but turned and walked away in defeat. I'd seen Daddy disarm any one he wanted and he'd primarily done that with action, talking loud, jumping up, but this time he ignored his victim and sent him away sad and deflated.

Daddy placed his wallet in his front pants pocket and adjusted the rearview mirror to get a clear look at me while he ate. I squared my eyes on my hot dog. Whenever I looked at Daddy his eyes were planted directly on me even as he and Mama talked about nothing between hot dog bites.

Mama gathered the trash to put in a plastic bag. I watched Daddy now because he'd become disinterested in glaring at me—he looked outside the car at the folks that moved around the parking lot. The smell of onion stunk up the car and I rolled down the window to get some fresh air.

"Where we going next?" I asked

"There you go again—what does it matter? When I was ah child nobody took me anywhere. Be glad you out the house," Daddy said.

Daddy loved to talk about when he was a child but I never saw any evidence he'd actually been one. Though Daddy loved baseball he never threw one ball with me, he didn't want me to learn about his garden, and teaching me to build anything was out of the question. As far as I could tell he'd always been an old man with old friends. Old Man Jeb and Uncle Robert were Daddy's only visitors and seemingly his only friends. But Old Man Jeb and Uncle Robert's visits involved business or some sort of outing. Daddy also had another brother he never saw. From my bedroom closet I listened closely to Mama and Daddy talk about his missing brother Tup Armstrong. From what I could make out he'd run away to Brooklyn with somebody named White Sam after they were run out of La Grange.

Uncle Robert and Daddy's business was to cut each other's hair. Uncle Robert didn't come by the house often—

Daddy said he was busy being a schoolteacher at some boy's college across town. I learned much later the college was Morehouse. When he did come, he and Daddy transformed the tiny den into their personal barbershop. Daddy's La-Z-Boy chair was moved to the side and two kitchen chairs were placed in the center of the room. Whoever went first was covered in ceremonial white cloth to protect him from flying hair. No other persons were permitted to enter while Daddy and Uncle Robert cut hair. Sometimes they'd share a beer or two.

Though Daddy was old he had a head full of thick hair. Once I overheard Mama say to her brother, Uncle George, "Amos's thick hair matches his thick skull."

I liked Uncle Robert. He was handsome and wore crisp dress shirts. He wasn't talkative except with Daddy. When I passed by the den door he'd smile warmly and he never bothered me.

Old Man Jeb and Daddy went on fishing trips, which like the haircutting had ritualistic overtones. They always drove Daddy's dull gray Chevy truck filled with a dozen or so fishing poles, artificial bait, tackle boxes, and a hearty lunch packed by Mama. Daddy owned up to twenty-five poles—he even owned a pocket fisherman. He and Old Man Jeb always left before the sun came up and they wouldn't return until after the sun went down. To change how they set up their trip would jinx their ability to catch fish.

I never liked Old Man Jeb. He wore old workman clothes that were never clean and he smelled like mothballs and red clay. But his teeth were the scariest—some were rotten, the rest were gray. On the days before their fishing trips, Daddy packed the truck while Old Man Jeb visited and watched. Sometimes Old Man Jeb would call me over to sit in his lap. I never did and each time he asked I'd run off to find Mama. I never saw Daddy sit and talk to his friends, like Mama sat and talked with our neighbors Miss Lucendy, Miss Dorothy, Ms. Inez, and Miss Hazel. Mama's friends were the opposite of Daddy's, none of them bothered me while I played at their houses and they even allowed me to listen in as they sewed, drank homemade brew, and updated each other on the neighborhood gossip.

DADDY PULLED out of the Tasty Dog 2 parking lot and headed in the opposite direction of home which made Lorraine and me smile and giggle. Though I didn't know where we were going, we were on our way somewhere other than home which, in my book, automatically made it an adventure. Out the window I could smell the dewy night's air especially as we drove away from the direction of both Tasty Dogs. I watched Daddy as he turned onto Peachtree Street toward downtown Eleven Light City.

On the edge of downtown everyone in our car was silent. I could hear the car engine and the tires scrubbing across the road as we meandered into the heart of the city. Out the window I could see a few tall buildings with their lights on and I wondered if anyone up there watched us as we drove along. I had a taste for a Dairy Queen Peanut Buster Parfait and its layers of ice cream, hot chocolate syrup, and peanuts. Sometimes after we left the Tasty Dog we'd go for ice cream. I wanted to ask, but I held my tongue because if I asked Daddy he might do the opposite, he might decide to take us home, which would punish everyone in the car. Daddy would rather not have ice cream if that meant he'd shown me he was the big boss.

While Daddy drove he seemed happy and in control. But it wasn't that long ago that Daddy lost all control—the day he found out I'd played house with Karla Lyons in a doghouse he'd built. Sometime after our first meeting in Mrs. Heart's burgundy van, our mothers had become fast friends at a Haugabrooks Academy PTA meeting. Once Mama told Mrs. Lyons about her childcare business she became a customer.

To MAKE extra money beyond his plumbing job with the city, Daddy built doghouses, and folks placed their orders and deposits in advance. Daddy did most of his building in the early hours and on the weekends—those times had no children to get in his way. The doghouses were built with gray wood slabs, tarred roofing, and small amounts of cement. They were put together crookedly with few nails, they might have collapsed except for the cement. While they waited for their future owners' pickup, they were the perfect places for the girls and me to play games. Mama even agreed we could play in them as long as we waited until Daddy went to work.

Lucky for Karla, Needa, and me, the older children—the nine and up crowd—weren't interested in the doghouses. The girls and I shooed away the younger ones if they tried to get inside. We'd block them out with our backs in the opening. When the young ones felt left out they'd poke our backs but we'd jump outside and run them off. Of course they'd come back, and we'd run them off again. Soon they'd go on to play chase games, swing, or mess around in the dirt. When Mama wasn't looking, the children poured water from the spigot into an old bucket to make mud pies. If Daddy caught them he'd be madder than a raccoon fighting to protect her young. But it was Daddy who left the knob on the spigot and his old bucket nearby.

Uncle George heard about Daddy's new enterprise and wanted to see the doghouses for himself. From the porch I could hear him talking to Mama.

"So this is the artist's work? Boy, I hate to say it but they are some kinda of raggedy ole huts," Uncle George said and laughed loudly.

"Yes, they are," Mama said. "But they are perfect for his customers' mutts and for the children to amuse themselves in the yard."

"Well if I know my brother-in-law, he doesn't want those children in his dog shacks," Uncle George said.

"Probably not, but what he doesn't know won't hurt him," Mama said. Uncle George groaned like adults do when they feel worried.

On the way out of the house Uncle George called me and I ran to get a hug, even though his apron was soiled with blood from his meatpacking job.

"How's school, kiddo?" Uncle George asked.

"I like it. Yesterday we went downtown to the museum to see paintings and sculptures," I said.

"Is that right—you moving up in life? You're gonna know the whole city before you're eleven."

"Mm' humm," I said.

"I brought you some steak. Yo' mama gonna cook it up tonight." I hugged Uncle George again, he was so sweet to Mama and me—but I didn't like steak.


The games we began to play inside the walls of the doghouses became something different. At first we played with Karla's Barbies because she insisted trucks and G.I.

Joes were for boys even after I told her that Mama had said it wasn't true. But when Karla's dolls returned home filthy, Mrs. Lyons wouldn't let her bring them. Maybe it was out of boredom or some other force but we began to play Doctor & Nurse, which we sometimes called Mama & Daddy. Karla played the nurse and I played the patient. Needa used her back to block the door opening while she pressed her eyes on us.

"Onnie, where does it hurt?" I pointed to my knee. Karla rubbed it to make it better. The warmth of her touch gave me chills. I looked close as she moved toward me. Slowly and without words I moved toward her. Then without warning we stopped. The game froze. Our eyes locked. Gravitation must have pulled us back toward each other. We continued to move until our lips pressed. I rubbed my lips back and forth slowly, without technique. Karla followed me. On occasions I'd crawled on my hands and knees between collards and cucumbers in Daddy's garden to spy on my neighbor Joe-Joe while he kissed his hairy-armed girlfriend Say-Say in their backyard. They locked lips and sometimes juice from their mouth would get to their chin before they wiped it with their hands. I was determined that a juicy mouth wouldn't be my fate. Karla and I continued to rub lips many long seconds, and to kiss Karla Louise Lyons was like kissing sunshine—warm and sweet to my lips.

Needa watched with eyes as wide as headlights. When it came Needa's turn to kiss me she twisted her head and then said, "Yuck." Somehow we knew the two sisters shouldn't try.

For weeks, when there was a doghouse Karla and I practiced our kissing games. Sometimes I was the Mama. "Where does it hurt?" I asked. Karla might point to her arm.

"You need a kiss?" She nodded her head yes and I'd kiss her arm to make it better. Then we would kiss each other to make it best. Over time we got better at kissing. We rolled our tongues around in each other's mouths. After school while Mama watched *The Young and the Restless* I'd pay close attention. Soon I added a head roll to kissing Karla—the soap characters leaned back and swiveled their heads more than they seemed to roll their tongues.

At school I'd see Karla in another part of the yard with her class and we'd wave at each other. Somehow we knew we could never kiss each other in front of our classmates. No one could know other than Needa.

When the doghouses were picked up by their new owners or not built yet we played pretend cars, raced, or swung on the swing set in the backyard. Once in a while there were two doghouses to choose from and Karla, Needa, and I would take the bigger one and leave the smaller one for the younger children.

One afternoon Needa decided she wanted to kiss me. She placed her lips on mine and moved slow. She stopped and tried it once more—this time she held it a little longer. When she finally released her lips from mine, her face soured as if she'd smelled spoiled sauerkraut. Karla warned Needa, "Don't tell Mommy we kissed Onnie, she wouldn't like it. She might give you a spanking for being with us. Okay Nee-Nee?" Karla pointed her index finger in Needa's face.

Needa paused while the information washed over her. "Okay, Kar," she said with a head nod. She shrugged her shoulders, then she joined the other children in the yard and left the kissing game up to Karla and me.

KARLA and I were always careful to watch Daddy drive away. We listened for his rumbling truck to turn out the driveway and down the street before we went into a doghouse. Each newly built doghouse sat in the same area of the backyard, near Daddy's prized tool shed. Though this area was off limits, it sat only twenty-five feet from the back door. Daddy must have imagined he had some superhuman force field that would keep us out. But Daddy was silly—even Batman had to share his cave with Robin. Still, every so often Daddy would repeat his doghouse rules.

"Don't y'all go over yonder bothering my doghouses," Daddy would say, pointing to the tool shed that sat ten feet from where we played. "It's off limits to you chillins!"

"Yes, sir," every child within earshot would recite.

After Daddy was gone Karla said, "Mr. Amos sure is mean!" Then she frowned, turned her nose up, and grabbed my hands while we walked toward the doghouse.

Our game started like all the games before, with a short discussion. Being the doctor was my favorite because it seemed doctors had the most permission to touch. "Where's the pain?" I asked. Karla touched a spot I hadn't examined before. She smiled and I looked puzzled. To be sure I asked again, "Where's the pain?"

She pulled her shirt up and touched her belly directly this time. My eyes and mouth opened wide. She gathered the tips of my fingers and moved my hands toward her belly. My body temperature warmed itself in the balmy doghouse. "Kiss it?" I asked.

"Mm' humm," Karla said with a head nod.

Karla rubbed my hair as I kissed her belly. The children that ran and played outside the doghouse sounded as if they were in a distant field. Karla pulled off her shirt, and I looked onto a prepubescent body same as mine. I rubbed my hands over her bare chest. We kissed and I lay on top her placing my hands between her back and the scratchy wooden floor. Now we giggled and kissed some more. From the far-away field came a muted cry that our ears refused to hear. Our lips kept kissing. But soon the cries were right on us, and the magic that held the air dissipated like ice on a hot Southern day. Karla pushed me off then fumbled to get her shirt on.

"He's coming back! Mr. Amos is coming up the drive-way! Get out of there! Get out of there!" I heard Needa clearly now.

Karla pulled her shirt down and I rushed to straighten my shirt and shorts. I could hear Daddy stop the truck, open his creaky door, then slam it shut. Needa stood frantic outside the doghouse. "Hurry up y'all!"

Daddy spotted us as we exited. Now Karla, Needa, and I stood immobile outside the doghouse while Daddy scam-pered toward us like a Confederate soldier who'd lost his horse. My first impulse was to run away but experience had taught me that you get it sooner or later. Plus, where would I go? The only thing to do was explain.

Needa, without my logic, took off running and calling, "Miss Susie, Miss Susie, Mr. Amos is back! He got his belt off to whup Karla and Onnie!" The ten or so children that were outside had even better logic—they secured them-selves on the back porch and hid behind the rocking chairs.

"Now what the... what you chillins doing in that doghouse?" Daddy said without sweating from the heat. He looped his strop and held it loose in both hands. Then for both a sound and fear effect, he snap-popped it.

"Daddy, we weren't doing nothing! We just wanted to see what it look like inside," I said as I erected my head and shoulders and held firm to my story.

"Yeah, Mr. Amos, Miss Susie said we could go in there and see the inside," Karla said with a little singsong in her voice and a twitch in her legs.

Daddy stood, gray shirt untucked, and without a belt his britches contemplated a fall with one wrong move. Daddy's lean body possessed no butt to speak of. His horn-rimmed glasses rested forward on his sizable nose. In his hurry he had left his trusty cap in the truck. He could smell blood and so could I. The first lash crossed my back and landed on my butt. I covered my mouth to muffle a loud cry. He whipped the strop around and landed it across Karla's legs. She screamed like a siren. He stung us like a hornet, and masterfully repeated the maneuver on the same spots on both our bodies—all in one big WHISH.

"I won't do it again, I won't do it again!" I shouted while dancing double Dutch, hoping to get fewer licks. Daddy's agile fingers wove Karla and my hands together as one, and he held us so we couldn't run.

Mama appeared on the porch, looked quickly through the cloud of dust at the bodies held together then yelled, "Amos! What'chu doing to those girls?" She moved as fast as her prosthetic leg and real leg would take her, Needa traveling by her side. Some of the children stayed close by Mama but with enough distance to run if Daddy came their way.

"Now Susie, I done told 'em time and time again not to get in those doghouses or near my tool shed. I ain't gonna have chillins not listening to me," Daddy said firmly.

"Amos, let the girls go, they won't run." Mama stood both defiant and at ease, like she'd take Daddy on if she had too.

"Miss Susie, how Mr. Amos know they were playing the

kissing-doctor game?" Needa asked as she looked up at Mama with an innocence that could kill.

I looked at Needa without a blink and then I saw Karla put her hands over her eyes.

"What's she talking 'bout, Susie?" Daddy said, scrambling to grab our hands again as we flapped our arms like fledglings.

"Wait Amos, I don't know." Mama directed her question to Needa. "Needa baby, what did they do in the doghouse?"

Needa looked at Karla and then at me and tilted her head and shrugged her shoulders, then started her chirp. "Well they..."

"Don't!" shouted Karla. "Shut up!" she screamed.

At this point silence was my best defense.

"Quiet Karla—go on Needa, tell me what they do in the doghouse," Mama quizzed.

If tigers and lions were loose in the backyard, it wouldn't explain the fear I felt. Karla held her head low as Needa spoke like a prisoner just released after weeks in solitary.

"Umm—they kiss and touch like doctors and nurses," Needa said while she held tight to Mama's hand.

"You brat, you kissed Onnie, too!" Karla said in hysterics.

I thought she could have spared me my second count of the kissing-doctor felony. Needa shrugged again but said nothing.

"See, Susie! See! You see what they been doing. I ain't raising no nasty bull dagger." Daddy lifted his belt but this time Karla and I ran behind Mama and joined the children who'd left the porch to secure a spot next to her. We all stood as close as we could get.

"Amos, that's enough beating for one day. I told the girls they could play there. I had no idea they...well they're just children. I'll handle it," Mama said with decisiveness then shot off another question. "Why'd you come back anyway?"

Daddy worked hard to keep his pants up, get his belt back on, and answer Mama's question. His brain snapped to. "I forgot ah plumbing tool I need at work." Daddy huffed off to examine the doghouse then redirected himself with a pointed finger. "I don't care what you told 'em, I told 'em not to go in there. If she turns up ruin, ittah be yo' fault, letting her run wild committing unnatural acts and what nots."

Mama scooted us inside the house, gave Daddy a final disarming look, and trailed behind us. All I could think of on the way inside the house was that bulls had horns and I didn't.

Outside we could hear Daddy fire up his truck and drive off. It backfired like a shotgun. I sat on the sofa in a daze. Needa consoled Karla who sat next to me. Mama moved about the kitchen. She brought us lemonade to ease our trauma. She rubbed our backs and used a warm cloth on the places we had gotten licks from Daddy. Just as I finished my lemonade Uncle George knocked on the back door. He entered jolly, "Hello there, anybody home?" He had arrived with enough brittle candy for everybody. He also gave Mama prime steak and hamburger meat.

"How's my favorite niece?" Uncle George asked as the other children and I abandoned the sofa to get a hug. I held onto Uncle George's knee as a few tears fell freely.

"Amos gave Onnie and Karla some licks with the belt for getting in the doghouse," Mama said.

"That's crazy, hitting 'em for getting in those raggedy doghouses? But I told you," Uncle George said. He gave each of the other children a hug. He picked me up and centered a kiss on my forehead. "Amos knows these children can't hurt those ole huts." Uncle George put me down and held my hand, swinging it back and forth.

"Yeah, I know, but he doesn't want them inside. It's my fault. I gave them permission, but then he found out Onnie and Karla was kissing in there," Mama said.

"So what, they're just children. Good grief!"

"Okay George, that's enough in front of the children," Mama said, ending the conversation.

I felt protected when Uncle George was around. He was big and strong, his wire-framed glasses made him stately and smart looking. He was a combination of a knight, a football player, and a teacher. On quiet Saturdays he'd sit and talk about where he had been stationed in the Navy. He had never seen war but he'd travelled to London, France, Germany, and San Francisco. And though Mama was the one that said, "Black folks live all over the world," it was Uncle George who told me, "You can live anywhere you want."

Mama forbid us to go near the doghouses and said, "No more kissing game. Kissing is for married folks."

Late that night I could hear Mama tell Daddy off. "Build a fence around your doghouses and that precious tool shed, but I keep these children for a living, it helps run this house as much as your plumbing job. I'll be in a lot of trouble if you can't keep your hands off them. Let me handle what they do." I wondered if I was included in "the children." I didn't hear Daddy say anything but I guessed he looked like a scolded child.

A LIGHT RAIN fell on Peachtree Street, and the wet conditions slowed Daddy down, though he drove fast enough that it seemed we raced with the streetlights. But it was Mama who liked to drive downtown at night. As we rode, Mama examined restaurants, skyscrapers, buildings, and theaters with a sense of knowing. She'd seen her city grow over the years and she took pride in its development. Mama periodically turned to look at Lorraine and I and with each turn her eyes reflected the streetlights. I smiled back at Mama, and so did Lorraine. Daddy continued up Peachtree Street until we reached the affluent white neighborhood of Buckhead, and this is where he turned back. Many times he'd driven us through Buckhead and beyond but this seemed to be Mama's personal city limits. Daddy made a few turns and we landed on North Avenue and on into the Fifth Ward community, where Mama and Daddy both grew up. It was a scary neighborhood, even in the daylight, but Mama and Daddy weren't afraid and somehow this made me proud. Outside Mama's old house she and Daddy talked about how when they first moved here they didn't have electricity, running water, or scariest of all, a way to lock their doors, but they managed to be happy. It took me until I was an adult to understand how this was possible. Daddy took us down Hunter Street on through the well-to-do black community of West Lake. Although West Lake was only two miles from our house it might as well have been as far away as Buckhead.

Lorraine slept on the way back, but I was glad I didn't because it was on these late-night drives that I got to hear Mama and Daddy talk candidly about their past, their hopes, their feelings. They talked like I wasn't there. I could imagine Mama reading and studying by candlelight. Running around the yard playing with Uncle George and their other brother Uncle Duecer. Daddy pulled in the driveway and I shook Lorraine to wake her. On the drive that carried Mama and Daddy back in time, Daddy seemed to forget he was mad at me. To my childish eyes he looked happy. Still, no matter how hard I tried I couldn't imagine Daddy was once a child, not even in my wildest dreams.

## 3/ I DON'T CARE DON'T HAVE
## NO HOME

A battle brewed on the horizon of my thoughts the Friday Lorraine told me I was adopted. The knowledge made me angry with Mama, not Daddy. I figured Mama had wanted me and Daddy had gone along. And in the ways children form their truths and build their logic, I knew Daddy couldn't tolerate me because he never wanted to share Mama. As for Lorraine, I didn't mean to punch her in the jaw but being a baby butch, she squared me back in the chest, which landed me on the lawn where we rolled around and grunted more than we passed licks. Still, moments before I punched Lorraine, we were fantasizing about how much fun it would be if I lived with her and Mr. Handsom.

"Come and live with us, Miss Susie and Mr. Amos not your real parents anyway."

"What?"

"Yeah, they got you from a woman who already had too many children."

"Liar!"

"I heard Daddy and Miss Susie talking while you were running errands with your daddy," Lorraine said.

Mr. Handsom stopped us from continuing to fight and roll in the grass. "All kinds of people are adopted. And you two act more like sisters than I do with my blood sisters. Now make up!" I hugged Lorraine loosely and she did the same. Instead of going next door to my house I walked around the block. It was 1972, I was ten years old, and all my life Mama had neglected to tell me I was adopted. And she'd allowed Lorraine and her daddy to know more about me than I knew about myself.

Mama woke early on Saturday mornings to bathe and command the house. Even with a prosthetic leg Mama moved smoothly and quietly. Her false leg was constructed partly of wood and fiberglass, and it fit over the remaining part of her upper thigh and knee joint. The leg stayed on with an elaborate strap system that crossed her body like a patrolman's belt. Though her new prosthetic leg seemed antiquated, the only other alternative was crutches.

I never heard Mama complain about having one leg. At six years old she arrived in Eleven Light City with both legs. She'd jumped from the train happy and hopeful. Mama was happy she wouldn't have to be a dirt farmer and glad to know she could go to a better school. Once she started she was the smartest in her class.

When Mama was seven, after school she'd sneak off with her best friend Ella Mae to play at the railroad depot. One day while they ran around in between train cars, Mama's left foot got stuck between the tracks. In a freak accident the train car shifted, settled, and locked onto Mama's foot. All in one moment, one snap, her leg was useless. Mama lost the lower part of her leg and had to walk on crutches until she got a prosthetic as an adult.

On this Saturday morning, I rested my hand on the smooth, lacquered doorframe. The astringent smell of Jean Natés bath bubbles filled my nose as I peeped through the cracked door jam. I watched Mama turn off the water and get in the tub. It was a skillful maneuver. She sat on the side and put her right leg in. Then she braced herself with a crutch in her left arm, and reached over and held onto the lip of the tub with her right hand. Slowly she lowered herself inside. Plop went the sound of the water. Once in the tub, a calm came over Mama's face, and though Daddy's loud snores filled the quiet spaces of the house, it still felt peaceful. All of Mama's muscles seemed to melt down inside the tub. She leaned back into the bubbles and steaming, hot water.

I pressed my ear toward the opening and listened awhile, but all I heard were the crackling sounds the bubbles made once they began to evaporate. Again I peeped through the cracked door and Mama was still resting. This was the precise moment I was waited for to ask Mama if it was true—was I adopted?

I knocked but I didn't pause for Mama to respond. I wanted answers. I opened the door and my heartbeat sped up fast like one of those windup monkeys playing the cymbals. Mama smiled but I returned a toothless grin and Mama studied my face.

"What's wrong?"

"Am I adopted? Lorraine said you told her daddy."

Mama's eyes grew big and flashed a kind of wildness I was seeing for the first time, but she gathered herself just as quickly. "You were handpicked, chosen by me and Daddy to be our daughter. That makes you extra special. Most folks get what they get but we chose you."

I locked eyes with Mama and feeling bold with knowledge said, "I don't care 'bout being special. Why didn't you tell me?"

"First off, Miss Missy, I've told you time and time again not to say I don't care. Not caring about something doesn't mean a thing—it doesn't have a place to be or a home where it belongs. So stop saying it! And we hadn't told you because it never seemed to be a right time." Now Mama rested her arms on the lip of the tub.

"Well, where's my real Mama?"

Mama craned her neck up. "I am your Mama."

"But where's the Mama that had me?"

Mama leaned back and took a breath. "She moved away. She wanted us to be your parents. She couldn't give you the home you deserve."

"So she just left me here?" I asked with raised eyebrows.

"No, she didn't just leave you here. We brought you here when you were three days old," Mama said with attitude in her voice. Then she leaned toward me and continued with a more gentle voice.

"A mama is the person that takes care of you every day, watches over you, feeds you when you're hungry, and makes you chicken soup when you're sick." After she finished she released a big sigh that deflated her chest.

"Did she have other children? Do I have brothers and sisters?" My heart sped up again.

"Yes, but I don't know where any of them are now. Your birth mother had one girl after you and she was adopted and loved just like you," Mama said breathily.

I examined her while she spoke, even judged the story she told. I decided that day I'd question everything I saw and heard Mama and Daddy do. Now I could see our physical differences clearly as if a lightning bolt had hit—my medium-brown versus her chocolate-chocolate. In height, she was five-two versus my five-four, even at age ten. And I didn't look like Daddy either. His big nose, his thin lips, his small eye—nothing mirrored me.

"What's her name?"

"Ruth Ann Lewis," Mama said.

I turned and walked out, then pulled the bathroom door closed and stood there with my back against it. Then I pushed myself away and stood in the hallway with a heavy heartbeat. I wondered, where did Ruth Ann Lewis live? Where was my real daddy? I eventually asked Mama. She didn't know where Ruth Ann lived, and she didn't know my real daddy. The missing father was the worst. Even folks with broke-down daddies knew who they were.

Mama always talked about how great this city was. She'd arrived in Eleven Light City by train at night, and coming from a small country town like Monroe, she was captivated by the city lights. Apparently those same lights didn't fascinate Ruth Ann.

I stayed in my room the rest of the day into the evening. Mama came to see if I wanted something to eat, but I wasn't hungry. I discovered I could feast on anger for hours, even days. In the late evening a pebble hit my bedroom window. I looked to find Lorraine outside.

"Hey, Onnie, why don't you come over to my house? We can play records and talk," she said.

"Not today, Raine. I don't wanna play."

"You still mad at me?"

"No, I just don't wanna."

For weeks I sat on the front porch instead of playing in the backyard. I wanted to be away from the daycare kids but I also wanted to distance myself from Mama and Daddy. During this time even Daddy teetered on being kind, he didn't stare and he stopped threatening me. Once he even patted my head as he walked down the front stairs. While I sat out front I began to wonder if my real mama wanted to come and pick me up. Did she drive by to see if I was okay? Did she remember my birthdays and send me messages in the mail? Maybe I just never got any of the letters or gifts she sent. I told myself to sit out there and call to her if I needed help, and perhaps, just perhaps, she'd hear me and come. She never did.

One day a car slowed down as it approached the house. The car moved slow and steady, it felt altered, like a dream. A woman younger than Mama looked intently in my direction. She had four children. Three of them seemed older than me, and one girl looked younger. The two boys and two girls looked like ghosts in the front and back seats of the car. The woman drove past. Her eyes looked familiar as they pressed against mine through the driver's window. Her mouth hung open in surprise. I stood up so she could see me. I held a stare that traveled with the car until it drove out of sight. Seconds later I shook my head and wondered if I had daydreamed it all.

Weeks later I gave up the front porch and returned to the backyard and playing with Lorraine. Though at the time I couldn't articulate it, I knew somehow that if Ruth Ann wanted to find me she would.


I STARTED the school year excited because my new school, Hills Elementary, was in our neighborhood. Finally I could walk back and forth to school on my own without being bussed off to Haugabrooks Academy. Most days I didn't think about being adopted. That was replaced with the excitement of going back and forth between home and school unsupervised.

Mrs. Baseltine B. Bradley, the principal at Hills Elementary, seemed to tower taller than eleven feet when she stood on the moveable wooden blocks she called a podium in the middle of the school's foyer. With the eyes of a magistrate she looked down with X-ray vision to examine each child that entered her domain. She made it her business to read and remember all the reports on students' wrongdoings. She conducted unannounced visits to our homes to see where and how we lived. Her visitations appeared positive to parents, teachers, and administrators, but Principal Bradley used the information she gathered to control and embarrass any student sent to her office for misbehaving.

"Maybe if you stop being such a little fool, act like you got some sense, you might claw your way out of the Dixie Hills ghetto apartments," she was reported to have said to more than a few students.

Principal Bradley, an uppity-faced outsider who lived in a modest brick house in Collier Heights, believed the working-class folks who lived in wooden houses in Dixie Hills were better than the folks who lived in the Dixie Hills apartments, but neither was better than she. In her mind, the homeowners wanted the American Dream, while the apartment dwellers did not. She believed she was born in what W.E.B. Du Bois called the Talented Tenth, and she saw it as her duty to steer us, the dimwitted blue-collar flock, in the right direction.

Principal Bradley also believed that the girls of the day needed fewer women's rights, liberation, and left-wing gobbledegook and more home economics training. We needed to know how to cook for our future husbands or present-day fathers, depending on our fate in life. On the first day of school she closed the assembly program with,

"And remember girls, a lady is as a lady acts. Keep your dresses down and your pants zipped up. And you know I prefer you to all wear dresses." Then she gave us a menacing smile, which revealed only one tooth in the corner of her mouth.

My new fifth-grade teacher, Mrs. Ada Spivey, was one of Principal Bradley's appointed staff sergeants. She was a barrel-shaped woman with a mustache who drove a black four-door Lincoln Continental and told us that President Nixon drove one just like it. When she walked, each of her buttocks took turns rotating up and down, pressing in on each other like rolls of floury dough. She took the liberty of cleaning out her nose with her right index finger as she spoke to the class. And if her porcupine wig moved out of place it was nothing for her to turn it a complete 360 degrees to position it just right.

From the swing set, I could hear Miss Lucendy talk to Mama on our back porch. "Susie, that ole Mrs. Spivey was my girl Say-Say's teacher seven years ago. She's ah uppity moose-face woman who wears her dresses too short for her old husky legs. She ought to know she's too old for all that." Miss Lucendy did a head and neck roll as she put her fists on her full hips. "As for that Principal Bradley, her old husband ran off a decade ago. What she know 'bout being a lady? She hasn't had practice with a man for years."

On the first day of school, Mrs. Spivey didn't even try to contain her laughter at the homemade Shirley Temple–style dress Mama had forced me to wear. Mama had been on a campaign to femme me up since the kissing-game fiasco. From her little metal desk at the front of the classroom, a boisterous and comical laugh sprung from Mrs. Spivey when I entered. The classroom followed her lead. They fell over in their seats with the teacher's approval.

Mortified I sat in the last row, in the corner closest to the window where I could see the trees and the squirrels.

Mrs. Spivey cleared her throat before she lifted herself up to speak. "Well I see that some of us think we're going to a cotillion or perhaps we're a princess for the day. Whatever the event, no one gets special treatment in this class. It doesn't matter where you live or where you came from. We are here to learn, children, and learn we must. I've got my education signed, sealed, and delivered. Now it's up to you to get yours." There was complete silence except for the pitter-patter of squirrels that played freely along the windowsill. I sank a little lower in my chair in an attempt to not be seen. While I slumped in the chair I wondered how Mrs. Spivey got her education delivered in a sealed box.

THE CAFETERIA WAS a large rectangular room where children buzzed with excitement. Some lined up to get their food while others sat down with their lunchboxes to eat. The fourth and fifth graders ate during the same lunch period—the fifth graders, being older, got choice seating. I'd decided to sit downwind of Mrs. Spivey at a table with Lorraine and Charleston. I'd known Charleston since we were four years old and even now at age ten he was still a notorious crybaby, which is why Lorraine had appointed herself his personal how-to-get-tough teacher. We sat in a row of three with Charleston in the middle. Mrs. Spivey sat drinking her glass of milk on ice, barricaded behind tinted eyeglasses. The dark lenses allowed her to watch all our moves covertly. "So how was class?" Lorraine asked.

"Well—if you don't count the teacher and the class laughing at my dress, hair, and shoes, it's been good so far," I said as I ate my peanut butter and jelly sandwich.

"I think your baby-doll curls are pretty, Onnie," Charleston said. I smiled while Lorraine snickered and ate. "I heard that Spivey lady was mean as a rattlesnake. She might even *bite* you," Charleston's eyes grew large as he willed himself into a trance.

"Snap out of it, Charleston. Ain't nobody got to be afraid of that old Mrs. Spivey. She's just fat and a little crazy," Lorraine said eating the fruit cocktail dessert that came with the day's lunch. Charleston rolled his eyes and moaned.

"You know that dress is funny looking," Lorraine said.

"Lorraine!"

"Well I'm glad your girl Karla didn't see it, you know with her moving and all."

"She'll be back after her mother's better. She'll be back," I said.

"But her mom's cancer..." Lorraine said.

"She's my pen pal. I should know, she's coming next school year," I said loudly.

Lorraine's eyes bugged large like a cartoon character. "Shhh—okay."

I leaned back and whispered. "That Mrs. Spivey is mean to me."

"What you gonna do about it? We're big girls now, we're ten going on eleven. My daddy says nobody likes everybody. But don't worry, you got me and crybaby over there," Lorraine said with a snarl.

Charleston protested, "Hey!" Lorraine and I laughed out loud, which caused Mrs. Spivey's head to move in our direction like she was a rusty robot that needed oil.

I couldn't pinpoint why Mrs. Spivey hated me, but she

did, and her venom leaked out each time she spoke. Weeks turned into months and Mrs. Spivey developed a habit where she'd announce to the class my shortcomings.

"Onnie Armstrong! You'd learn something if you'd shut your mouth and pay attention. Silence is golden."

"Onnie Armstrong! Keep it up, and you'll end up living with your Mama in Dixie Hills forever."

I hated when she said my full name, and I hated even more when she brought my Mama into the classroom. And forever seemed like a lifetime away. Granted, I did talk, but not much more than the other children. To stay seated at a desk all day long bored me. The two thirty-minute play-times weren't enough. I needed to breathe and learn outside. I needed variety. Plus, I talked to keep alert and awake, but Mrs. Spivey didn't see it that way.

Sometimes she'd chant a mantra directed at me. "Armstrong! Armstrong! Armstrong! An empty wagon makes a lot of noise," she'd say and turn back to continue the day's lesson. If loud noises came from others in the classroom, Mrs. Spivey blamed me. If I protested she'd either threaten to send me to Principal Bradley's office or make me sit in the dunce corner.

On the walk home I talked to Lorraine and Charleston about my troubles.

"That Mrs. Spivey is a black widow spider. Just like the ones we're studying in class," I said, holding my books close to my chest. "And I'm stuck in her class like a fly caught in a web. And—she talks too loud."

"She probably can't hear that good, you know she's old," Lorraine said, looking carefree dressed in blue jeans and a red sweater.

I rolled my eyes at her, then looked in the distance at a group of boys playing football in the street. I wasn't dressed nearly as comfortably in my white button-up shirt, a jean skirt, and Mary Jane shoes.

"Maybe you should bring her an apple. I saw that on *Leave It to Beaver*," Charleston said. A few car horns blew as the boys' football hit a moving car.

"That old witch don't need no fruit! She needs to be in a cage with monkeys in the zoo," Lorraine said, then stopped to laugh. She finished and put her arm around my shoulders. "But you get so upset, Onnie. Just be cool and that old bat will find someone else to bother."

Lorraine might have been right, but then again she was the one that had told me all the teachers at Hills Elementary were young and cool.

After the children were gone Mama phoned Mrs. Spivey. I stayed in my bedroom and waited for the verdict. Mama opened the door without a knock.

"Well, Onnie Marie Armstrong. That Mrs. Spivey might not be sweet, but she says you won't shut your mouth in her classroom. All day long you talk, talk, and talk. She says you even talk to yourself if no one else will. So while I don't like her calling you names, and I told her so, you have to learn when and where to talk," Mama said with a long hard look from my bedroom door.

"Her class is so boring," I said and leaned back on my twin-size bed. "We never go outside and have class like we did at Haugabrooks. And my class is so big everybody doesn't even get a turn to read, and she only calls on me when I'm doing something she doesn't like."

"You wanted to go to Hills Elementary, remember, after Karla moved. It's a public school, not a private school, so the classes are bigger, and there's more competition for the teacher's attention. So stop talking in class and do your homework."

While we walked to school I reported to Lorraine and Charleston what had happened. "I'm glad she didn't tell Daddy."

"Me too! But Mrs. Spivey not supposed to call you names," Lorraine said.

"I know. I wanna get her back."

"How?" Lorraine asked.

"Maybe by putting one of those spiders in her desk drawer to scare the bejesus out of her," I said.

"I don't know, Onnie, that's against the rules," Charleston said.

"Charleston, we're almost at school. Go on to yo' classroom," Lorraine said.

Charleston glared at Lorraine for a while but walked on.

That morning I decided to work hard at not talking. And though I was well behaved, Mrs. Spivey seemed as spiteful as ever. But I didn't care because Lorraine and I had a plan. Maybe I couldn't stop her from calling me names, but I could scare her and that would make me happy.

After lunch the class went to the playground. Lorraine's class usually came after mine. My class lined up to leave and when I passed Lorraine she high-fived me, which meant our plan was in motion.

The class rested their heads on their desks. Mrs. Spivey read stories to us after lunch and P.E. It seemed to be the only time she was peaceful. Maybe because this was the only time the entire class stayed quiet. Mrs. Spivey pulled the desk drawer open. I laid my head on my desk but cocked it to the side with my eyes cracked open. She pulled the book out without a scream. But how could that be? She started reading from *Roll of Thunder, Hear My Cry*, and still no screams. We were at the part where the fires were raging, and it sounded like the fire would burn down the farm—it sounded like it would burn everything. I looked again and saw the spider had traveled up Mrs. Spivey's pink knit sweater. I screamed so loud Mrs. Spivey dropped the book, then she saw the spider. The whole class raised their heads quickly. But instead of a loud squeal, Mrs. Spivey only gasped, then flicked the spider off her sweater.

She motioned for some of the children to get a jar and put the spider back inside. But what happened next completely surprised me.

"Well, Miss Onnie Armstrong, your powers of observation are good after all." Then she said the impossible: "Thank you." She smiled big but didn't show any teeth.

The next day Principal Bradley loomed over me in the school's foyer. "I hear you helped Mrs. Spivey yesterday. And I see you wear dresses and skirts more than the rest of these girls. Be warned, though. I know a bad seed when I see one." Principal Bradley said before turning to walk into the school's main office. I watched until she disappeared from sight then held my books tight around my chest and moved unsteadily toward my classroom.

## 4/ BATTLES WITH BADASSES

The sun produced a crooked light as it fought to enter with me into Portable Number Seven, my new classroom. It was 1973 and I was eleven. Miss Isabel Pearlman was my new sixth-grade teacher and Shirlene Tallas my new nemesis. On the first day of school, Shirlene pushed me because I sat at a desk she thought she might like to sit in and this before we were given seat assignments. The war had commenced.

Shirlene was round and multilayered in fat, and looked as tall as she was wide. She was shaped like a twisting tornado without the movement. She wasn't known for her intellect, beauty, or physical ability. She wasn't considered for plays or the chorus. If, in fact, she'd actually sung in the chorus, she would've been placed in the baritone section, to bring forth the low tones of bass violins and trombones. What Shirlene did best was create fear. She could say ordinary words in ways that would frighten even the bravest souls. Her sharp-eyed stare even unsettled adults. Teachers would demand homework, but after a stare or some roughly turned words they wouldn't expect to receive what they had requested. I saw her power and appreciated the masterful ways she wielded it. I even admired it, but I refused to submit.

Miss Pearlman was raised and schooled up north in Ohio. She knew very little about the South. She hadn't seen or eaten collard greens before she moved to Eleven Light City. I imagined her Jewish heritage taught her a lot about survival in foreign lands, different from black folks' survival but just as effective and even more so in the South. Southern customs, manners, antebellum rules, and dress codes never affected Miss Pearlman the way they did those of us that grew up in the midst of their physical and mental grip. Miss Pearlman didn't believe girls should only wear dresses and skirts like Principal Bradley and her flunkey teachers. Nor did she believe girls could only be teachers and nurses. "Civil rights and equal rights are about choices. Find your passion and you'll get your goals," Miss Pearlman said. "My passion is teaching you." This was the first time I'd heard teaching and passion in the same sentence.

On a warm fall day Karla arrived at my front door, her father had dropped her off. It was the perfect Saturday to visit. Daddy was off on one of his infamous fishing trips with Old Man Jeb and would be gone all day. Mama told Daddy that Karla and her father were coming, and I guess Daddy had hightailed it to Lake Winnipesauke to fish because he was scared Mr. Lyons might come to settle the score. Shortly after Daddy hit Karla and me Mrs. Lyons found another daycare for Karla and Needa.

Mama allowed me to open the front door. Karla had grown taller over the years. She'd also grown small breasts but I tried not to look at them. I'd decided nothing was worse than a girl who liked girls acting like a big-head boy looking at a *Playboy* magazine. I had discovered how boys acted around these magazines when Lorraine stole a few copies from her father. Lorraine, Charleston, and I examined the pages of the scantily clad vixens with wonder and awe. Charleston foamed saliva at the corner of his mouth and temporary lost his ability to speak looking at page after page of large-breasted women with and without bras. He even resorted to trying to steal the already-stolen magazines.

Karla smiled and reached to hug me and I hugged her back. Mama left to prepare lunch. Mama had agreed to allow Karla's visit but had set some ground rules. Karla and I could play and talk in my room providing the door was open. We could also play and talk in the backyard. "I'm guessing you and Karla are over that kissing stuff. Y'all are almost teenagers now," Mama said. I acknowledged what she said but didn't agree, though Mama thought I'd agreed with my head nod.

Karla looked around my room, examining my collection of forty-fives. She moved on to my jar of marbles and my *Archie* comic books lying on the shelf. Then she sat down on the twin bed across from me.

"I didn't think you'd ever come back," I said.

"Mama was really sick and Daddy needed to work so we had to live with my Aunt Sarah."

"How was Athens?" I asked.

"Country, a little slow, but cool in a way. There's a big university there. I may go when it's time for college."

"College—that's a long ways off. When'd you start planning for college?"

"I guess while living in Athens, while Mama recuperated," Karla said.

"Did they save 'em?" I asked, folding my arms tight around my chest.

"No—the doctor took them to save her."

I didn't know what to say. I'd never known anyone that had surgery and certainly not cancer. Who knew Mrs. Lyons would lose both breasts? Now I looked at Karla's breasts. We both got our training bras from JCPenney. Our mothers, on separate occasions, took us to be fitted. I was so embarrassed that some strange woman and Mama were standing there, looking to see if my bra fit properly, but it was the pulling and tugging of the new bra while it was on me that was the worst. My mind wandered back and I hoped Karla wouldn't lose her breasts—they looked nice. Nice enough to touch, but Mama was in the kitchen and I didn't know if Karla had grown out of being a kissing girl. But Karla caught me looking at her chest and smiled. It was then I knew she still liked girls, or at least me. I whispered, "Mama's listening from the kitchen." Karla pointed for me to close the bedroom door. "Can't—Mama's rule." Karla motioned for me to join her on the twin bed where she sat. I did and quickly we felt each other up and kissed, all while remaining upright. I put my hand under her shirt to fondle her breast. She giggled and I thought I'd done something special. We got good and heated when we heard Mama coming from the kitchen. I was never so grateful for hardwood floors and a small house that carried sound—Mama's prosthetic leg made a clump sound when it hit the wood floor. By the time Mama got to us I was back on the other bed and Karla was leaning back across from me laughing while she turned the pages of a comic book. "Girls, you ready for lunch?" Mama said. We smiled broad and silly then nodded yes.

After Karla moved back I'd hoped she'd land in my homeroom, but she ended up in Lorraine's while I was stuck with Shirlene. Still, Miss Pearlman's classroom buzzed with activities like debate team and poetry club, fun projects like painting a section of the class wall, and trips to the state fire-prevention contest. The only part I didn't like was reading out loud. Though I liked to read, especially my encyclopedias at home, it was hard for me to read in front of the class. I'd run over the words, I'd read words not printed on the page. In general I was unable to find the rhythm to read the words smoothly. At some point Shirlene saw the unskillful way I delivered readings as the best reason why I wasn't hot stuff—my disability was proof I wasn't any better than her.

The Pathway was a sandy dirt lot that forked off the school's main road. We called it the Path for short. It was the quickest way to go to and from the Dixie Hills apartments by foot from Hills Elementary. Mama reminded me, "I know you and Lorraine like to go down that path but frankly it's safer and quicker for you both to just take Tiger Flowers Drive home."

"Yes, ma'am," I said. Of course her demands made the journey through the Path more desirable. After school Lorraine said she was going home down through the Path. I reasoned that Mama would want me to travel home with someone she knew rather than by myself. Of course I could have walked with Charleston, but he wasn't as much fun as Lorraine. When Lorraine and I asked Charleston to join us on the walk home via the Path, he ran off ahead of us down Tiger Flowers Drive. We took his running as a no.

The Path's sandiness reminded me of a beach, though no beach I knew of had red clay underneath. Still it was fun to get sand in my shoes. Lorraine and I stopped to unwrap the candy we had kept hidden in our pockets all day. Not only did we break the No Candy rule, we were also instrumental in undermining the Dresses Only law. Lorraine never wore a dress and I had stopped at the beginning of sixth grade. I was still labeled the troublemaker in Principal Bradley's eyes, not Lorraine, but that was due to Mr. Handsom, who told her, "The city taxes I pay give me the right to decide what clothes my daughter will wear to public school." This also implied he paid her salary. Mama never said anything to Principal Bradley but she decided pants kept me warm and protected my legs when I ran and played. And after I told Mama the boys looked under girls' dresses, I only wore dresses for chorus recitals and picture day, and those days I also wore tights.

The Now and Later I put in my mouth burst a sweet and sour watermelon. Lorraine and I started down the Path, kicking sand as we went. We zipped around with our classmates happy like baby bumblebees, free to wander. I turned to smile at Lorraine but suddenly my head snapped back, something was clawing deep into my scalp, pulling hard at my roots. I pressed my heels down into the sandy path to get my footing. I swung wide but the pain from my head stopped me from getting free. Shirlene gripped my Afro even tighter, and I feared she'd snatch me bald before I could get away. She grunted as she spun me around uncontrollably. Her head flapped in the wind and in a moment of exhilaration she lessened her grip. I managed to get my head loose only to discover I'd entered a kiddy gladiator's arena. A high school boy used a four-by-four to draw a large circle in the sand, making the arena official. Shirlene and I were enveloped by kids from both sides of the Dixie Hills community—the apartments and the houses—as they chanted, "Beat her butt. Beat her butt." Lorraine picked up my book bag and my notebook and pencils, but left the trampled candies for the ants. I tried to get myself together, stand up without stumbling. Lorraine couldn't help me because Shirlene's brothers' friends were there to protect her.

"I'm g'wine to beat your butt," Shirlene said with flaring nostrils. She circled her arms as if they pedaled a bike. "Then I is g'wine to send you home the way folks 'pose to when they live in the Dixie Hills houses." Shirlene spat on the ground, and then continued, "You ain't no better than me and you can't even read."

I looked around and hoped she'd keep making speeches while I found a way to get away. But Shirlene circled the arena and growled like a bulldog tied to a post in the Southern heat. I circled to keep her away, and mirrored her motions to show I was ready for battle. I wasn't. Shirlene pounced, got hold of my shirt sleeve, then pulled with a force that toppled me over. She moved on me with more speed than I'd ever seen her exhibit on the playground or during P.E. class. One moment later she had me in a head-lock. Without a pause she shoved me down to the Path's hard, red-clay bottom. That day, Shirlene used my body to wipe the Pathway clean to victory.

On the walk home down Tiger Flowers Drive, named for a famous black boxer, Lorraine tried to console me. "That wasn't fair fighting, Onnie. She's twice your weight and her bad-ass brother's gang stood next to me the whole time," she said, losing control of her breath. I shook my head like a wet puppy to get the sand out. I brushed off my pants and shirt while Lorraine continued to talk. "Plus, she came from behind. You didn't even see her. It wasn't fair, Onnie. The whole thing wasn't fair." Lorraine sulked as she talked. I licked my wounds and continued to dust myself off. But not even the great Tiger Flowers himself would have been able to hide my torn shirt, dirt-soiled jeans, and bruised knee from Mama, who was always ready to inspect.

The next morning Daddy cornered me in the kitchen. "I hear tell you was in a fight. I hope to gawd she looks worse than you. If you fight, you better win," he said as if he told his gospel. "'Cause if you come home beat, you gonna to get another beating. You gotta to learn to fight yo' own battles. Ain't nobody gonna fight 'em for you." Daddy's words penetrated my insides where they settled themselves into the truth of my situation—I was on my own.

A week later I stood on the basketball court where dust stirred. This would be the last year we played basketball with the boys, after this they grew to think of girls as the lesser sex and playing sports with us was futile and useless. Lorraine and I played with them in the morning before school and during my class's playground time. Daryl Sterling was a plain brown boy with light brown eyes and the posture of a weasel, he teased me as we played ball.

"So I hear Shirlene whip your b-u-t-t!"

"I whipped hers, too," I said.

"Yeah, but she won," he said.

What could I say? She had whipped my butt and she had won.

That day during my playground time I pretended not to watch Shirlene while she watched me. Karla and Lorraine warned me to stay away from Shirlene. "Just run if you see her coming, Onnie," Karla said over the phone. "You need to get a pocketknife like me, then show it to her and she'll wobble off," Lorraine said, showing me her blade. She only carried that blade for three days before her daddy confiscated it. Still, sometimes trouble has a way of finding you even when you're not interested, even if you run or carry a blade.

I continued to pretend I didn't see Shirlene as she followed me inside the main building and to the restroom. As I finished and left the stall to wash my hands, Shirlene appeared out of the shadows with squinted eyes. I returned the same eyes. She stepped wide just inside the entrance to the bathroom. She stood like a gun-toting cowboy without holsters or guns. The music of some old Western played in my head. The sunlight shined brightly off the polished tiled wall and surrounded us in a glow. We both felt in our glory. I moved slowly toward the doorway and Shirlene used her body to prevent me. Without words I heard the battle cry and jumped to run either into her or out the door to safety. Landing into Shirlene felt like hitting a bed of bricks. My first attempt didn't move her but with another blow I rammed her to the ground. Unable to move I watched with fear as she managed to get up from the tile floor. As she got to her feet I rammed her again, this time into the wall where we struggled in a wrestler's grip.

Some girls who'd tried to enter the restroom had sounded the alarm that there was a battle being fought there. Miss Pearlman arrived first and held the kids outside the doorway. Shirlene and I bounced off walls and stalls as we struggled. We stood almost in a truce breathing like animals in a Spanish bullfight. I gave one final blow as we charged toward each other. This time our heads butted and I landed on the floor while Shirlene landed butt first in a can filled with soiled paper towels, smelly toilet paper, and other assorted garbage. Landing in the can wasn't the final blow, being stuck was.

Shirlene wiggled to loosen the can, but without success. "Get me out of here," she demanded in one of her forceful voices, but it was delivered without the usual punch. Frightened and titillated I gulped in air while I watched her continue to struggle.

Miss Pearlman stepped into the restroom from her guard post and the kids from the playground poured in to see the spectacle, she looked at Shirlene and then me. Shirlene took the opportunity to tell her part of the story.

"Miss Pearlman, that Onnie Armstrong pushed me in this trash can," Shirlene said as if I'd stalked and chased her inside.

"Shirlene, we can either talk about it now and then we can go to the office to see Principal Bradley or we can return to the classroom and settle it there," Miss Pearlman said firmly. "It's your choice." Shirlene's silence answered, I choose the classroom.

Other teachers came in to clear out the mass of students. Miss Pearlman gave me a little wink when she pulled my arm to help me up. One teacher called the custodian to get Shirlene out of the garbage can after teacher after teacher had tried unsuccessfully. Neither Shirlene nor I were expelled due to some miracle or blood oath Miss Pearlman secured with Principal Bradley. Perhaps the victory went beyond me.

From that day on I never again fought at Hills Elementary and Daddy never beat me for being beat up. Lorraine bragged to whoever would listen that I was her best friend. Karla and I secretly stole lip-locked kisses when we got a chance. The school embraced me as some type of dragon slayer—a hero of all things. But Principal Bradley saw things very differently. "Just another badass from Dixie Hills," she said under her breath when I passed her in the school's foyer.

## 5/ WATER BONDS

From my bike I watched the vibrant world of the Dixie Hills apartments unfold before my very eyes. Young and old women in colorful headscarves sat on their porches and watched small children play nearby. A group of ragtag boys competed with smaller kids on the swing sets and seesaws. A flurry of pay phones rang nearby and those same preteen boys ran to pick them up. An old barber yelled from his shop door warning the boys about the downfall of kids running the streets. It was a sunny Saturday morning as I rode past these sights with happy feet and an excited heart. I'd turned thirteen and I was in eighth grade at Frederick Douglass High School, surely I was old enough to ride my bike away from Mama and Daddy's watchful eyes.

Both Lorraine and I received brand-new ten-speed bikes for our thirteenth birthdays, which were one week apart, and Mama officially granted me permission to ride my bike away from her Safety Areas. But Mama's permission came with the stipulation that I shouldn't ride into the Dixie Hill apartments.

My mind moved fast.

"What if we want to ride over in the West Lake area?" I asked.

Mama stopped cutting vegetables and looked up at me from the kitchen table.

"Then go around if you have to go over to West Lake," she said with a firm stare, then returned to her work.

"The only other way is up Tiger Flowers Drive and it has such a steep hill to ride up," I said, hoping that Mama would change her mind.

"Onnie, you can ride down Joe Louis Street and avoid Tiger Flowers Drive and those ole projects. Ain't nothing in those apartments but trouble. Plus you got a ten-speed—won't it help you climb hills?"

I'd forgotten that one of my petition points for the ten-speed bike was that it would help me climb the Dixie Hills. But Mama remembered everything.

Unlike me, Lorraine had permission to ride in the Dixie Hills apartments long before she got a ten-speed. Back then she rode her long-handled bike with the glittery banana seat. Lorraine's daddy said in his booming voice, "I grew up in the rumble-tumble streets of New York City Harlem USA in the 40s. Now that was scary! Those tiny Dixie Hills apartments ain't no real ghetto 'cause this ain't no real city." Then Mr. Handsom leaned over the front stoop, slapped his thigh, and burst out in laughter, "Ho, ho, ho." He sounded like the Jolly Green Giant.

Truth be told, back when I was twelve I'd already snuck and rode through the Dixie Hills apartments. I rode my old three-speed bike and Charleston rode his dirt bike. The two times we rode there, Charleston, the chicken shit, wore his baseball cap low on his head so no one could identify him.

"We can't be stopping or nothing. My mama said folks shoot you up here if you look at 'em the wrong way," he said.

When I slowed down to see people up close walking or playing, or old folks sitting around, Charleston kept going. When he noticed I had slowed he shouted back for me to come on, then rapidly flapped his legs. That was my first time in a notorious place where guns allegedly went off and so-called illegal deals went down. I'd only heard gunshots on the Fourth of July and New Year's Eve, and all of those shots came from old men in their backyards on Carver Drive and surrounding streets. One of those men was Daddy, bringing in the New Year with Mama and me tucked inside the house far away from the windows. Charleston and I rode directly toward the afternoon sun away from the bad, bad Dixie Hills apartments, and then, like now with Lorraine, nobody even noticed us.

This time as Lorraine and I rode I got a better look at the apartments. They were made of red brick, not wood or aluminum siding like most the houses on my street. These apartments sat flanked by a sea of green walnut trees, entrenched on a hillside where they were grouped close and stacked together like children's building blocks. Unlike what Mama said, these were nice-looking buildings. Lorraine looked back, smiled, and pointed for us to turn left toward the apartment where her friend Hiawatha Lightfoot lived. Karla said she'd sneak out once her daddy got engrossed in the baseball game—the Braves against the Dodgers.

Outside Hiawatha's apartment I jumped off my bike and saw patches of balding brown grass amid muddy red dirt, busted-up sidewalks, and strewn trash. Lorraine said it looked like the part of the Bronx where her cousins lived, near Yankee Stadium. I didn't care that the apartments were unkepted. They had a buzz of excitement with adults and children moving here and there. It wasn't quiet like my street. A group of unkempt children huddled near the edge of the door that led up to Hiawatha's apartment. Their focus was an old water hose that they were using to fill up balloons. Neither the balloon kids nor the adults moving around seemed to care what we were doing, unlike the busybody Old Folks Mafia on our street. Lorraine said she liked it that way. I hoped Karla would show up soon, she'd like the view and the excited feeling of the Dixie Hills apartments.

Hiawatha lived on the third floor of the apartment building. We walked our new ten-speed bikes up the three long flights of stairs. One long climb and one short ring of the buzzer brought Hiawatha to the door.

"Hey Raine," Hiawatha said. "I see you had a sweaty climb."

"No big deal. What's happening, chick-a-dee?" Lorraine asked, but only after she'd looked at Hiawatha from head to toe. I laughed to myself when I heard that chick-a-dee line. It was straight from one of the W.C. Fields movies that Lorraine watched with her daddy. "Oh—this is Onnie."

"Hey Hiawatha," I said with a blush that neither Lorraine nor Hiawatha noticed.

"Hey Lorraine's best friend," Hiawatha said. "Wipe your feet and come in. You can leave the bikes in the hallway or you can put them on the back porch with ours."

"Careful, Onnie. Pick it up high so it won't get on the carpet," Lorraine said in her bossy voice.

I took several small deliberate breaths as I struggled to

keep the bike's tires high enough, but the back tire grazed the living room carpet just as I entered the kitchen. Only sweat from my forehead actually stained the beige carpet, though. I could smell toast and butter, but that came from the crumbs on the kitchen counter after Hiawatha's snack. A Marvin Gaye song, "Let's Get It On," played on the radio. I walked through the kitchen behind Lorraine and Hiawatha and then onto the back porch where we placed the bikes. From there I got a close view of the thickly layered green trees. The black metal staircase crisscrossed itself to the bottom creating a maze with other intersecting porches, none of which had gates that locked.

"Hey, y'all," I called back from the kitchen. "Will the bikes be okay out here?" But Lorraine and Hiawatha didn't answer. They'd made themselves cozy on the sofa in the living room where they stared into each other's eyes, made goofy smiles, and cooed like content babies. Lorraine finally registered the question.

"The bikes are fine. I ride over here all the time," Lorraine said.

"But do you leave your new ten-speed on a unlocked porch?"

"I just did—crybaby," Lorraine flung her hand in the air and looked back at Hiawatha.

Hiawatha got up and walked toward the kitchen. This time I got a good look at her. Her body was curvy but lean, her face sculpted with big, oval eyes. Hiawatha seemed older than us, more girly and mature. She landed next to me and I aimed my eyes back toward Lorraine.

"Onnie, don't worry about the bikes—they'll be fine. I'll get us milk and gingersnaps," Hiawatha said and pointed back to a fluffy-looking chair next to the sofa.

As I got closer to Lorraine she rolled her eyes but smiled and rubbed my back when I sat down. "You worry too much, Onnie. Chill, be cool."

"It's my new purple bike," I said and returned an eye roll without the reassuring back rub. Then I fell into the cushy chair's coziness.

As I got comfortable Hiawatha called from the kitchen, "Raine, come and help me bring out the snacks." After Lorraine left the living room, I could hear giggles and muffled words. The apartment smelled of honeysuckle and sandalwood. Hiawatha's place was opposite from the outside, it was clean, organized and neat. And though I had felt a rush of excitement before I entered, inside I felt safe and calm.

FINALLY HIAWATHA and Lorraine returned from the kitchen with glasses of milk, gingersnaps, and big, shit-eating grins about their faces. I was mad they had taken so long but if I could neck with Karla in my kitchen with Mama gone I'd ignore Lorraine like she'd ignored me. I sat cooped up while Lorraine gave Hiawatha goo-goo love eyes. I was surprised that Lorraine actually ate— it must have been hard to concentrate on biting the cookies and looking at Hiawatha at the same time.

"So where's your mama?" Lorraine asked, grinning and purring as she spoke. She fluttered her eyelashes like a butterfly's wings while she ate.

"She went to the grocery store. That Fig supposed to be here with me. But he's running the street with those badass boys that hang out with Cannonball. He never listens to Ma," Hiawatha said with a sigh.

"You talking 'bout Shirlene's cousin?" Lorraine asked.

"Yeah—you know him?" Hiawatha said.

"Naw, but I heard he's a wannabe thug."

I listened while I ate my gingersnaps. "You think he'll come here?" I asked.

"Mama doesn't want boys in the house while she's gone —Fig's not that crazy," Hiawatha said. And in that moment I felt relieved and shot off another question.

"Where did you and Fig get your names?"

Lorraine gave me a glance that I couldn't read, but Hiawatha spoke openly.

"Ma is one-quarter Cherokee and three-quarters black. Papa is half black and half Cherokee. Grandpapa named us."

I wanted to ask where her Daddy was but that seemed impolite. I looked close to examine her features—her nose, her lips, her coloring—but Hiawatha looked like a light-brown-skinned black person. She did have what some black folks called Good Hair because it didn't need straightening with a hot comb or chemicals. Mama always said, "You got hair on your head? Then that's good." As far as Mama was concerned, only the women who elected to scalp it off to the shortest nappy Afro had bad hair. I believed Hiawatha had Indian blood. Still, everybody claimed Indian blood, but I didn't know one full-blooded Indian person who lived in the Dixie Hills community.

Hiawatha continued, "Grandpapa said Fig's head shaped like a fig, and when he was born he was a light shade of green." Hiawatha's chuckle bounced off the wall and echoed in my ear. The pitch of her laughter was only outmatched by Fig, who burst in with a pack of his wild buddies dressed in camouflage pants with bandanas across their foreheads, a trail of cigarette smoke following on their heels.

"Well looky here, Watha's girlfriend visiting again." He looked to survey the living room. "And she brought another he-she for protection." Fig watched me out the corner of his eye but directed his fiery words to Lorraine while he moved toward her and Hiawatha.

"Thought I told you stop coming around here slumming, little boy-girl. You don't live up here," Fig said. He stood with a half smile as he pointed his crooked pinky finger. His gangly crew giggled like children on the playground.

"I ain't no boy-girl, you putz," Lorraine said with a semi-Harlem accent.

"Fig, Ma said Lorraine's welcome here and Onnie too. Raine helps around the house more than you do. Leave us alone," Hiawatha said and stood with her arms folded.

Fig looked back at his buddies and slapped them five on the black-hand side then turned back and smiled like the Grinch. "Y'all fools know I'm kidding, but Ma never said you and she-him could hug up on the sofa. You think 'cause you turned thirteen you grown enough to date this baby dyke," Fig said. Now he stood close enough to smell the aftershave Lorraine wore with her daddy's permission.

"You're fifteen but you act ten," Hiawatha said with her face in Fig's.

Fig laughed at Hiawatha. Lorraine jumped up. Scared, I jumped up, too.

"Fig, you want a piece of me? You want a piece?" Lorraine said bravely while I was concerned for her health. There were three of us and four of them, and while I believed in women's rights, and Billie Jean King did kick Bobby Riggs's butt in tennis, the facts were they were older, bigger, and stronger. They were boys and unless one of us could turn into Captain America we'd get our butts beat. As we stood in a weak stance one of the boys ran to the kitchen and returned to report his findings.

"Fig-Man you got two new bikes out here," the punk said with a big ole smile.

"Man what'chu talking 'bout? I ain't got no new bikes," Fig said, still watching us, but then ran to see what his partner saw. He returned. "Oh, those bikes. Yeah, those is my bikes all right," Fig said with a wink.

"They aren't your bikes, they're mine and Onnie's," Lorraine said. She pushed past Hiawatha who managed to grab her arm before Lorraine could actually leave the living room or get close to Fig.

"Well then you won't mind if we run errands while you two visit with my darling little sis," Fig said and laughed his best imitation of a mad man. Then he and the other two boys ran to get our bikes, and Hiawatha's.

Lorraine tried to run after them but Hiawatha jerked her by the arm and then flung both her arms around Lorraine's waist and gripped her hard. The punk that had discovered the bikes now stood in front of me with one hand on his crotch and the other pressed hard against my shoulder. "Chill—unless you want some of this," he whispered while the other three confiscated our bikes. I grimaced and stretched my neck to see what Fig and his gang were doing. "Shit," I said and jumped to retrieve my bike but the boy used both his hands to shove me down in the chair. "I see you a wild cat. I may need to come back and see 'bout you." He shoved me down one more time before he ran out the back door hot on the trail of Fig and his crew.

"Let me go! Your brother's getting away with our bikes!" Lorraine shouted.

"He'll bring them back, he's got nowhere to go," Hiawatha said, releasing Lorraine.

Lorraine and Hiawatha went to the kitchen and I followed. "Well, they're gone. No bikes, no badass boys!" Lorraine said. "You should've let me go."

"Why—so you could get beat?" Hiawatha said. Lorraine kicked at a piece of trash that the wind had blown in when the boys went out.

"What if he trades them?" I asked. "I heard folks trade for drugs and money."

"He won't do that," Hiawatha said. "Fig plays bad but he's just a little chicken."

"I tell you what, I'm gonna beat his butt when he gets back," Lorraine said in a low, solemn voice.

I sat back down in the same chair the punk had pushed me in. Neither Lorraine nor Hiawatha said anything about the punk that had held me down and played with his crotch. Maybe they hadn't seen him in all the commotion. I took a long breath and sighed.

"We ought to go find our bikes," Lorraine said.

"How will we find them? We don't know where Fig hangs out," I said.

"And—I'm not going with you," Hiawatha said. "We can't mess around in these apartments."

I was glad Karla hadn't come. She didn't know anything about ghetto life. Neither did I, but somehow I felt I could protect myself from the punks that threatened me. In some ways they weren't any worse than some of the men that attended church. Those men and these boys both wanted to have power over girls and women.

While Lorraine laid her head in Hiawatha's lap, rubbing her forehead, I leaned back in my cozy chair and flashed back to a time when another man, not Daddy, had controlled my destiny.

BEFORE I GOT HOODWINKED into joining the church, I was a free agent. Back then Lorraine was often my church cohort. On Saturdays I'd go with her to ask her daddy's permission, and he would laugh and say, "So you two good Christians going to church to be with the Lord on the Sabbath? Sure, Raine, you can go, but I got one question. What color did you say Jesus was?" Not wanting an answer, he'd smile without showing teeth, a smile so wide that the corners of his mouth would press his cheeks against his eyes. Then Mr. Handsom would walk off humming some old song like "The Battle Hymn of the Republic."

Lorraine and I always sat a few pews in back of Mama. She never seemed to mind as long as we were in earshot of the Lord's words. The pageantry of the black church wasn't lost on us—we soaked up all of its drama. We watched with eager eyes at the sideshow that always began with the Minister of Music, Mr. Woodruff McCree, Jr. He was both a music man and a minister-in-training. He played the organ or piano, mindful to use the one that gave a given song the most grandiosity, which meant all his arrangements were festive.

Mr. McCree often wore an emerald and topaz pendant that held his white robe and green satin cape together. It bound the two fabrics around his neck below his larynx. Just as he made the organ crescendo, his nightingale voice fluttered out. He'd hold the notes for as many bars as needed then he'd drop them as he'd picked them up. This drop signaled the choir to begin its short processional from the back of the church. They sang as they swayed and rocked toward the choir stand. Then Mr. McCree steamed up his vivacious voice. He sang a solo whose musical notes moved amongst the choir's clear, clean chorus. By the middle of the song his body was steamed up and hot. Eyeliner and makeup ran from his eyes and face to meet each other at the bottom of his neck in a pool of colorful sweat. The mixture lodged itself on the collar of his white robe. Always on point, he continued to play to the glory of the Lord amidst the puddle of sweat and runny makeup that oozed about his face.

On the fateful Sabbath that I got double-crossed, Lorraine was fortunately absent. After the choir performed and all the hymns were sung, I felt as I always felt—it was time to go home, but the Reverend Thaddeus Glover had other plans.

Until now I'd successfully avoided the invite to be baptized, the offer to be dunked in the pool of water that lay stagnant underneath the pulpit, but Reverend Glover, a new man of the cloth, had replaced the recently deceased Reverend Cecil Campbell at Woodward Baptist Church. Both Reverend Campbell and Reverend Glover were good at getting an invite to folks' homes. Once there they'd eat everything in sight. Over the years, I learned this was a trait was common among reverends.

Reverend Campbell, my first minister, had been a frequent Sunday dinner guest. Mama's heart sang with joyous pride when I recited Psalms 23 at age four while the ham cooled along with the collards, candied yams, macaroni and cheese, black-eyed peas, and cornbread.

"The Lord is my shepherd, I shall not want," I said with the passion of a four-year-old poet. "He maketh me to lie down in green pastures."

"Well! Well!" announced the Reverend.

"I will fear no evil, for thou art with me," I said.

"Speak the gospel, girl, speak the gospel," Mama pressed.

"Surely goodness and mercy shall follow me all the days of my life, and I will dwell in the house of the Lord forever —amen."

"Amen, little sister, amen! You're a good and faithful servant," said Reverend Campbell in his best minister's voice.

Mama's pride for my accomplishment seemed to send holy chills up and down her when I completed the verses I'd learned in Sunday school.

Mama always wanted me to come to the Lord on my own, and from age four until now Reverend Campbell had seemed fine with my soul. So what was Reverend Glover doing when he invited all of the non-baptized children to the front three pews?

My first instinct said run outside and hide until service was over, but Mama, being Mama, lived her life a few steps ahead of me. Her eyes locked on mine hypnotically and pulled me forward. I felt forced to leave the safety of the back pews to come to the front pew where the church's fire and brimstone both laid souls to rest and brought them to Christ.

Reverend Glover stood in front of the congregation like a stone statue of some forgotten apostle from the lost books of the Bible. The good Reverend had arrived from east Georgia. He stood before us in the whitest robe with the fluffiest sleeves I'd ever seen. I could see heaven inside that fabric but the glare produced black spots if I looked too long.

Statuesque, the Reverend stood with a voice that rang then cracked like the Liberty Bell. It rang the sound of freedom that only salvation could produce. His neck jutted in and out like that of a long-necked rooster in a barnyard filled with new chickens. With each point that he made about our pending salvation his neck jutted out more in excitement, then it would freeze to hold that position as if the children in the congregation had said, "Simon says—freeze." Then his neck would pop back to its set point as if those same voices had said, "Simon says—unfreeze." Acknowledgement was what the Reverend sought. A firmly stated amen released his neck each time.

We seemed doomed to Sunday ridicule if we refused the water, but would get public praise if we accepted it. One by one, children gave themselves up to forces unknown, Jesus and the Holy Ghost, for forces known, their parents and the church. I was the last to submit to being submerged in the stale water under the pulpit.

The next week Mama and our neighbor Miss Hazel worked together and sewed my white baptismal dress. Each time I tried it on, one of the pins that held the fabric together would stick me. On baptismal Sunday all of the future Christians, and the already baptized, wore white: the choir, the Mother's Board, the deacons, the reverends, and us—the newly appointed lambs.

Choir Number One, Mama's choir, brought tears to the congregation's eyes on most Sundays that they sang. But on the day of deliverance we found ourselves flooded with more than the usual tears when they led the shaky-voiced, off-tune rendition of "Take Me to The Water."

*Take me to the water*
*Take me to the water*
*Take me to the water, to be baptized.*
*They say I should love Jesus*
*They say I should love Jesus*

*They say I should love Jesus, but do I?*
*None but the righteous*
*None but the righteous*
*None but the righteous shall see God.*

"THE HOLY GHOST is in this place, this morning," sang Reverend Glover. "Now can I get a witness?"

"Alleluia." "Glory be." "Praise the Lord and amen," were the congregation's synchronized and standard responses.

One by one we were dunked in the water as if we were caged victims in a glass box at a roadside carnival where a bull's-eye thrower hit the target with each throw. When I stepped into the water it was surprisingly cold, even hostile. I moved slowly toward the Reverend guided by a deacon. All eyes were on me, as I stood, cold, beside Reverend Glover. He stood facing the congregation. He placed his left hand on my forehead and his right hand on the small of my back.

"I baptize you in the name of the Father, the Son and the Holy Ghost," the Reverend proclaimed. It was as if he were reading me my rights before I was tried, convicted, and sentenced to my watery prison. The Reverend dunked my entire upper body by the small of my back. Water entered every crevice as he discovered that I was heavier than I looked. He found it difficult to return me from the water. The few seconds played like long minutes in the caverns of my consciousness. Was this God's will or a prank performance from Reverend Glover to congeal my connection to God? One divine yank later I was brought back to the surface. I blew water from my nose. As I regained my breath the congregation let out a hearty shout of celebration and the claps filled any space without sound in the small church.

I was never certain if they clapped because I didn't drown or because now I was free from sin. The baptismal celebration forced me to wear all white, almost drown, and to get wet in frigid water, which only aided in revealing my most private parts to lecherous old men and badass boys. But the congregation had another understanding. In their minds I now had my own personal bond with the white savior—Jesus.


WHEN HIAWATHA's buzzer sounded off I knew it wasn't Fig, though it sounded like trouble from the erratic way it was pressed. Hiawatha asked who it was and to my surprise it was Karla, she'd arrived a few hours late but right on time. I went to help her get her bike upstairs. It was easier than my bike because it wasn't a ten-speed. Hiawatha insisted we take the bike to her room, even though this meant the wheels would be on the carpet. In Hiawatha's room I popped the kickstand out, and Karla and I sat on the edge of Hiawatha's bed to talk.

"What took you so long?"

"After I got my chores done Daddy said I could go riding to see you," Karla said. "I didn't tell him you were at Hiawatha's house."

"How long you got?" I asked.

"Dad said an hour but I better be back before he calls your house looking for me."

"That's plenty of time," I said, closing Hiawatha's door. Lorraine inquired from the living room why we had shut the door and when were we coming out. "Lorraine! Take a chill pill. We're hanging in here for a minute." I smiled at Karla. I didn't hear Hiawatha say anything so it must have been okay. Lorraine probably pinned Hiawatha down on the sofa as soon as she knew I was going to stay in the bedroom with Karla.

Karla told me how goofy her daddy looked sitting in the family den wearing a Hank Aaron cap and jersey, both with the number 44. We giggled and Karla fell back on the bed and our laughter grew bigger. I leaned on my side and Karla rested on her elbow. Without ceremony we kissed and without the fear of parents intruding I laid on top of Karla. In the past we'd only practiced kissing and touching but something felt different. We took our T-shirts off and pressed our training bras firmly together. Karla unsnapped her bra and I unhooked mine faster than usual. Though I thought the women in *Playboy* were beautiful topless, Karla was more so—and she was real.

It was official. I was something different than what Reverend Glover said young girls should be. I had broken a few of the Reverend's rules. Here I lay with a girl, we weren't married, and I'd lusted after her beforehand. We wrapped ourselves around each other like noodles while our eyes embraced. A boom sound from the living room startled us and we jumped to find bras and shirts and put them back on. We'd just fastened our bras when the door slammed open. I threw Karla her T-shirt but with intruders she feared pulling it over her head. There I stood with a T-shirt half over my bra. My eyes focused to clearly see the culprit.

"I told you I'd come back to see 'bout you." It was the punk from earlier.

Out the corner of my eye I could see Lorraine and Hiawatha sitting on the sofa very still and calm. In the flash of time it took my mind to ask why wouldn't they come to help us, I spotted another boy with a switchblade holding them back. Still, Hiawatha shouted, "Earlee, Fig gonna beat your ass for this!"

"Fool, keep those bitches quiet like I told you," Earlee said.

"Earlee, we don't want trouble," I said.

"Well you got it," Earlee said and unzipped his pants to reveal his bulge. Karla let out a scream that I hoped would bring the police, but instead it brought a girl—tall, lean, and muscular. She slid through the open door with a pillowcase of items from Hiawatha's house.

Though masculine, she moved like a tigress at night with her prey already cornered.

"Felicia, where were you?" Earlee asked.

"Man—I told you I wasn't coming and leaving empty-handed," Felicia said and slammed the door shut. "Pussy ain't the only valuable thing." Felicia moved quickly to slowly rub her hands across Karla's arms, which were held tight around her chest. Felicia grabbed Karla's crotch and I leaped up like a jackrabbit to jump Felicia but Earlee bull-dozed me onto the bed beside Karla. "My girl," Earlee said. "Way to cop a feel."

Earlee pressed hard on my shoulders while I kicked at him as hard as I could. He kept saying, "Lay still, bitch," but each time he said bitch I fought more. Felicia laid on top of Karla, which made me crazy in a way I'd never felt. "Baby girl, you so soft. Bet you softer inside," Felicia said. Earlee pulled out his penis, which I thought would be bigger, but it was still hairy and scary. He struggled with my jeans as I kicked like a deranged billy goat. "Wildcat, you gon' like it if you relax," Earlee said. Karla's bra was off, though she fought to keep it on. Felicia licked her tongue all over Karla's breasts. "Taste good, too—sweet like candy."

Here we were, trapped. Maybe like the girl that had been raped and her body dumped in the woods near Hills Elementary School. After that, all our teachers had insisted we walk home in pairs. Most did but we seventh graders were on our way to high school in the fall, we felt we could take care of ourselves.

Scared witless, my brain scrambled to know what to do, so I prayed and kept kicking. Earlee managed to get my jeans unzipped. Now on top of me, he jostled his hand down, inside my vagina, and then pressed both his shoulders against mine. Earlee squirmed to get his penis inside me. Once it was, I yelped out a loud yodel that made Karla go ballistic like a rabid dog. Karla bucked up and Felicia toppled over on the floor. Karla kept kicking until her foot squared the side of Earlee's head. Still kicking, Karla's heels half kicked Earlee in the mouth, enough that blood oozed from it. Felicia struggled to get up then grabbed her bag of stolen goods. "Y'all is some crazy bitches. I'm out!" Felicia headed for the door to exit.

The punks in the front room followed. Earlee lay rolled up on the bed with his head in his hands. Karla helped me up and we scooped up our clothes. Hiawatha now outside the door shouted "My God!" when she saw us tumble out the bedroom. She ran to get a wet towel from the kitchen. Lorraine went to get Fig's baseball bat. Bent over, Earlee stumbled and wobbled out the bedroom, holding his head and moaning. By now Lorraine had positioned herself to swing the bat at Earlee's head, while Hiawatha stood with her mama's prized kitchen knife. "You get out of here, asshole," Hiawatha said. Earlee, dazed, mumbled, "Hos," but left, too chicken to even look at us.

Hiawatha examined me and Karla wiped me with a warm cloth while Lorraine paced the floor with the bat still in her hand. I went to the bathroom to wash up. I wasn't sure if I'd been raped until I saw blood in my panties. I'd never seen blood there before since I hadn't started my period. I didn't know how I'd explain the scratches on my body to Mama. Karla knocked on the bathroom door. "You okay?" Through tears I said I was, but I was lying.

My mind ran a hundred miles a second while I sat on the sofa in the living room. A cloudy numbness overtook my body and my head slumped back while the room spun around. If Daddy ever found out he'd say I had no business up in those Dixie Hills apartments anyway. Mama might agree but she'd also want to kill Earlee. But I'd already learned I was on my own. Mama told me that nice girls kept their legs closed and that was the end of our conversation about sex. Kids at Hills Elementary School bragged about having sex, sometimes reporting doing it at school. Still the overall belief in our school, community, even church, was that good girls weren't supposed to know anything about sex.

Lorraine paced back and forth in front of the sofa. Filled with adrenaline she wanted to bust Earlee and Felicia up. Probably any big-head boy or girl in the Dixie Hills apartments would do. Karla sat next to me with one hand on my forehead while the other hand rubbed my back. My mind went back and forth on if I should go home or not, but of course I would, where else would I go? Still I didn't want to go back without my bike.

The booming sound that came up the stairway made me twitch uncontrollably, but I managed to bolt off the sofa and Karla followed. I grabbed a small chair, and Karla got a broom. Lorraine started to swing the wooden bat, and Hiawatha grabbed a chipped field hockey stick. The key turned quickly once and the door opened. There stood

Hiawatha's mama, Miss Lightfoot, with her keys in one hand and Fig's ear in the other. Behind her, one punk struggled with three bikes. The second punk struggled with Miss Lightfoot's groceries. Somehow Fig managed to hold onto the grocery bags he carried. Miss Lightfoot led him first to the kitchen so he could put the bags down. The punk with groceries followed and the other punk propped our bikes on the wall in the living room. Miss Lightfoot steered Fig toward us and we sprang back in surprise.

"Apologize, boy—and do it before I get my belt," Miss Lightfoot said as she twisted his ear harder.

"Ooowww. Ah, ah—sorry y'all," Fig said. The two punks stood in a tattered line and watched dumbfounded from the sidelines.

"Sorry for what, boy?" Miss Lightfoot pulled harder.

"Sorry we took your bikes," he squealed like a pig about to be slaughtered. Miss Lightfoot let go and Fig fell to his knees but he elected not to pray. Instead he rolled into a ball toward his bedroom.

Then Miss Lightfoot turned to the boys in their frazzled lineup. Before she spoke she gave each boy the stink eye. Then she pointed to them separately. "Boys, go home. And if I catch either of you in my house again, I'll shoot you— each one of yah."

As if we were being directed, we all gasped in unison. The punks ran out and didn't look back. They moved like their upper bodies were frozen or stiff like boards of lumber. Lorraine and I both went to see if our bikes were okay and they seemed fine. Hiawatha wanted to tell her mama about Earlee, Felicia, and the assault but Lorraine said Miss Lightfoot would never let them see each other again and I said Mama would keep me in the house forever.

Miss Lightfoot called to Hiawatha from the kitchen.

"Baby, get me the phone book—that Fig lost his keys again," she said, and I realized that's how Earlee, Felicia, and the punk got into the apartment. Miss Lightfoot settled in to use the phone in the kitchen. Hiawatha huddled with us in the living room. "Shit, I forgot they stole from us. Y'all better go. I need to tell Fig what went down while Ma's on the phone."

Lorraine looked worried but Hiawatha said she'd only tell them about the robbery and that her Ma wouldn't blame us—if anybody, she'd blame Fig. "That Fig is scared of Mama, but not of Earlee."

"What's Fig gonna do?" I asked.

"He might beat his ass or tell Cannonball. He's the one they all worship," Hiawatha said.

"Cannonball must really be a badass if he knows Earlee," I said.

"Everybody in the Hills knows Earlee and Felicia. We call them the Crazy Cousins but they're not cousins, they're sort of boyfriend and girlfriend. They'll steal the wings off a fly," Hiawatha said.

Lorraine, Karla, and I sat with our mouths wide open, with this new information we felt even less safe in the world. We gathered our bikes, waved goodbye to Miss Lightfoot, who was on hold with a locksmith, and scurried out the door.


THE SIDEWALK outside Hiawatha's apartment was abandoned. The scruffy children relocated themselves across the street where they played like wild things in an unleashed fire hydrant. With buckets and water guns they targeted each other, and then us, as we peddled hard to avoid getting soaked. With my back completely wet, a throb of pain released from between my legs. I peddled harder to keep up with Lorraine and Karla. At Karla's house I watched as she entered the back gate. Just before she went inside Karla and I just looked at each other—no words were needed—then we gave a wave goodbye.

In my driveway Lorraine held my hand for a brief moment. From under her breath I heard her say sorry. I pulled my hand away fast, afraid I'd cry before Mama got to examine me.

In the backyard Mama stood hanging clothes. Daddy and his truck were still off the premises. There was times when our house sat holy, anointed, and soundless. Unlike when I was a baby girl it now unsettled me, but when the house was in a fury—Daddy fussing at me or arguing with Mama—I longed for no sound. I wheeled my bike quietly and approached Mama from behind, but she turned from the clothesline and saw me before I spoke.

"How was your ride?" Mama asked as she reached down to pick up wet clothes from the basket.

"Okay, we rode so fast near school I fell over in some bushes. I got wet, and got some bruises," I said and I waited for Mama's verdict.

Mama gave me a quick look over. "I see the scratches. I'll put some bacitracin on them. Take a quick shower and we'll put a cold compress on those bruises," Mama said as she continued to hang clothes.

After I got in the house tears fell from my eyes. I wanted to turn back and say that Earlee stuck his penis inside me. Let's go find Daddy and tie Earlee up and beat him down. Let's hang him over the edge of Stone Mountain until he pees and shits his pants, and then let's take pictures to show everybody in the Dixie Hills apartments. But I couldn't tell Mama, and Daddy already said I had to fight my own battles. And I didn't want to be the girl in the news, the one folks pointed at and whispered about her plight. So Mama would never know and would always believe she'd sent her only daughter out in the world to ride her new purple bike and that the daughter had returned to her, save a few scratches, the same girl that had left.

## 6/ PLAYING IN FOG

As the airplane descended, the sun peeped through the fog and it made the buildings of San Francisco glow like some heavenly city Reverend Glover claimed all saved souls would ascend to after death. I imagined the good Reverend had flown to San Francisco for some church convention and decided to describe it as heaven. After all we, his congregation, were country bumpkins who'd never flown in a plane. From the window the Pacific Ocean took on a blue-green color. Nearby the Golden Gate Bridge looked red, not golden. We landed with some thumps, bumps, and screeching wheels, and my ears were blocked thicker than the morning's smog. This didn't look like Eleven Light City—but Mama insisted that was a good thing. Good for me to get away and see something new and have other experiences. I hadn't agreed or disagreed but my heart was not convinced.

Outside our gate stood Uncle Duecer. I recognized him from the family pictures Mama had on the buffet in our small dining room. Although I'd never met him he looked like an older version of the young man in the army uniform stationed at Fort Benning and even older than the kid in a photo with Mama and Uncle George. There they were in black and white smiling for the camera at a country fair. Uncle Duecer was three, Mama was five, and Uncle George was seven. Mama liked telling the story of the Monroe County Fair because it was the first time she'd had ice cream on a cone. Mama had swirled her tongue to lick the cone clean then was shocked to learn she could actually eat the soft wafer.

Uncle Duecer was dressed in nice slacks, polished black shoes, and a sports jacket with a crisp white shirt, he looked like Harry Belafonte with a Clark Gable mustache. At first I thought Uncle Duecer travelled alone. My eyes opened wider once I realized the white woman that stood next to him was his wife Irina. She was dressed in a summer dress, flats, and a thin sweater. They were married professors, which Mama made sure to tell me anytime it crossed her mind. What she hadn't bothered to tell me was Aunt Irina was white. Back home, black men were careful not to look too closely at a white woman, let alone date or, heaven forbid, marry one. All hell would break loose on both sides of town, but maybe black and white couples lived in California. Still it didn't matter who my uncle married but it did matter that Mama and Daddy kept things from me. To them news, information, and the ways the world worked was for grown folks. Children were told things they absolutely had to know, like how to stay safe and keep out of trouble. Still it was the summer of 1976 and I was fourteen, when would Mama and Daddy think I should be told the race of my new aunt?

But Mama had made it her business to tell me about Elsee, Aunt Irina and Uncle Duecer's daughter. She'd only told me to make a point as apparently Elsee was a couple of years older, a straight-A student, and a really good dancer. From afar Mama liked what she knew of Elsee, someone that could be a role model for me. Now I knew Elsee was probably white, just like Aunt Irina, because I overheard Mama when she told Daddy that this was Aunt Irina's second marriage.

Uncle Duecer and Aunt Irina gave me big hugs. He smelled like aftershave and she smelled like honeysuckle. I was taken aback by their warmth, especially Aunt Irina's. Though Southerners prided themselves on being generous of spirit and warmhearted, in other words, know no strangers, as Mama would say, city-Southerners sized up unknown folks before they displayed their Southern hospitality. Perhaps to Aunt Irina we were Uncle Duecer's kin and he'd told her all about us, and that knowledge made her warm and willing to hug an unknown black child she'd just met.

We all walked along the airport terminal. The smell of sourdough pinched my nose and it was at that point I knew I was hungry and already missing Karla. Before Mama sprang California on me, she'd promised that we'd go on our summer vacation to the Great Smoky Mountains and that Karla could come. When I reminded Mama of what she'd promised Mama said, "Yeah, well, the plan changed." Then Mama looked at me directly. A look she held to reassure me she wouldn't change her mind. To put a positive spin on things Mama added. "And think—your first plane ride," which she said with a firm smile that bore no teeth.

As much as California was Mama's so-called attempt to give me a vacation and grant me freedom from mandatory summer school it was also Mama's way to cool Karla and me down, to break the spell of our connection. I overheard

Mama tell Daddy it just wasn't natural for us to spend that much time on the phone and at each other's houses.

When I called Karla to tell her I was going to California I thought I heard her cry. But Karla only admitted that she'd moaned because she felt sad.

"Will you be okay out there?" Karla asked.

"Yes," I said. "You will, too!" I said with a surge of optimism. "Don't go up in the Hills—that way you won't see those crazy fools Earlee or Felicia. I'll be back before you know it." I imagined Earlee and Felicia were swamp monsters and as such they never left the marshes of the Dixie Hills apartments.

Through the airport I walked behind Mama, Uncle Duecer, and Aunt Irina while they talked. At baggage claim Uncle Duecer wanted to know how Daddy would fare at home by himself. Though Uncle Duecer had offered pay for a hotel room Daddy still refused to come with us to California.

"Don't you make no never mind 'bout Amos. He can't always have his way. I wanted to spend time with my baby brother, and Onnie needed to meet her uncle, aunt, and cousin Elsee," Mama said and motioned me to get her luggage off the rolling rubber belt.

In the car the cool air that came through the back window was the opposite to the warmth of the sun, which produced a bright light and sharp blue skies on the drive from San Francisco to Berkeley. Now the fog laid itself over the bay, which allowed me to peep out the car window and see all the tall buildings in downtown San Francisco. Aunt Irina pointed to a building that was shaped like a pyramid except for the two triangles coming out the sides. It turned out the winged slabs were added to the Transamerica Building so it wouldn't fall down. Aunt Irina reported out that the Egyptians are the only people who'd successfully built pyramids. I wondered what they knew that we didn't.

When Lorraine returned from her trips up north to New York City she loved to detail the spots she visited and the buildings she'd seen. Stuff about how far you could see across the city from the top of the Empire State. Or how tall the two towers were of the World Trade Center, anything but talk about her missing-in-action mother. She'd spent her last trip with her three aunts in Harlem because yet again her mother was a no-show. When I got back I planned to brag to Lorraine about the Transamerica Building but I'd leave out the part about the slabs holding it up.

We travelled across the Bay Bridge headed toward the East Bay. Out in the hazy water a few ships sat languid. One, a naval vessel, anchored close to a pier. It must have been filled with men busy at work. Once Uncle George was stationed out here in the Navy during the Korean War. A woman he loved had lived out in San Fran and Uncle George might have stayed except the woman died in a car accident. Now I wondered if she was a white woman. Uncle George was still a bachelor who lived in Eleven Light City and brought us steaks on Fridays after work.

As we came across the Bay Bridge I saw houses stacked on the Oakland hillsides and wondered why the folks inside weren't afraid that they might come tumbling down. I'd overheard Mama talking to Uncle Duecer about how deadly earthquakes could be in California. The glass from the houses' windows reflected the sun and the glare made me squint my eyes as we drove down the freeway.

The exit we took showed signs that pointed to the Berkeley Marina, which excited me. Perhaps Uncle Duecer and Aunt Irina lived on the water. But we turned away from the Marina and landed on their street, Alcatraz

Avenue. I was happy to discover they lived in the flatlands of Berkeley, not in a house made of stilts, but as we drove the roughness of the neighborhood became apparent. At a red light a group of black boys gathered themselves. I watched as they flashed and flipped their fingers into incomprehensible symbols. A tinted-windowed car drove up to the boys then stopped. One boy moved his hands faster than a magician doing a card trick as he exchanged something with the car's driver. The car quickly pulled off. I continued to watch the crowd of boys when one spotted me, grabbed his crotch, and licked his lips. The traffic light turned green and Uncle Duecer pulled off but flickers of Earlee's face pressed atop me tickertaped its way across my mind.

I replayed the long moments I tried to fight him off before and after he entered me. Now every boy that stood or walked on Alcatraz reminded me of Earlee—his sneering face, his ashy hands, his nappy Afro, his musty odor, and his gray teeth. I readjusted my eyes but each time I saw Earlee in the face of a boy. I shook my head and I said to myself he doesn't live here, he doesn't live here, he doesn't live here. Sweat popped from my forehead and I heated up though it was cool in the car. Involuntarily my body lurched forward and Mama, seated next to me on the back seat of the car, clutched my arm and asked, "What just happened?"

Not willing to talk about Earlee or my fears with Mama I told her something bit my leg. Mama eyed me a few seconds but returned to sightseeing. We pulled up to the house and Uncle Duecer jumped out the Subaru wagon and opened the burglar-bar gate that surrounded their house and tiny bit of land. Once inside the gate I surveyed the street and now I saw regular-looking people going on about their business. No boys within eyeshot. Still I knew they were only blocks away.

Uncle Duecer and Aunt Irina lived in a wood bungalow that was painted pale green with a dark green trim. It was larger than the houses in Dixie Hills though the porch looked Southern with four wooden rocking chairs.

Inside the house felt completely different from where the boys stood on the street. Uncle Duecer dropped his keys in a dish and he and Aunt Irina stole a quick kiss. The living room had a small fireplace with a fluffy sofa, and two red leather chairs. The dining room was painted a pale yellow. Framed posters of California nature—trees, vineyards, and coastlines—filled those walls. I could see Uncle Duecer's house didn't have the traffic of daycare kids running in and out. It didn't smell like baby poop and the hardwood floors were shiny and not scuffed up.

Aunt Irina opened a few window blinds to let in more sunlight and I saw them laugh and kiss again. Now Mama turned her head. Perhaps she wanted to give them privacy. But I watched, calculated their gestures, and discovered they were in love. They'd been together five years, married for two, and they were still in love. I searched my memory but I couldn't recall a time I saw Mama and Daddy kiss or hug. No moments where they acted like lovers and just smiled at each other. Once, Mama was a young bride of sixteen, while Daddy was twenty-four. Although Mama miscarried two children they had been married for over forty years. Maybe after ten years of marriage folks stop kissing and being in love.

Uncle Duecer and I carried Mama's and my luggage to a back bedroom. He instructed me to carry mine to a small home office down the hall from Mama's room. I checked it out while Aunt Irina made coffee in the kitchen and Uncle Duecer and Mama laughed in the living room.

After a while I heard a tap on the door. I opened it and

found Uncle Duecer. "It was your Aunt's idea to give you her home office while you're here."

"Oh—should I...?"

"I wanted you to know we're so happy you came. Use those empty drawers for your clothes and make yourself at home. Oh, and Elsee will be home after her class."

"She's in summer school?"

"No, she's in dance class, she loves it. I hope you and Elsee will become good friends. You could be a good influence on her. We'd like that. Oh, we're having lunch soon," Uncle Duecer said and exited.

I listened to the sound of Uncle Duecer's footsteps as he tapped down the hall. He was a spry walker. As I reached for my luggage I marveled at what Uncle Duecer said, "A good influence," and wondered if he'd told Mama. Now I took items out of my blue plastic Samsonite luggage —long-sleeved T-shirts, sweaters, jeans, and a picture of Karla. I'd even packed the musk cologne that Karla gave me for my birthday. I quickly placed my clothes in the drawers. Mama would be surprised that Uncle Duecer saw me as a good role model. Maybe Mama sold me better to other folks than she did to me. From the daybed my eyes travelled along the walls of Aunt Irina's office. Books were everywhere. Stuffed in corners, on bookshelves, in the closet, and stacked on the wooden desk next to a typewriter. I ran my fingers across the spines of the books as if I played the scales on the piano. I looked around and decided I wanted a room just like it.

After we'd sat down to tomato soup and grilled cheese sandwiches the front door flew open then slammed shut. Strident footsteps clamored across hardwood floors. When Elsee entered the dining room, Aunt Irina's mood shifted and I gathered from her folded arms she didn't like Elsee being tardy. At the table I watched Elsee as she half smiled but got a good look at me before she sat down.

"Did you wash your hands?" Aunt Irina asked and Elsee glared back as if to ask, seriously, before she nodded—yes. "Then introduce yourself."

Now Elsee looked at Mama and me, "Nice to meet you, Aunt Susie and Onnie."

Elsee didn't look anything like Uncle Duecer, which made sense he was her step-daddy. She was a *Seventeen* magazine type of white girl with long, auburn hair, a sharp nose, and pouty lips. She looked like Aunt Irina spat her out and I wondered where her real daddy was. Elsee wore a colorful scarf around her neck, a long-sleeved leotard top, and leggings under a pair of denim short-shorts with combat boots. I imagined she'd spray painted her combat boots silver to pretend to be a bad ass like the boys in the Dixie Hills apartments or to drive Aunt Irina crazy.

At lunch Mama and Uncle Duecer talked about the old days after they'd first arrived in Eleven Light City from Monroe, when although they'd moved to the city they still didn't have electricity in the shotgun shack they rented in Fifth Ward. So after Mama did her schoolwork she taught Uncle Duecer how to read the Bible by kerosene light. Mama said that was why she had bad eyes and why she wore glasses to this day. Uncle Duecer said though he missed Mama and Uncle George he didn't miss Eleven Light City and its country backwards ways. Mama defended her city and told how much it had grown and changed. The budding city skyline, good schools for black folks, and how a smart black man could build a business. But Uncle Duecer had the last word on subject when he said he still couldn't live in peace with the wife of his choosing in any neighborhood in Eleven Light City. Mama begrudgingly agreed with a very slow head nod, grimaced lips, and closed eyes. They continued to talk and Aunt Irina listened on while Elsee watched me as much as I watched her. As lunch ended and the conversation died down Elsee did something that I'd never do in a room full of adults, she directed a question to Mama.

"Aunt Susie, I want to take Onnie downtown Berkeley to see the sights. What do you think, Onnie, you want to roll with me?"

Aunt Irina spoke up, "Elsee, Onnie might be tried after the flight."

"No, I'd really like to go," I said.

Elsee didn't look at her mom. She looked directly at Mama and then toward me.

Uncle Duecer waited for Mama's verdict. And Mama, being the same ole Mama, said, "You girls can do that tomorrow or the next day. Let Onnie settle in and we'll see."


A FEW DAYS went by and Mama relaxed into her new surroundings. She'd become as laid back as the bay breeze that eased across the flatlands of the East Bay. Mama's new morning routine included reading the *San Francisco Chronicle* at breakfast while she drank coffee and ate an egg on toast. Now Mama didn't have to jump up to cook for Daddy or me. She didn't have to prepare Daddy's lunch or plan the next meal. She didn't have to change some stupid baby's stinky diaper. Or create a lunch from scratch for a daycare kid whose mother conveniently forgot to bring one. Mama didn't have to serve anyone. Mama was free. She'd only called Daddy once to let him know we'd got to California safely. I noticed Mama didn't stay on the phone long and she even smiled at me as she hung up the phone.

After dance class Elsee again asked Mama if she could show me Telegraph Avenue and when Mama answered, "Go get your jacket and you girls should be back before it's dark." I all but fell out of the red leather chair where I sat reading the day's funny pages.

The walk down Alcatraz took us away from the blocks we drove past on our way from the airport. Still there were sprinkles of frowny-faced boys posturing out on the street. One or two catcalled Elsee and she flipped them off as we continued to walk. "Ohh, come on chica, you know you like it," one boy insisted. I looked back to make sure none of the boys followed us. Elsee was either brave or crazy acting that way, I didn't have enough information to decide. Maybe this was my new normal, looking over my shoulder to make sure some boy wasn't close enough to do something to me. But at least this group of boys' faces didn't turn into Earlee's. I looked back again and saw that the boys stayed hugged up on the corner lamppost and my fear radar lowered.

On Telegraph Avenue we walked past old hippies that played Beatles tunes on worn-out guitars as young hippies roller-skated a jig or two and sunbaked street kids sang along, all while they held out plastic cups and asked for money. I'd never walked on a sidewalk filled with so many people and so much trash and debris. Elsee said Telegraph Avenue was filled with more people during day but at night a lot of the homeless and panhandlers migrated to People's Park. Blocks up from the hippies we landed in front of a shop named Annapurna 1969. Inside I discovered it was a head shop that sold accessories for smoking tobacco and reefer. I'd learned about shops like this from Lorraine's daddy. He didn't smoke reefer as far as I knew, but Lorraine and I had gone with him to pick up loose-leaf tobacco that he smoked in his carved-wood pipe. Inside disco balls glittered from the ceiling and incense perfumed the air. Statues of Hindu and Greek goddesses were strewn in with books on astrology, numerology, mythology, and women's fiction.

A group of disheveled college boys huddled near a glass case where they examined hookahs and bongs. Elsee said they were science and math geeks from UC Berkeley. I kept my eyes on the variety pack of boys. I'd never seen boys of different races hang out together. Once I saw they weren't interested in us I ignored them. I walked with Elsee to the store's counter where a curly-haired boy with a nose ring smiled big when he spotted her. Elsee leaned over the counter and gave the boy a long luxurious kiss. And I thought so much for the guided tour of Berkeley.

"Oh Joss-Z this is my cousin Onnie. The one I told you about," Elsee said. She swung my arm as if we were kids on the playground.

"Far out," Joss-Z said. "You taking her to People's Park?"

"No, that's boring. She doesn't need to see a bunch of drunk homeless kids and high old hippies."

"Hey! They're my family, I still hang out there."

"You couch surf now. You'll get a place soon," Elsee said and looked at me. "Plus, I haven't figured out what Onnie's into yet," she winked like I knew what she meant.

While Elsee and Joss-Z made out I headed toward the goddesses section. Out the corner of my eye I looked to find where the geeks were now. The disco balls that spun overhead near the reefer papers mesmerized them. In the goddess area I spotted a T-shirt of a goddess named Lakshmi, maybe Karla would like it. Mama wouldn't, she only liked characters from Bible stories and the soaps operas she watched. Plus Mama didn't wear T-shirts. Now my eyes roamed over the store to the women's fiction area. Down below was a sign that read: "Lesbian Pulp." I gasped under my breath and put the T-shirt down. I looked around as if I'd been caught stealing. Elsee and Joss-Z still made out while the geeks pretended not to watch. With no one else in the store I surveyed the lesbian books. Titles like *Lavender Love Rumble*, *The Odd Kind*, *Lesbo Lodge*, *World without Men*, and *Twilight Girls* populated the section. I snatched one book up, something about nurse's quarters. I read quickly but nothing happened. Just a lot of talk and no pictures, I thought I'd see naked women like the ones in Lorraine's daddy's *Playboys*. The story moved very slow, page after page of a lot of women looking at each other, breathing deeply, and talking about getting a nurse on an empty bed, in an empty wing, in the empty part of the building. I thumbed through more pages but didn't find the real action.

On Saturday nights Mama allowed me to stay up and in my bedroom I watched *Twilight Zone* reruns on my small black-and-white television. Week after week characters started off normal but would ultimately end up in some bizarre warp of time or place. In Annapurna 1969 I had entered my own twilight zone. Even without pictures maybe I'd buy one of these books. Or maybe not—it might be easy to hide it in Aunt Irina's office. I decided to return the book to the shelf because with a title like *Nurses Out to Get You* on the spine and a cover page with a nurse sporting a lacy bra and a nurse's cap while she pulled up her stocking as another nurse watched off in the distance would be a vision that would either send Mama to the hospital, or me, after Mama finished beating my butt.

Next to the lesbian pulp I spotted a book called *Rubyfruit Jungle* by Rita Mae Brown. I examined it closely. It was about a Southern gay girl like me. It didn't have a half-dressed woman on the cover, only a simple flower.

Lorraine might've discounted it because the girl was white and poor but this story was closer to my life than the nurses running around the hospital looking for empty beds. This one I had to buy. I looked to see where everybody was. Now the geeks were at the counter ready to purchase a bong. I guessed they'd get high in their dorm rooms tonight. Elsee ran over and I threw the book down.

"Hey Onnie, Joss-Z got a friend we can all go party with before it's dark. You want to go?"

"What friend?" I asked as Elsee picked up the book I'd thrown down.

"Oh," Elsee said. "Never mind."

"What?" I asked. "What!?"

"So you got a girlfriend?" Elsee asked.

I hesitated then answered. "Kinda—not really—Karla..."

The geeks left the store with their bong wrapped up in a brown bag. Now Elsee waved *Rubyfruit Jungle* in the air. "Baby, can we take this one home?" Elsee asked.

"Yeah, no problem. I'll tell the manager I took it," Joss-Z said. "Now bring those lips back over here."

I watched again as Elsee and Joss-Z's lips acted like magnets. They were desperately in love and I realized how desperately hard it was to watch them. Something about it wasn't natural. On the way home Elsee was full of questions and answers. She wanted to know how long I'd known I was a lesbian, how many girls had I been with, and if I was truly in love with Karla.

I told her I'd always been this way and that I hadn't ever told anybody though a few friends knew because they were like me too. I told her that I hadn't told Mama or Daddy, though they suspected. And I said Karla was sort of a girlfriend but not really. Now Elsee turned into my self-appointed teacher in the matters of love, like Lorraine had been Charleston's self-appointed teacher in the ways of not being a scaredy-cat.

We sat on bench at a bus stop near the corner of Telegraph and Alcatraz while Elsee looked at my horoscope in the *East Bay Express*. She revealed the real meaning as to why I came to California. Apparently I was supposed to meet a tall, mysterious stranger who'd help me find my way to true love and Elsee was meant to be my guide. When I asked to see the horoscope Elsee tossed it in a nearby trash bin and said, "Never mind, I know where I should take you to meet the right Drag King—ah I mean the right stranger." And she whisked me down Alcatraz before the sun set as I wondered, what was a Drag King?

WE WERE BARELY inside the house before Elsee ran off to call Joss-Z and I went into the kitchen where Mama, Uncle Duecer, and Aunt Irina sat civilized with tea and biscuits. Mama was so unhurried and relaxed it was hard to recognize her. Gone was the perpetual frown line on her forehead. She'd let go of that steely-eyed look produced anytime I returned home but that especially came to life if I ask to go somewhere or do something with my friends. But now in a matter of days Mama transformed herself, and those stale facial expressions and the mad dash to cook or clean was replaced by quiet moments where Mama sipped tea and talked.

"So how was it?" Mama smiled.

"It was fun. Folks sang, played instruments on the street, and there were lots of bookstores," I said. I remembered *Rubyfruit Jungle* was tucked between my panties and jeans. It rested just above my butt covered by my jacket.

"Oh! Bookstores. I see Elsee has rubbed off on you,"

Mama said with her pinky finger pointed airborne while she held the teacup.

"I read all the time," I said.

"Not when Karla's around. Y'all stay holed up looking at each other," Mama said.

Uncle Duecer and Aunt Irina busied themselves as they ate little sandwiches and smiled at each other. I looked hard at Mama. I tried to stare her down but she returned no facial expression, she either didn't care or refused to notice. "Okay then, I'm tired, I'm going to my room," I said and turned to leave the kitchen.

"Your Aunt Irina made you a sandwich when you get hungry," Mama said and poured herself another cup of tea.

I locked the door of Aunt Irina's office and lay on the daybed. I wanted to telephone Karla but Mama said it would be rude to call long distance on Uncle Duecer's phone. Instead I popped open *Rubyfruit Jungle* and started to read. It was funny how a book could produce a sense of danger inside me. Goosebumps covered me as I read and couldn't wait to tell Lorraine all about it. I knew she would insist that some white girl could get away with stuff we black girls wouldn't be allowed to. Still as I read I imagined there must be hundreds of girls like us, maybe even thousands, black and white girls hiding from the world. Maybe most of the gay girls lived in California.

Hours later Mama's ratatat on the office door startled me and I sat up erect. I shoved the book inside my pillowcase. I jumped to open the door where Mama was holding a look of "did you mean to lock the door?" but said nothing.

"Just wanted to say night before I went to bed," Mama said and looked around at all the books. "You know Aunt Irina gave you permission to read any book you want."

"Yeah, I might get one," I said.

"That would be nice. See I told you you'd have fun and see new things," Mama said, excited but with a sleepy look.

I nodded my head and pretended my eyes were about to close.

"Well—go to bed and I'll see you in the morning."

I closed my eyes and Mama left the room. I listened while her artificial leg clumped down the hall then I waited until she shut her bedroom door. I sat and listened for the sounds of the house to go mute. Mama always wanted me to be off somewhere reading books, encyclopedias, magazines, but she didn't read novels. She read the newspaper every day, sometimes the occasional *Ebony* or *Jet* magazine, and on Saturday nights she read her Sunday school lessons. During the week, before bed, Mama read the Bible. She so often fell asleep while reading it I imagined it was like Mama's own version of a sleeping pill. Tucked under the covers with my eyes wide opened I continued to read about the crazy antics of a Southern gay girl into the wee hours of the night.

Each day Uncle Duecer and Aunt Irina took us to see different parts of the Bay Area. We drove across the Golden Gate Bridge and picnicked in Mount Tamalpais State Park. After lunch Mama and Uncle Duecer sat and talked under the redwoods while Elsee, Aunt Irina, and I hiked a few dusty trails. California was in a drought and Aunt Irina said it was important to stay on the trails and not to walk on any green areas, that way we wouldn't hurt the grass or small plants that needed water. At the house she'd also schooled Mama and me on how to use the toilet. If it's brown flush it down, if it's yellow be mellow. Which was a nice way to say if you shit—flush, if you pee—don't.

We'd gone to Fisherman Wharf, which Elsee whispered was a tourist trap, and ate at a no-name seafood restaurant as we watched the sea lions wrestle for the best spot on a barge out in the bay. A lion or two looked just like Daddy with their large shiny foreheads, balding hairlines, and out-of-control whiskers. We also rode a cable car up Nob Hill where we visited a souvenir shop. I watched Mama while she plucked a new penny out her purse. She handed it to the guys that made art with them. Mama smiled broad as she showed me the miniature cable car now embossed on the penny. As we left the shop I wondered why Mama thought Daddy would want some embossed penny from a place he'd refused to come to. We almost went to Alcatraz but Mama didn't like the idea of going to a place that was once a prison. Elsee looked relieved. She said it was a big old stupid rock in the bay and that there wasn't one thing exciting on it.

On most of our excursions Elsee would find a time to be excused to go to the restroom, or say she wanted to show me something nearby. After she got permission she'd find a pay phone and call Joss-Z. When I asked why she called him so much, she said, "We're in love, we need to be connected." Which is why Elsee didn't believe I really loved Karla. If I loved Karla I'd find a way to call. I'd get a roll of quarters and use a pay phone. I'd sneak and call her in the middle of the night when everyone was asleep. I'd simply find a way, if I were in love. I didn't have a comeback for Elsee. Maybe I didn't love Karla the way she loved Joss-Z.

Some days after we were done being tourists and after we'd finished dinner, Elsee, Aunt Irina, and I explored different parts of the Berkeley Marina while Mama and Uncle Duecer sat on bench and watched the sun set over San Francisco. With Mama's artificial leg she couldn't possibly walk the entire marina, only small parts, and I wondered if that made her sad inside. Uncle Duecer sat there with Mama in his typical cool and laid back demeanor. He was the only man I knew who was willing to sit and talk for hours. But maybe he did it because he missed Mama.

Still, when we were tourists I'd watched Uncle Duecer as Elsee made up excuses to call some dance-class friend but instead called Joss-Z. And after Aunt Irina granted her permission, Uncle Duecer's chilled-out manner grew into a furrowed brow at Elsee's antics and Aunt Irina's choices. Maybe Uncle Duecer couldn't reprimand Elsee because he wasn't her blood father, or maybe because he was a tall, black man. Elsee's real dad, Chip, was out of the picture. He was off in some place called Point Reyes practicing free hippie love and living off the land. Elsee said he showed up every two years on Father's Day looking for a gift. If Mama heard that she'd say Chip was a deadbeat dad who'd shunned his responsibilities. Chip's behavior also fell under one of Mama's favorite sayings: "He don't have a pot to piss in, or a window to throw it."

Even with our busy tourist activities Elsee maintained her dance class schedule. One day before Elsee ran off to class she pulled me aside to tell me she'd made a plan for us to go to place called Ollie's. There, Elsee said, I'd meet the mysterious stranger who'd teach me about true love and I imagined I'd get to meet the person named Drag King. But I didn't get any more details because Elsee was late for class. Now my mind ticked back and forth between excitement and terror. I wondered if I actually needed to be taught about love. Maybe that was something you learned as you went—if you loved someone, wasn't that true? I wished I could talk to Karla and ask her what she thought about

Elsee's plan. But Karla might not want me to go. If I could ask Lorraine she would have dismissed Elsee as a lunatic before she had all the facts.

With Elsee gone I canvassed the house and found Uncle Duecer grading papers on the patio, Aunt Irina reading student manuscripts at the dining room table, and Mama sitting on the front porch with her morning coffee and newspaper. Mama looked so relaxed and at ease. For days now, after I'd finished reading *Rubyfruit Jungle* I played with the idea of whether I should tell Mama I was gay. Just go up to her and say "Mama you know what? I'm gay. I like girls and I love Karla. Deal with it!" and then step back and wait for what came next. I'd speculated that it could go one of two ways. Mama could slowly lose it, steaming herself up like a hot teakettle then out of nowhere she'd pop her top and proceed to helicopter her arms around and across the side of my head. Or—she'd have a new attitude, that of the cool, laid-back California Mama, the one who drank Earl Grey tea (no sugar please), and who ate fancy shortbread biscuits while she listened to Cuban jazz playing on the KPFA radio station. California Mama would smile then draw me in to hug her and she would even allow me lay my head on her bosom for several long seconds as she cooed, coddled, and congratulated me for being so brave, so fierce.

I decided it might be the right time to tell Mama because I'd determined that's where the character Molly Bolt went wrong. I figured if Molly had told her mama years before she went to college it wouldn't have come as such a shock when the university called and said Molly was expelled for having sex with a girl. With California Mama alone on the front porch there wouldn't be a better time, especially with Daddy thousands of miles away. Even if

Mama called him and told him I was a big ole dyke he wouldn't come and get me. He hated California and I'd also guessed he was too afraid to fly.

I opened the glass-framed door and looked in Mama's direction, she smiled and motioned for me to come over. I sat down in the rocker next to her. Now I could test the waters, see what kind of mood Mama was in. As I searched the street for stray boys that lurked about Mama started to talk. Apparently Daddy called two nights ago and he was fine. When I asked why she didn't tell me yesterday, Mama flipped her hand in the air and said she didn't remember. Now silence separated us.

I looked in Mama's direction while she looked off toward the street.

"I wished I'd given Karla Uncle Duecer's phone number," I said as I turned to look off in the area that Mama found so interesting. A young mother and daughter walked hand in hand smiling and laughing down Alcatraz.

"Why? Mama asked. "She's not family."

"No—but she's...she's my best girl friend, friend girl," I said and held my breath while I kept my eyes directed toward the street. A group of boys all clustered together like oatmeal walked by talking loud and slapping five. They didn't notice us.

I could feel Mama's beady eyes on me, as she watched and waited for me to say more. But no sounds found their way out. And without words I kept my eyes cemented on the sidewalk with no one in sight. Mama touched my arm and I flinched but that didn't stop her from gripping it to hold me in place while she started to talk.

"When I was young there was a girl at church I really loved. Her name was Ruby, she was the Reverend's daughter. She was pretty, smart, and she dressed so nice. She smelled like a bouquet of flowers. Ruby and me did every-thing together, if you saw one, you saw the other running around church. We were best of friends up until we were sixteen and we both ended up married. But ours wasn't real love, like between a man and a woman. We was infatuated —girlhood love. It's just a phase, you'll grow out of it," Mama paused and took her clutched hand off my arm. I felt a chill come over my body that had nothing to do with the California breeze. I shook my arm to get the blood going. Mama continued, "Anyway, your goals are go to college and make a career. Be a teacher, become somebody. You don't have time to be in love with anyone. I wish my Mama could have helped me go to college. Without schooling, girls in my time got married in their teens, so I married your father."

For what felt like an hour we sat in silence. Mama always decided what I'd do and how I'd do it. She never asked what I liked or what career I wanted. She never complimented me when I did well in school or performed in a church play or sang in the school chorus. No hugs of encouragement, no kisses of affection. Mama hadn't hugged me since I was in kindergarten. Now Mama lifted herself up from her rocker. "I'm going inside, it's too cool out here for me," she said. I watched her as she clopped off the porch. I wished I'd said more. I wished I'd shouted the word lesbian if for no other reason than to have Mama's eyes grow big like flying saucers.

I stayed on the porch and remembered when I was in the seventh grade we'd studied poets from Langston Hughes to Walt Whitman. I was assigned Emily Dickinson to report on. As I researched her life I first discovered the word "lesbian." Folks speculated she was gay. They based it on the letters she wrote to her childhood friend and later sister-in-law Susan Gilbert. In her thirties Emily became a recluse and spent her days taking care of her mother. I didn't know how someone got away with refusing visitors and staying in one room, but that was the part I reported out to my class. I wouldn't dare say the word "lesbian" to a room full of seventh graders. Still when I looked up the word in the dictionary the definition described me, a female homosexual with sexual desires for someone of the same sex. And though "lesbian" sounded better than "dyke," "bull dyke," "bull dagger," "he-she," "shim," "boy-girl," and "funny girl," it still didn't sound cool.

THE NEXT MORNING I stood outside the kitchen and eavesdropped while Aunt Irina explained to Mama how she broke up Joss-Z and Elsee. Aunt Irina said this gave Elsee more freedom, which allowed her opportunities to explore other interest like dance and creative writing. Aunt Irina went on to say Elsee had more friends and seemed happier now that the dreadful, skateboarding dropout wasn't in the picture. I couldn't believe what I heard. I could have burst Aunt Irina's little bubble but that would hurt Elsee. Plus, if Mama followed Aunt Irina's advice I might get to see Karla more often. The idea that Mama would accidentally help me spend more time with Karla made me smile devilishly.

"Morning," Uncle Duecer announced from behind me and I snapped my head back. "On your way to breakfast?" he asked. Uncle Duecer put his arm around my shoulder and escorted me inside the kitchen. As we entered Aunt Irina and Mama both paused and examined me closely. I guessed they wondered if I'd overheard their conversation. They looked at each other while Uncle Duecer kissed Aunt Irina on the cheek. Now Elsee burst through the saloon-like kitchen doors just in time to redirect everybody.

"Onnie, good news, did they tell you? Mom and Aunt Susie said it's okay for us to go to Mama Bear's for the community potluck. You game?" Elsee asked.

"Yeah," I shouted then bit down on my toast with jelly refusing to make eye contact with Mama.

On Friday evening Elsee and I walked up Alcatraz Avenue on our way to Mama Bear's bookstore. The walk didn't yield the usual faces of boys that hung out on the corner of Alcatraz and Telegraph. Instead a younger brothering, a less imposing brood, sat and practiced what might become their profession, talking shit and shooting the breeze, but these young-uns didn't say anything as we walked by. During my first few weeks in California whenever I walked by boys on the corner I felt a throbbing fear that ached inside my bones. Most of them contorted their faces to mimic wild animals like lions, tigers, and bears—faces that would scare sensible people. But Elsee said they were full of hot air and bravado. Now I'd grown used to seeing the various boys on the corner. Though I always examined each boy, I wasn't as afraid they'd try to do something to me. I no longer compared any of them to Earlee or transposed his face onto their bodies.

One of the older boys, now missing, I'd grown to understand wasn't menacing—he was just loud and maybe hard of hearing. He was talkative like old folks back home, the ones that attempted to have conversations from their front porches with people walking down the sidewalk. Elsee said his name was Reuben. He sort of looked like a giant baby because he didn't have hair anywhere visible. Reuben got used to seeing me, he'd catcall Elsee as he sat amongst a sea of rough boys, "Yo chica, what it be like?" But as I passed he asked, "What'zup Li'l E?" I'd nod, but under my breath I took to calling him Big Baby Rube.

Outside the door of the bookstore Elsee said, "This is Mama Bear's bookstore, now let's leave."

"But, I thought we were going inside," I said.

"Hell no—we're not old lesbians or little children, this was an excuse to get out of the house," Elsee said.

Ollie's was only three blocks up from Mama Bear's down Telegraph Avenue in the opposite direction of Annapurna 1969. Outside the club doors the music pumped. Elsee and I were standing and trying to peek inside the club's smoky glass façade when Joss-Z walked up. Once Elsee spotted him she leapt up in his arms like a trained monkey. The usual lips locking and lips rubbing ensued. I watched them for a hot second, and then I scanned the street to see if anyone else watched. If Karla and I tried kissing on the streets of Eleven Light City I guess we'd be arrested, beat up, or sent to juvenile detention. Now I spied a very tall man who watched the lovers. He took one whopping stride as he stepped over the velvet rope outside the doors of Ollie's.

"You kids lost?" He asked with a voice that crackled between deep and deeper.

"No we want to—uh, go inside," Elsee managed.

"Y'all some young things, what you know about this place?" He asked.

Elsee elbowed Joss-Z who gave her a baggie of pot. "Here's our entry fee," Elsee said like she knew what she was doing. "I'm Elsee, this is Joss-Z, and this is my cousin Onnie."

I couldn't believe she told this strange man our names—it wasn't very smart. Elsee was acting like a country bumpkin. Hadn't Aunt Irina taught her not to talk to strangers?

"The name is Brown Elvis," he said as he stepped forward, snatched the bag of pot, sniffed it, then secured it in the front pocket of his white jumper. Now I had a moment to look him over. He sported pink cowboy boots, pink-framed eyeglasses, and a Mohawk with pork-chop sideburns.

Brown Elvis smiled. "You two girls can go inside but the surfer boy can't."

"Why not? I'm the one that got the pot," Joss-Z said.

"For this very reason. Boyfriends can't come in with their girls. That's a fight waiting to happen. You can go cool out until the girls come out. You copy?"

Elsee jumped into action and pulled Joss-Z and me to the side.

"Baby," Elsee said. "Onnie's visiting, we won't get another time. Go hang out in People's Park and meet us back here in two hours."

Joss-Z's face drooped then he frowned, and although he sulked and kicked his feet in the air he still reluctantly left the bar for the park. With Joss-Z gone Brown Elvis waved us inside and I noticed he'd polished his nails Pepto-Bismol pink. In the foyer of the club the music blasted in our ears even louder than outside. Brown Elvis stood close by and I could now see his sideburns were glued on—he wasn't a he, he was a she. Brown Elvis peeped over her pink glasses to survey the club like a periscope surveying the waters off the San Francisco Bay. "It's all types in here, she said. Stay away from the butches—some of those alley cats are fresh out of prison, or just fired from the post office or something crazy. You and Hippie Barbie need to keep your noses clean. Don't start no shit, don't be in involved in no shit, don't smoke no shit, don't drink no booze! Now go on and dance, come get me if there's trouble. Do you copy?" Brown Elvis asked with arms folded and waited for our reply.

"Yes sir...I mean ma'am or sir, yes...yes." I said and Elsee shouted out, yes. Brown Elvis stamped our hand with a neon yellow marker—yellow for No Alcohol. She pointed us toward the belly of the club, the dance floor. Once inside Elsee grabbed my arm and we headed toward the dance floor, pushing past a group of people. Once there I felt like I was in a movie with all the flashing lights and the hubbub. As I looked around I wondered where was the mysterious stranger, and what important information would he or she reveal to me about true love? Elsee grabbed my hand again but this time spun me around. I tried to dance like a regular person but Elsee wouldn't let go, she was stronger than she looked. Now she spun me around in mini circles like a plastic ballerina in a jewelry box. Then out of nowhere Elsee let my hand go and my head spun from dizziness. I lost my balance, fell into people dancing, then landed butt first on the dance floor. I watched Elsee as she flitted off dancing and flapping her arms like she originated the Funky Chicken and the Hustle. A Jheri-curled woman with a light mustache helped me up. It was hard to hear over the music but I gathered she wanted to know where was my butch and could I buy her a drink.

"I can't buy alcohol," I said. "I'm not legal."

"What? Well spot me some green. My money's funny."

Before I could say, I don't have any money, a more feminine woman dressed in a tight dress and heels approached.

"Quovitas! You can't even be for real, going after Fresh Fish up in this piece," the woman said with her hand on her hip and revealing a full top row of silver teeth.

"Now baby—if you wait a minute, this nice young lady 'bout to buy me a drink."

But as Quovitas was talking I'd already started my exit to go find Elsee. I searched the entire dance floor. I went into the unisex restroom, which was dingy and gross. I went to the back patio and then I stood at the bar looking at all the people. I contemplated going to get Brown Elvis when a girl and I locked eyes. I froze in place. She smiled and came over to get water. She reached past me to get a glass and I got whiff of her, she smelled like a cologne sample from a fashion magazine. There she stood with her glass of water.

"My name is Jemma," she said and I wondered if she had a girlfriend.

I shook her hand and cleared my throat. "I'm Onnie."

"Southern accent?" Jemma asked.

"Georgia," I said. "I'm on vacation with my mother."

"She let you come to Ollie's?" Jemma asked.

"No, well, I came with my cousin Elsee but she's missing in action."

"Oh—she's probably holed up in a dark corner on the edge somewhere," Jemma said and smiled. And for a second I tried to imagine Elsee holed up with a girl but the idea wouldn't solidify, she was so in love with Joss-Z. I smiled back at Jemma and it felt like I just cheated on Karla. Jemma had warm brown eyes. She held back her short crinkly hair with a headband. She had on a yellow, short-sleeve blouse and a jean skirt with Mary Janes on her feet.

"You have a girlfriend?" Jemma asked.

I paused before I answered as if I watched the second hand tick down on a stopwatch. "Kinda," I said.

"Oh kinda—how old are you?" Jemma asked.

"I'm fifteen," I lied.

"You look younger," Jemma said. "I'm sixteen."

"How you'd get in?" I asked redirecting her.

"Same as you, with a gift for Brown Elvis," and we laughed.

Jemma was in good spirits to be heartbroken. Some college girl named Susan called it quits. The name Susan sounded so boring and unoriginal, but to listen to Jemma, Susan was hot stuff, butch and buff, like she liked her lesbians. That let me know I didn't have chance. I wasn't a girly girl but I wasn't muscle bound or masculine either. And although Jemma and Susan's relationship had only lasted three months, Jemma said three months in the gay world was like two years in the straight. If that was true then Karla and I had been together as long as two grandmamas who'd met in preschool.

Now Jemma had an idea. "I'll help you find your cousin if we dance first." And off we ran to the dance floor like kids at the park with nothing but time.

Time had zoomed past when Jemma and I finally left the dance floor to get water. The bartenders kept several icy pitchers filled at the edge of the bar. Even if I wanted to buy a beer or a glass of wine the bartenders wouldn't allow it. They only served people with pink stamps. Jemma had had wine there before but Susan always bought her drinks. Now I wondered if Susan would show up and start trouble if she saw me with Jemma. As we drank our water I spotted two boys kissing across the room. As the one boy turned I recognized him, it was Big Baby Rube. He spotted me and motioned his boy to move toward us. Without word I pulled Jemma and ran toward the front door.

"Where we going?" Jemma asked.

"Those boys following me," I said and I ducked down a dark hallway still holding Jemma's hand. Now I could hear Reuben shouting, "Lil' E what's up?" The hallway dead

ended and there was no place to go. Now Jemma and I tried
to open any door.

Jemma yelled, "I found one," and we ducked inside.

Mama talked about places where girls and women
should never find themselves. Down dark hallways, alleys,
or empty buildings, just to name a few of the places in her
cautionary tales. But here we were in a dark room, down a
dark hallway, in a dark lesbian club. The room was lit by
candles and it was hard to see but over in the corner was a
small bar and across from it was two rag-tag sofas that
Mama would say didn't look sanitary to sit on. On one of
the non-sanitary sofa sat Elsee sandwiched between two
men with her short ruffled skirt hiked up high enough for us
to see her red panties. In my mind I couldn't imagine why
Elsee needed to come to a lesbo club to meet men.

"Elsee!" I shouted. "I've been looking everywhere for
you, and you've been in here the whole time?"

Elsee waved her hand like she was on a cruise ship that
just left the shore, then slurred. "Hey Ons-lee these are my
friends." Elsee squeezed them both in closer.

"Susan!" Jemma shouted. She pointed to the person
who looked like James Dean—he sat on Elsee's right. Elsee
repositioned herself and straddled her leg across James
Dean's leg. On the other side of Elsee sat someone dressed
as a dapper pimp with a wide-brimmed fedora. Elsee leaned
in and rubbed the pimp's thigh. In a flash Jemma ran toward
Susan just as Reuben pushed the door open and said, "Oh
the drag kings on tonight? Hey girrrrls." Now Reuben
rushed toward me, I didn't know what to do, so I stood in
place while Elsee acted as if I weren't in the room.

"Lil' E I didn't know you was family! I suspected Big E
over there. That surfer boy is her beard," Reuben said. "Oh
—this is my man, Switch." I acknowledged him but turned

back to see Elsee and Jemma have words. Susan was in between Elsee and Jemma while the pimp woman watched from the sofa. Jemma jostled Elsee down on the nasty sofa then she ran after Susan who'd decided to exit the room. Elsee slumped upward but fell back. Now I knew she was drunk. Reuben and Switch helped me get her up and as we walked her to the door the pimp woman asked, "Where you going Sunshine?"

Near the front of the club I propped Elsee up because she couldn't stand on her own. While there I saw Jemma, who mouthed sorry as she waved goodbye. Susan glared my way and for some reason I winked. I watched long enough to see Susan small her eyes back at me, but now she moved through the crowd headed toward the bar with Jemma on her heels like a lost baby lamb.

At the door Brown Elvis laid into us. "Now how you gonna get this drunk girl home?"

I looked at Reuben and Switch who looked at Brown Elvis. "Man we can't get caught up in this white girl's bull-shit. Her daddy would fuck us up," Reuben said and continued. "He's already told us to stay clear of girly over here, now how I'm gonna show up at his front door." And with those parting words Reuben and Switch disappeared back in the club.

I stood with Elsee as Brown Elvis called one bouncer to watch the door and another to go get coffee from the bar. I wanted to yell at Elsee but she'd just finished spitting up in an empty fried chicken bucket and I thought she'd already had embarrassment for one night. The bouncer returned with coffee and handed Elsee a cup of black, muddy joe. Elsee took one smell and tried to pass it to me. "You heard Brown Elvis," I said. "You need to drink it." Elsee downed the coffee and looked at me like she been given cod liver oil.

But afterwards she looked better. The music continued to pulsate from the dance floor as it hit against the wall. Elsee held her coffee in one hand and her head in the other.

Brown Elvis returned with street clothes on. She'd discarded her club persona but not the color pink. Her blouse was pink and she'd kept on her pink cowboy boots. But I was so happy she'd put on blue jeans and a matching jacket. Too much pink makes you look like a clown or a silly toddler.

My mind first said yes when Brown Elvis offered to drive us home. But my second mind landed on no—it wasn't a good idea. Elsee voted to get a ride but in a night filled with the unexpected I refused to get in a stranger's car. Elsee gave in and we stepped out the club into the fog.

Outside Ollie's the fog rolled in slowly from the Bay. I could see fine but the skies were covered in a slate gray. Plenty of folks moved on the sidewalk and cars drove up and down Telegraph Avenue. A gang of young hippies flashed peace signs as they rustled past us on the sidewalk smelling like weed. One even offered to help us get Elsee home. I guess we looked a sight with Elsee leaning on our shoulders while she wobbled a bit. But Brown Elvis shooed the guy on and he ran to catch up with his tie-dyed friends who would all land at People's Park before the night ended.

Somehow we found our rhythm and Elsee leaned on us less. I prayed we wouldn't find any of the Alcatraz boys holding up the corner. Luckily we didn't. It was too cool to just stand outside. A few blocks from the house I could see the walk had done Elsee a lot of good. She mostly stood up on her own steam but she held my hand just in case. We were minutes away from the house and I had a question for Brown Elvis. I'd already realized Elsee made up my horoscope, there was no mysterious stranger to point me toward true love. Still Brown Elvis seemed smart, so I asked, "Your folks know about you?"

Brown Elvis looked at me and didn't say a word. I looked at Elsee who now managed to stand on her own, but barely, and she said, "Nobody told you to get in her business."

Brown Elvis looked around the street, back at me, then at the house and said, "I don't talk to my mother or father about my personal affairs. I came here from N'awlins to go to UC Berkeley and I stayed. I live on my own and I don't answer to anyone."

I looked at Brown Elvis and swallowed hard then she continued, "Be yourself, live where you want, and you'll be fine. Do you copy?" She asked.

I answered yes just in time to see Elsee teetering up the steps toward the front door, but before I could stop her she rang the doorbell like she didn't have keys. Aunt Irina, Uncle Duecer, and Mama poured out onto the porch. Brown Elvis saluted the adults on the porch and walked off down the street. Uncle Duecer ran past me shouting, "Now see here, Mister."

Aunt Irina asked, "What happened?" and Mama insisted I get inside right now, while Uncle Duecer watched Brown Elvis vanish into the fog. Inside Aunt Irina and Uncle Duecer took Elsee to the kitchen and Mama took me to the living room.

"Who was that man, and where have you two been, and is Elsee drunk?" Mama fired off her questions like a machine gun while pointing her finger in my face.

I took a deep breath. "I don't know if Elsee is drunk— I'm not. We went to the potluck then hung out at the bookstore. And that wasn't a man it was a woman and she was at the potluck," I said and stood back.

A tornado of emotion ran all over Mama's face and when it landed Mama exploded and moved as fast as she could up on me spitting as she talked. "You must think I'm a special kind of crazy." Mama's eyes almost closed as she sprang her neck to get even closer to my face. "But I'm three times a nigger: I was a nigger baby, a nigger girl, and now I'm a grown-ass nigger woman, you can't fool me. I don't know where you been, but I know a man when I see one." Mama had to sit herself down, she'd run out of steam. "But I tell you what, you won't go anyplace else without me. Now get out of my sight."

I was almost free until Aunt Irina came in to tell Mama where we really were. And when Mama heard we were at a lesbian bar she didn't care that Aunt Irina apologized because Elsee had been to other lesbian bars without permission. Mama didn't hear the apology, she only heard I'd been to a lesbian bar. Mama's face fell a few inches as she glared at me. The look on her face was far worse than when she thought I'd hung out with a mysterious black man. Mama looked like the world was ending, like her plan to bring me to California to get me to stop my lesbian ways had in fact been foiled. Mama wasn't the puffed-up mad person blowing out a lot of hot air that she was just moments ago. Now Mama's eyes caved in their sockets as weariness spread across her face and left her ash colored. She turned her gaze toward me, a defeated, disappointed, and sad look. I watched as Mama walked off. And now I listened to the slow clump, clump in her steps. I listened until she shut her bedroom door, and that sound jolted my insides and pinched my heart.

LATE IN THE night after the house was asleep Elsee came

to my room. Aunt Irina took the telephone out of her bedroom, and banned her from all activities, even dance class. She said the No Dance Class idea was Uncle Duecer's. Elsee also apologized, saying, "Sometimes I get a little crazy having to be the perfect daughter." She continued but I tuned her out like the static from a too-faraway radio station because I knew she'd do it all again if she were given half a chance. Once everyone was asleep I crept to the front porch and sat out in the chilly night's air. No one stirred on Alcatraz Avenue except a stray cat I heard purring nearby. With the fog mostly lifted I could see stars in the night's sky and a sprinkle of lights illuminated from the houses on stilts in the Berkeley Hills and for no reason in particular I liked looking at them.

## 7/ DRIVING LESSONS

Against Mama's wishes Daddy taught me to drive. In theory it was a kind gesture, a father teaching his daughter a skill set, yet in practice generosity was not Daddy's strong suit. In the end Daddy taught me to drive in order to spite Mama. Still I imagined he wanted to be my hero and finally teach me something I'd always wanted to do, maybe even offer that learning to prepare me to get my learner's license when I turned fifteen. The Saturday morning Daddy approached me I sat doodling on a notepad on the back porch.

"After yo' Mama and me get back from her errands, I'm gonna take you to practice driving."

I watched Daddy, examined his intent, but dared not stare, ever careful not to ask too many questions or say too much. I waited the right amount of seconds, and then said, "Okay. Did Mama say...?"

"Yo' mama ain't got nothin' to say 'bout it."

I held my notepad in one hand, my pencil in the other, and sat up in the rocking chair. "Yes, sir."

It was Mama who controlled the household and set the

rules in it. She decided when we'd go shopping for groceries, clothes, or appliances. She decided when and where we'd go on vacation. We'd gone to Florida for Daddy to fish, to Disney World for me to play, and to Washington D.C. to see the monuments and check up on democracy. But I guessed us romping off to California was the last straw and Daddy needed to prove he could also wield power.

Once upon a time when Mama and Daddy were first married Daddy controlled Mama, even took up the sport of hitting her—but only twice. Mama said that's how many times it happened before she ambushed Daddy in his sleep and poured hot grits on his chest. Now Daddy saw Mama as his home-base boss because she managed our lives, the checkbook and the household finances, though Daddy's paycheck was clearly the larger earnings over Mama's daycare business. I guessed Daddy had forgotten about his inability to read or write. So when Mama insisted that Daddy not teach me to drive, he decided that second that he would.

I'd fantasized about driving down Peachtree Street without Mama or Daddy. I'd stop when I wanted and do what I wanted. Other times I dreamt I drove Lorraine and we hung out for hours driving all over the city. I could also see myself on a date with Karla, that is before she broke up with me. She said I took too long to come back from Cali. I dried my tears on my pillow after the umpteenth phone call went unreturned and in my fantasies I replaced Karla with random cute girls from school. I'd take one of my new dream girls to see a movie like *Foxy Brown* and I'd hold her hand when the fight scenes scared her. Driving meant I could not only get away from Mama and Daddy, but could also roam well beyond the streets of Dixie Hills.

I stood just inside the back door and watched Daddy

make his announcement to Mama. "We getting ready to go, Susie," Daddy said and paused for Mama to say something. But Mama didn't say a thing and I wondered if she'd heard him. She didn't bother to look in our direction, instead she unpacked groceries from Kroger's and household items from Kmart. She put milk, meat, and cottage cheese in the refrigerator, and saltines, Vienna sausages, cereal, and paper towels in the cabinets. Mama continued to ignore Daddy as he walked toward me unhurried but in an agitated way, slow and deliberate like John Wayne.

"We'll see you later," Daddy said, and flung his hands in the air, then gave me a push out the back door. I fluttered and stumbled down the stairs while I tried to see Mama's reaction. Daddy sped ahead of me, then I heard Mama say under her breath, "Bye."

I watched Daddy walk toward Mama's silver-gray Chevy Caprice in the driveway. Daddy wasn't a traditionally handsome man—he wasn't tall, though one wouldn't consider him short, he didn't have broad shoulders or a spark of charisma. He was average in every way and now that he was older, he had the posture of an old man—rounded back and dangling arms, but if you caught Daddy in the right mood, on the right day, and he smiled wide and big, he would reveal one gold tooth on the right side of his mouth, just like Mama. In those moments Daddy was handsome because he looked happy.

Daddy unlocked the car door and I got in the driver's side. I rubbed the leather steering wheel—I loved the way it felt in my hands. I squished my butt onto the seat and found just the right spot. The air freshener that hung over the rearview mirror smelled of sweet pine and it permeated the car. The fragrance pinched my nose and I threatened to sneeze, but I didn't care about minor discomfort. I was in the driver's seat getting ready to pull off. Daddy sat on the passenger side, rearranged his apple cap, adjusted his eyeglasses, put his seat belt on, and began his list of instructions.

"First thing, put your seat belt on. I shouldn't have to tell you again. Next, adjust your mirrors so you can see the cars behind you. Now turn the key, start the car, and pull off slowly—slowly," Daddy said, looking forward.

But this wasn't the first time Daddy had let me drive. On occasions when we were out by ourselves running Daddy's errands to Sears and Roebuck to get parts for his lawn mowers, electric hedge trimmers, or fishing rods, I'd get to drive around the parking lot. And on quiet streets near our house, Daddy would let me drive the straight ways, but Daddy's broadcast to Mama made me learning to drive official.

I pulled out the driveway slowly, stopped at the end and looked both ways, then pressed the signal and turned left out the driveway. Daddy moved in close, adjusting his body to be more in the middle of the front seat than on the passenger side. He hovered close enough that I could feel his hot breath on my forehead, and hear his heartbeat grow fast and faster. I guessed Daddy had zeroed in on me as a precaution. Just in case he needed to quickly slam his foot on top the brake or steer the car from oncoming traffic. All his activities made me nervous, so I worked even harder to keep my mind alert and my eyes on the road.

At a stop sign Daddy said, "Don't go until I say so," and he put his hands in the air. "Okay, no cars—let's go...And for Christ's sake keep your eyes on the road."

I'd often heard Daddy fussing about his bossy bosses to Mama, "Those ole Mr. Charlies work us like dogs, my colored crew gets the hardest jobs on the coldest nights.

And those white boys don't know a lead pipe from a hole in they heads, but they get the easy jobs, they don't ever get tested."

I imagined Daddy was ordering me around just like those white foremen did him on his job. Still, Daddy was one of the city's best plumbers and when Daddy and his crew landed in the communities of Eleven Light City to work on the busted-up or frozen pipes, they worked boss-free. Daddy must have felt liberated when he traveled the Eleven Light City streets without those white foremen. One day I'd have that same feeling, but without Daddy.

DADDY HAD me drive until we meandered and landed at the Eleven Light City Water Works, his place of employment. "So far you done good. Park here," Daddy said and looked around. "I'm gonna get my check, you wanna come in?"

"Can I get one of those peanut brittle bars?"

"Yeah, iff'n the machine have some."

The work facility was large and impressive with dozens of huge metal cylinders that wrapped themselves around each other like a church pipe organ. Chemically treated water traveled through them out to the city's homes, schools, churches, and businesses. Below the large steel pipes sat row after row of what looked like narrow swimming pools that contained the untreated water. The murky liquid inside them lay motionless and stiff, it smelled like swampy fish water. The odor blocked my ability to use my nose until we went inside the plant. In bold block letters the sign outside the entrance read WATER WORKS INC.

I was surprised to see Daddy move around the building like he was king. He moved seamlessly and without fear as his feet glided across the plant's gray concrete floors. He spoke to a couple of men, some white and others black, and they spoke back, but he didn't bother to introduce me. Everybody seemed friendly. Where were the Mr. Charlies on Saturday? I guessed those bossy white foremen didn't work on the weekends.

The inside of the building smelled better than outside, still it reeked of motor oil and dirt. Daddy's work clothes stunk just like the building before they were washed. Finally we got to an office walled off by glass where an old white man sat at a desk. The old man had a head full of white hair, just like Daddy's, except the white man's hair was thin and straight, and Daddy's was kinky and thick. He looked up and motioned Daddy to come in. Daddy walked so fast it was hard for me to keep up.

"Hey there, Amos. How you doing?" the old white man said, then shook Daddy's hand.

"Fine, Mr. Hambrick, came to get my check," Daddy said and smiled. I stood beside him, but Daddy didn't introduce me.

"Okay, let me look here. Got it. Sign your X so the accountant knows you picked it up. Say—who's this young lady?"

"Oh—this here's Onnie," Daddy said, not looking my way.

"The baby girl y'all adopted? Oh—ain't she cute, just like a brown baby doll," Mr. Hambrick said with a boisterous laugh.

Daddy smiled, nodded, and took the check from Mr. Hambrick.

"Well, I'll see you on Monday. Nice to meet you, young lady."

I faked a smile directed at Mr. Hambrick and ran to

keep up with Daddy. On the way out we went by the candy machine that was located in the back of the cafeteria. I spotted a water fountain nearby and drank some water while Daddy bought two peanut brittle bars, one for Mama and one for me.

On the way out Daddy saw one of his crewmen.

"Hey there, Amos, what you say?"

"Just here to get my check," Daddy said.

"Me too," the man said. Then he looked directly at me. "Well, well, well, who's this little lady—your girlfriend?" The man laughed, slapped his knee, and elbowed Daddy in the side, but then calmed himself down. "Alright man—see ya Monday."

"See you Monday," Daddy said. He laughed too, but never corrected the man.

Once we were out the building Daddy asked, "Do you wanna drive home?"

I walked on the passenger's side and looked over at Daddy, then firmly and solidly shook my head no. Why didn't Daddy correct that man? He knew I wasn't his girlfriend.

"Well, suit yourself," Daddy said. He put the brittle candies in his front shirt pocket, jiggled his keys, and unlocked the car door. Once Daddy was in the driver's seat he paused for several long seconds before he unlocked the passenger door to let me inside the car.

FROM MY FRONT porch I watched pigeon-toed Charleston walk up Dahlia Avenue. With each step one foot threatened to step on the other and I wondered how did he manage to be such a good footballer with two clubfeet? But his feet hadn't stopped him from growing and he'd shot upward toward six feet. He towered over me when he walked up to say, "Hey."

On the porch we sat and studied *Car & Driver* magazine, which his granddaddy gave him after he finished reading it. Over the years we'd learned the makes and models of most domestic cars: Chevrolets, Fords, Chryslers, and Cadillacs; some foreign cars: BMWs, Volkswagens, and Toyotas: even a few race cars: Maseratis, Ferraris, Jaguars, and British Leylands.

Charleston and I had always been natural competitors and we tried to outdo each other whenever possible. Long before high school, way back in elementary school, we would compete to draw the biggest, the best, and the coolest cars. Then we'd rush to color them the fastest. Sometimes we asked Mama to judge but Mama, a born diplomat, never declared a winner.

"Well, Charleston, this orange car is colored nicely, and Onnie, your car looks very fast with that smoke coming out of the tailpipes," Mama said decisively then went back in the house. I always thought she should side with me—wasn't she my Mama?

Now we sat and commented on the cars as they went by.

"That red Mustang is gonna be mine one day," Charleston said.

"A Mustang isn't as cute as a Triumph Six, that's what I want."

"You never saw a real Triumph in person. It's a British car."

"Yes, I have. I see them downtown when I'm with Mama," I said.

Charleston turned to a page in the magazine and

pointed to the new Mustang. "See, I'm for real you're just dreaming."

If looks could puncture a large hole you'd be able to see clear through Charleston's forehead.

After I got back from California, Lorraine busied herself with Hiawatha in the Dixie Hills apartments and though Karla never answered the phone her mother said she was busy with anything from piano lessons to going on outings with her sister Needa. Now I was left with Charleston to hang out with before school started in the fall. Although I liked Charleston, he wasn't easy to be around. He was what Mama called a "fore knower," he knew it before anybody else.

But, when I told Charleston that Daddy let me drive our Chevy Caprice he refused to believe me.

"Ain't nobody gonna let you drive a car. 'Specially your mama's pretty Chevy."

"I drive it all the time you silly boy. My daddy let me drive all over Dixie Hills."

"I ain't seen you drive, and I live off your street. I ain't ever seen a girl drive nothing."

"I've never seen you drive nothing. Where's your car, Mr. Boy?"

After a few weeks passed Daddy took me out to drive on a Saturday morning. Mama appeared to get used to my driving lessons, or she'd decided to ignore us.

Just before we pulled out of the driveway, I asked, "Daddy, can I drive down Dahlia Avenue?" Daddy agreed as long I followed the rules to drive slowly and with both hands on the steering wheel.

I released the brake, then pressed the gas gently to move toward the end of the driveway. I looked down the street both ways before I moved steady toward Dahlia Avenue. A little hill led up to and then moved down Charleston's street. His house was the eleventh house on the left side of the street. As I approached, I slowed to a crawl, then stopped in front of his house. Quickly I pressed the horn. Honk, honk—honk, honk. Daddy grabbed the wheel.

"Gurl, stop blowing that horn. You crazy? And didn't I say keep yo' hands on the wheel?"

"I honked to say hey to Charleston," I said.

Charleston came running to the door and my eyes locked onto his quickly. Charleston glared and I pulled off. Out the corner of my eye I looked in time to see Daddy smirk as I drove up the street. Maybe Daddy was proud of me or he liked outdoing folks as much as I did.

Early Sunday morning as I got ready for church I heard a horn blowing from our driveway. I went to the front door and found Charleston sitting alone in a sky blue Chrysler—he'd planted himself on the driver's side with his forehead shining bright above the steering wheel. The car hummed and purred as it sat idling. Charleston lifted his big head a little higher, then darted and rolled his eyes back and forth as he waved his hand out the window. The insane excitement I saw in his pupils was only rivaled by the sisters and brothers in the church when they'd received the Holy Ghost. Our eyes met then held each other in the knowing and accepting of winners. Seconds later Charleston backed the car out our driveway, and in a flash he turned up Dahlia Avenue and drove out of sight.

## 8 / PINK PIG

The wall in the girls' restroom at Frederick Douglass High School was sandblasted white. Days before, Southern gothic graffiti depicted Eleven Light City in bold aerosol colors. The clouds above the cityscape were tagged "Hot ELC '77." Down below a blackened underground filled with Day-Glo skeletons and dismembered body parts foretold the artist's version of Hades. Laced within this modern day hell was our school's motto: *Right is of no sex. Truth is of no color.* And in the far edge of the artwork were the initials PPP.

Our principal, Lester Bottom, was a nice man who ran a tight ship. Yet, all his kindliness went out the window at the school assembly when he announced his new mission was to find the vandals and lay down the law. Nobody knew anything, but teenagers were notorious for being tight-lipped and secretive when it came to authority figures. Plus, who wanted to be a snitch?

In that same restroom I sat fully clothed on a cold toilet seat in a metal stall. I missed looking at the bright colors as I peed. Unconsciously I sipped Mad Dog 20/20 from a

Tupperware cup. Like a grape Popsicle it was sweet but without the slushy ice. Alcohol rushed to my brain and in seconds I was heated up. Afterwards I felt loose and unfettered by Mama's constant input on how I acted, dressed, or where I was going and who would be there. Between the drops of wine I found solace—brief mindless moments of liquid calm.

A minute later I was forced out of my tranquil state by a repetitive ting-ting-ting. It echoed in the empty restroom and brought me back to the present. Lorraine was flicking her finger against the metal stall. "You better save me some," she said.

For a while I ignored the fact that Lorraine was there. And after a very long pause I said, "Chill out—I'm taking my last sip."

Always needing the last word she said, "'Bout time."

I could hear her fidgeting. I took one giant gulp then passed the cup under the stall. Lorraine popped the lid instantly and drank the Mad Dog like it was water to replenish her on a hot Southern day.

Lorraine had more practice drinking than I did. Mr. Handsom allowed her to have wine with dinner and when I visited he poured me a half glass. "Kids in France drink with dinner all the time," he said. But Mama wasn't cultured like the French. If she found out she'd lose her all of her religion, then with her new freedom from God she'd hang Mr. Handsom up by his toenails.

It wasn't like Mama didn't partake in spirits over the years. She and Miss Dorothy mixed their own home brew in the kitchen, starting the process days before. I was appointed to collect apples from our yard and Miss Dorothy's. Then I'd carry the mashed-up apples Mama had prepared over to Miss Dorothy's house, where she'd boil them up and let them ferment for several days. On the evening they planned to indulge in their concoction Mama and I came over and they'd add their Special Sauce. Mama said it killed all the germs. They called their tonic Lap-rope in order to fool me, but Mr. Handsom said it sound like alcoholic apple cider. Mama and Miss Dorothy shared it as they sewed and gossiped about other members of the Old Folks Mafia.

"Honey child, Lucendy done left her husband," Mama said.

"Truth be told, he tipped out on her first," Miss Dorothy added.

"Well—Jane Lee is heavy on the bottle these days," Mama said.

"Yeah she is. And Inez and Hazel know they ah little mo' than roommates," Miss Dorothy whispered then she and Mama winked and giggled.

I WAVED my hand under the stall to let Lorraine know it was time to go. She chugged the last bit of wine and passed the cup back with a small bottle of Listerine. At the sink I rinsed the cup, then swished the minty mouthwash between my teeth and tongue. Lorraine peed as I spat mouthwash into the sink.

I tied and secured the cup inside a plastic bag and put it in the bottom of my book bag.

Coming out of the stall and reaching for the small bottle of Listerine, Lorraine said, "I hoped you used soap."

"I'm no dumbass—smart-ass," I said as I threw my coat over my book bag and exited the girls' restroom.

The bottom floor of Frederick Douglass High School housed the fine arts classes—painting, sculpture, and metal work. The band, orchestra, and chorus rooms were also in the basement. Mostly creative types ran around but a long hallway also led to the boys' and girls' gyms. With liquid courage running through our veins, Lorraine and I glided passed a group of football boys wearing letterman jackets like we were John Travolta strutting down the boulevard in *Saturday Night Fever*. The boys glared as we went by but ultimately decided to ignore us. We were not girly girls. We didn't show up flashing our cleavage in padded bras or tight blouses, while wearing miniskirts positioned to collect roaming eyes from jocks, band geeks, mad Scientists, preps, chess Club members, pretty boys, or any other boy that ran around school. Yet being understated in our attire of Levis, dress shirts, and sneakers gave off hints of tomboy, which made us stand out even more.

I looked back to see where the boys landed—if they'd try to bum rush us—not that it had happened to us, but it could. I found they'd split off to talk to various girls near the glass doors that led to the gyms. Lorraine and I continued on and turned down the hall headed for the chorus room. I could feel my buzz intensify and I knew I'd have to concentrate as I walked. No wobbling, no unexpected gestures, just be cool and walk straight down the hall.

The chorus was my saving grace because it was the one thing I could go off and do after school without Mama turning into an investigator. The chorus room was always filled with excitement and energy like a Broadway show was about to start. Today would be even better than most because after class we were going downtown to Rich's department store to practice for the Annual Lighting of the Christmas Tree.

Lorraine and I sat next to each other in the second alto section. From where we sat I spied Karla as she came into the chorus room with her new posse, Glory Bug Reynard and May-May Atkins. Decked out in heels, tight jeans, and a see-through silk blouse, these days Karla was cuter than ever. She flashed her eyes my way but didn't acknowledge my wave. This wasn't the first time. After I got back from California Karla refused to acknowledge me when I rode my bike past her house. And she'd told Lorraine and Hiawatha she'd found Jesus, which made me laugh out loud because I didn't know he'd gone missing. God's gonna get Earlee and Felicia for their hateful-evil ways, Lorraine reported Karla had said. And though the anointed church girl told her parents about the assault, she'd only told half of the truth, saying Felicia jumped her on Fairburn Road before she got to my house. Periodically Mr. and Mrs. Lyons would drive Karla up and down Fairburn Road looking for the ghost that raped their baby.

Karla Louise Lyons proclaimed herself an official good girl—a nice girl, a church girl, an anything-but-a-queer girl, which automatically meant she couldn't be my girl. Now comfortably wedged between the high-class Collier Heights girls, Glory Bug and May-May, Karla formed a new identity that included dresses, makeup, *Glamour* magazine (not *Essence*, it wasn't chic enough), and boys. The neighborhood of Collier Heights housed some of Eleven Light City's elite blacks. They were business owners, lawyers, city councilmen, and architects. Douglass High sat smack in the middle of the blue-blood Collier Heights and blue-collar Dixie Hills.

I watched while she and her girls smiled and giggled at a group of funny-looking boys in the tenor section. I watched while she reapplied her lip gloss as the Collier Heights girls amused her with talk and animated hands. I watched until she caught me. Then I stared directly into her brown eyes and Karla turned her head toward May-May, who whispered something in her ear. Then they burst out in laughter.

"Ouch," I said and tried to rub away the pinch Vatray Hathaway gave me as he wedged his butt between Lorraine's chair and mine.

"I'm head of the second altos," Vatray said. "I gets to sit wherever I want, girrrrls," he said in a high-pitched voice that hit my ears like a school alarm. Lorraine laughed, while I was annoyed.

"Now don't get no attitude, Miss Girl," Vatray said and firmly planted his butt in my former seat and pinched me again. "You getting skinny—worried about that girl."

I shushed Vatray when I saw that Mr. McCree, our choir director, had entered the room. He tapped his baton on the podium like he was sending Morse code to the choir.

"Mr. Hathaway and Miss Armstrong we don't mean to interrupt you this afternoon. But the buses are on the way. And weeee," Mr. McCree swung his arm around in two big circles in the air, "need to warm up our voices." He paused. "Now then," he nodded and tapped the baton twice. "The scales,     Me-me-me-me-me-me-meeeeee—repeat."     And we did.

As we sang the scales I thought about Eleven Light City. Mama and others loved to talk about it being a big ole city, but to me it was as small as a country town. How else could you explain Mr. Woodruff McCree, Jr., from Woodward Baptist Church, Mama's church, being hired as our new chorus director? And like country folks he hired his friend, a retired schoolteacher and Old Folks Mafia member, Ms. Inez Du Bois, as his piano-playing posse member. For now I pushed all that away and allowed my mind to flow in between the buzz from the Mad Dog and the musical notes as we sang

"Ave Maria."

Two big yellow school buses arrived to take us to practice downtown. I grabbed my coat and book bag, and Lorraine, Vatray, and I walked arm in arm down the crowded hall. I could see Karla up ahead sauntering like she didn't have a care. In the bustling stairwell I lost sight of her. Just as I pulled Lorraine's arm, and she pulled Vatray up the stairs, Charleston called us out from the first-floor landing, "Oh lookey at the girls holding hands. You little Negros going to perform for the nice white folks downtown?" Then Charleston put his index finger in the air, circling it as he whistled, and the football boys blocked our path up the stairs. These were the same boys Lorraine and I had seen earlier.

Maybe the Mad Dog made Lorraine extra brave, she tried to push Charleston out of the way shouting, "Move, football head!" But Charleston wasn't that little shrimp from elementary school. His once puny frame had been replaced with the son of the Incredible Hulk's and I feared, rightly so, that his brain hadn't grown with it. Charleston placed the palm of his hand against Lorraine's shoulder.

Finding my voice, I shouted, "Charleston! We gotta go —call off your boys."

"You can go, but the freak boy with the mascara gotta stay," Charleston said. He released Lorraine's shoulder and she stumbled to the side. Charleston zeroed in on Vatray who said, "We don't want any trouble." But Charleston repositioned his stance and stood on the first floor landing like Moses looking off to the Promised Land.

One of his devotees shouted, "You shoulda thought about that 'fore you sprayed up the girls' restroom, we don't need no geek and freak making our school look bad," Willie James insisted.

I only knew his name because he'd had it stitched in italic script across the front of his letterman jacket, like Uncle George and Daddy had their names stitched on their work uniforms, albeit for different reasons. I wondered the appeal of announcing your name to random strangers as you walked around school or your job. The other boys were named Gregg and Tyrone. Tyrone spoke up insisting that if Vatray got away with this crime the next thing we knew he'd be in the boys' restroom spraying it up and trying to get a sneak peek at his johnson. The Mad Dog buzzed my brain, but for the life of me I didn't get the correlation of Vatray showing up in the boys' restroom with spray paint to get a look at Tyrone's penis.

Flocks of teens moved briskly by us as if we weren't there. Didn't they see Charleston and his football boys blocking our way? Maybe they scurried on because they didn't want our troubles.

I asked Charleston to let us go as calm as I could, but Lorraine shouted, "Yeah fool!" Charleston went on a rant about how we were still stupid lesbos and Karla had figured out how to be a real girl. And that she'd stopped dressing like a half-boy and running around with freaks. She even got a boyfriend, Charleston announced, which was news to me.

Since we were five years old I'd studied Charleston running around my backyard. He'd grown from having two left feet to being a football phenomenon. Scouts from the University of Georgia to the University of Southern California followed his football stats. Charleston wanted to follow in the footsteps of O.J. Simpson. But something about breaking rules mixed up with his newly formed muscles made Charleston a puritanical freak. And whoever painted up the girl's restroom, or acted queer, had broken the rules, and if he had to break some laws to keep others, that's what he'd do.

So there we stood cornered between the basement and the first floor by half-wit football heads daring us to move.

"Mr. Hathaway, Miss Armstrong, and Miss Handsom—what are you doing? This isn't the time to socialize. Go-get-on-the-bus," Mr. McCree said then turned his attention toward Charleston and his crew. "Oh—are you the football boys who agreed to hold the angels above the choir while they perform?"

Charleston nodded, yes, and I could see some wild plan formulating itself in his brain.

"But don't you have football practice?" I asked. Charleston said they were off for Christmas. Yet, as we headed for the buses I didn't believe for one minute Charleston was telling the truth about anything.

THE BIG, yellow school bus seemed to hit every pothole as it moved toward downtown Eleven Light City, though there weren't supposed to be any. The newly elected mayor promised during the campaign he'd make sure all them were patched, even if he himself had to help. True to his word he went out and filled in holes all over the city. Yet, with all the cars moving on the roads there were a lot of repairs to make. Daddy said there were more holes on our side of town than on the white folks'—because they got theirs fixed first.

From the back of the bus I had a clear view of Karla, Glory Bug, and May-May, all paired off with boys from the choir. Karla sat talking with a boy I didn't know. Vatray said his name was Hunter and that he lived down the street from him in Collier Heights. Karla brushed her fingers across Hunter's shoulder and I decided she wanted to date someone in a higher class. Hunter's daddy was a big-time judge and as far as I knew there weren't any judges, big or small time, living in our Dixie Hills neighborhood.

Karla and Hunter whispered to each other and whatever was said made the new love bugs laugh out loud and rub their arms against each other. Karla tilted her head and touched Hunter's shoulder again, and that was when I knew she liked him. Once upon a time Karla tilted her head the same way when she looked at me. Glory Bug sat behind Karla and nodded with approval anytime Karla turned and looked in her direction. I couldn't believe how open and affectionate Karla was with Hunter in public. From the seat across from me Vatray leaned over to catch my eye then shook his head and mouthed, losing battle.

I turned from Vatray in time to see the bus stop in front of Rich's department store, which sat at the southern edge of downtown Eleven Light City. We exited the school buses and a few security guards watched as we entered through the glass doors. Inside near the perfume bottles I spotted Karla and Hunter walking and holding hands and I wanted to scream out loud. I'd decided I should go say something when Lorraine and Vatray each got an arm and walked me in the opposite direction. Lorraine, Vatray and I walked toward the costume jewelry and watches. As we examined the cases Vatray said his daddy owned a real Rolex watch. I pretended to be interested and acted like I knew the watch existed before that very moment. With my inhibition made dull by Mad Dog, I asked Vatray if they were so rich why did he go to public school? It turned out his daddy grew up poor, attended public school, and had done well for himself. He owned a few nightclubs, financed business deals, and ran around with politicians like his cousin, Mayor Sharp. But later Lorraine said she'd heard Vatray had been kicked out of three private schools for inappropriate behavior long before he landed at Douglass High. Still Lorraine didn't know how he'd misbehaved. As Vatray continued to regale us with his knowledge of watches I observed the security guards as they pretended not to scrutinize our every move.

Mr. McCree gesticulated circles in the air to motion us to round up. He pointed toward the elevators and we walked toward them like he commanded. Several flights up the doors opened onto the Crystal Bridge where we'd perform. The glassed-in bridge connected the two buildings that made up the old and the newer additions of Rich's department store. From the Crystal Bridge, perched many stories above the city streets, the hordes of people below looked like worker ants on a mission.

Mr. McCree cleared his throat and I could feel one of his Negro Speeches bubbling to the surface. "We've been invited to this time-honored tradition. Isn't it wonderful to be chosen to perform here at Rich's Annual Lighting of the Christmas Tree? Years ago this wouldn't have happened to our all-black high school. So be grateful as we practice, and sing like you mean it."


Mr. McCree was preachy about black folks' struggles, but he was right about the invite. Mama told me that Rich's and the other department stores in Eleven Light City had a history segregation and not inviting black folks inside their doors. But in 1938 Mama was a teen and downtown was the best place to shop so she decided to venture there even though her mama, Cora Mae, wouldn't dare. The fear of how she and her children would be treated kept Cora Mae close to the black community of the Fifth Ward. But Mama was young and exceptionally bold for her time, daring to walk inside Rich's though she encountered "For Colored Only" signage each step of the way, from store entrances, in the dressing rooms, at water fountains, and in restrooms, still Mama remained undeterred as she navigated the postings with her task in mind.

The day Mama first visited Rich's she was accompanied by best friend Ella Mae. The girls must have interesting to watch as they entered the store, both on crutches. Mama recalled the vintage glass and gold-trimmed doors, which led to the main room that had high ceilings and crystal chandeliers. Inside there was plenty to choose from with counters filled with perfume, jewelry, scarves, gloves, handbags, and hats. Mama had never seen a room like this except in the movies. It made her think of being on a fancy set with Lena Horne, Dorothy Dandridge, or Ella Fitzgerald. At each counter Mama and Ella Mae waited their turn with antsy anticipation. They waited until all the white patrons were served, even if those patrons arrived after the girls. But when their turn came the clerks' demeanor was different.

"May I help YOU?" or "may I help you—girl?" came out of the mouths of bitter-lipped Southern women. But Mama came ready for battle and adventure as she went from counter to counter and got the help she wanted. Mama would lean on her crutches as she tried on hats and gloves, checked out handbags, or put on perfumes. Those visits to Rich's were where Mama built the habit of combining more fragrances than should be legally allowed. Mama was prudent and able with her monies. She built the habit of paying cash or she'd layaway items until she had the money. Mama's first layaway was a hat she'd wear to church. She came back to get it three weeks later. This time even the sales clerk was nice. Mama and Ella Mae left arm in arm, excited about her new hat, but on the way out a woman entered with her little boy, who pointed at Mama and said, "There goes another digger." He was so young he didn't know how to pronounce the word "nigger."

FROM THE CHOIR stand set up on the Crystal Bridge, we rehearsed "Ding Dong Merrily on High." Out the corner of my eye I saw Charleston when he arrived with his football crew in tow. They stood near the elevator doors. I guessed they came in a car—first-string football boys like them didn't ride on buses except to football games and only then because it was mandatory. When Mr. McCree stopped us from singing an off-tune stanza, I elbowed Vatray and he elbowed Lorraine. Willie James rubbed his fist in his hand and Charleston winked and then sneered.

Mr. McCree beckoned the boys to come over and pointed to the white angels and clouds. Charleston didn't notice their color, he was too focused on punishing Vatray. The cardboard cutouts were stapled on long sticks, like picket signs used to protest lunch counters. Mr. McCree wanted the angels and the clouds to float behind us as we sang.

"That's so stupid," Lorraine said.

"Goofy," Vatray said.

"Dangerous," I said.

"How?" Vatray asked.

"Because Charleston and crew can watch everything we do, they're a part of the performance now."

"Don't worry—we'll sneak away from those clowns after we sing. They won't spoil my surprise," Vatray said with sparks in his eye. In that moment I looked over to see Karla.

She stood off to the side without her Collier Heights entourage, while Hunter talked to a group of boys in the tenor section. I couldn't decide if she looked lonely or sad, maybe both, and I found myself wishing she could come with us tomorrow night.

ON FRIDAY EVENING, after the daycare kids were gone, Mama bathed. She put on her slip and then her stockings. She added an extra pair on both her real and artificial legs. It was cold outside but Mama didn't wear pants, she didn't even own a pair. She slid a dark, eggplant dress over her head, it was one of her Sunday best. I zipped her up. I sat nearby as she powdered her face and placed just a touch of rouge on her cheeks. There was no mascara or eyeliner, but Mama finished up her make-up routine with Queen Helene ruby red lipstick. Then Mama laid out a dark coat textured like pores in black sand. As her pièce de résistance Mama crowned herself with a wool pillbox hat like Jackie Kennedy used to wear, just like the church ladies still wore at Woodward Baptist Church.

I was happy Mama wanted to drive us to the performance, and because we were going together she wouldn't have her usual questions of who, when, what, and where? Mama and I were both excited for the night so we didn't fuss—not even once. Still Mama wasn't the best driver. I was glad that Daddy had turned the car around so she didn't have to back out the driveway. Yet it was scarier to be in the car as Mama merged onto the highway. Cars zipped past and honked their horns because she drove too slowly. But didn't they see it was an old lady at the wheel? As we continued down I-285 I got a full view of the city. It rose like a pop-up picture in a children's book.

After we parked in Rich's parking lot, I held Mama's arm and we walked slowly toward the front of the store. Outside folks had positioned themselves early to get the best spot to hear the chorus and see the tree light up. They stood behind wooden sawhorses that read POLICE LINE DO NOT CROSS. Some in the crowd covered themselves in blankets to stave off the cold, while others drank hot coffee or tea from thermoses. I wondered if their drinks were spiked to help keep them warmer. I would have done that if I could get away with it, but Mad Dog wouldn't taste right with coffee. Maybe Vatray would bring a liquid surprise along.

I knocked on the glass door and a burly, red-faced man walked to unlock it.

"You here for the performance?"

"Yes, sir," I said and handed him the paper Mr. McCree gave the chorus members.

"You're the student—who's this?" the security guard asked.

"My mother."

"She's not allowed—just performers."

"She's here with me and...Mr. McCree said..."

"Listen up—either come in alone or leave with your Ma," the security guard said, blocking the door. I gave the guard a hard look, then turned and walked outside into the cold with Mama. We stood close to the glass doors where there was heat coming out of vents above. Mama insisted she'd be fine outside. Still, I knew that guard didn't have to talk to us that way. Who did he think he was? Mama acted like she was on his side saying he was just doing his job but then she added, "But he didn't have to be rude about it."

I spotted Mr. McCree walking toward us dressed in a winter white cape, a black suit, and a white shirt. He was a bit Liberace mixed with Little Richard. Up close I discovered he was wearing face powder and clear lip gloss. Ms. Inez traveled close by and in contrast to Mr. McCree, she was dressed in a black suit and overcoat—it looked like something Daddy wore to funerals. She was plain faced with nothing on her lips.

Years before, from my front porch Lorraine and I watched Ms. Inez the day she moved in with Miss Hazel a few weeks after Miss Hazel's husband died. Even in my seven-year-old mind they seemed like a couple, close like Batman and Robin. Years later as I rode my bike on the sidewalk I watched Ms. Inez working in their new flowerbeds while Miss Hazel brought her lemonade. They laughed brighter than the southern sun. Mr. Handsom overheard Lorraine and me still discussing the two old women.

"Some women are feminine, others a little manly. And plenty women move in together after they're old and through with men. That doesn't mean they are a couple. It's just economics," he said. But I wondered what Mr. Handsom knew. Lorraine said he hadn't had a lady friend since her mother left.

Mr. McCree called my name and bought me back to the present. "Why are y'all out here?" Mr. McCree asked, as he waved hello to Mama.

"The security guard wouldn't let Mama come inside."

"We'll see about that," Mr. McCree said and flung his cape as he moved toward the front door. Ms. Inez stayed outside.

Mama and Ms. Inez exchanged pleasantries that involved hello and if they drove together they would've saved gas, but Mama landed on it wouldn't have worked with an unpredictable teenager, which seemed impolite and unnecessary but I let it go. I was too busy watching Mr. McCree talk to the security guard who looked unhappy.

Then a tall man in a crisp, dark suit pointed in our direction. Everything seemed cool as Mr. McCree walked back but then he said the store manager explained he couldn't protect his store if he allowed too many folks inside, so no parents.

"Does that include white parents?"

"Onnie!" Mama said.

"I get you're mad," Mr. McCree said, "but we'll have to take him at his word."

Still I knew that if an older white woman had showed up with her child, that security guard probably would have let her in. A funny feeling came over me when I hugged Mama bye. She seemed fine, but I watched as she moved slowly toward the crowd. Mama didn't like being out in the cold. She'd always made me wear multiple layers, touting, "You let your bones get cold you'll get the *hippy gees*." The best I ever understood this meant was if you didn't cover your body and exposed it to long periods of wintry weather you'd get some type of bone arthritis. And now I couldn't see Mama, she'd folded into the multitudes.

Lorraine arrived at Rich's on the bus with her daddy. I ran to the door to tell her about the mean guard, but before I could Lorraine announced, "Your mama and my daddy are going to get a good spot in the crowd." I released a sigh because Mama didn't have to be outside alone in the cold.

Karla, Glory Bug, and May-May walked into the store like they were on a catwalk. The security guards gawked at the girls like they were witnessing water being turned into wine. They were jailbait, black girls who were taboo for these backwoods white men, but if no one was watching these good ole boys would risk jail and turn their backs on the Dixie state flag if they thought they could have a taste of young black stuff.

Karla looked at me directly and I couldn't figure why until Hunter came and gave her a kiss square on the lips. Glory Bug and May-May led a group of others who clapped as if kissing was a miracle. It turned out Karla and Hunter were "officially" dating. They held hands as they window shopped at the counters in the store. Maybe they were looking for rings. Karla showed most of her teeth. She beamed with happiness as they marched around like the winners of *Ebony* magazine's Best Black Couples Contest. A little steam released from my temples as I watch them move about the store.

"Onnie!" Lorraine called. She pulled my arm and walked me in another direction. "Forget her. I hope Vatray brings us some MD2. You need a shot," she said. But before we could go far, the security guard who'd eighty-sixed Mama warned us not to go away from the group and then stood over us until we moved back.

The guards continued to monitor every heartbeat and every breath we made. Meanwhile I watched a freckle-face girl from the north side, the Buckhead High School choir, take a trinket here and earrings there, little items that wouldn't be missed until tomorrow. Mr. McCree had already warned us back in chorus room, "Those white folks going to be on us like white on rice. So if any of *YOU* got sticky fingers, keep them to yourself. I'm not going to be the laughingstock of the Eleven Light City school system with folks whispering I can't control my choir."

Our chorus members were far more afraid of Mr. McCree's wrath than of the police hauling us off to juvie. After Mr. McCree finished exploding like a human bomb any of us would have welcomed a police escort.

Vatray arrived just as we were lining up to go upstairs. I eyed the security guard as he intensely took in every one of

Vatray's moves. I helped him put his gold robe over his head. He looked frazzled— his pants weren't zipped, his Afro was messy, and his dress shoes were untied. Lorraine tied a shoe while Vatray rebuckled his belt. I asked what happened and how he got to the store. Vatray mumbled something about errands to run and was I going to keep asking him fifty-eleven questions and who was I—Perry Mason?

"Al' right, al' right—chill out. You know if Mr. M. hears he'll pull us out."

Lorraine leaned over, "Just checking—our surprise still on tonight?"

"Yeah," Vatray said. "I got some magic in my book bag."

VIA THE ELEVATOR we made our way up to the Crystal Bridge. The glass window gave us a scenic view of the city's lights. Some of the buildings were outlined with Christmas bulbs. Mr. McCree had us position ourselves on the choir stand and I could hear Mayor Jarvis Sharp speak from the street below. Vatray didn't puff up his chest or act proud as I'd thought he might with his cousin the Mayor running things. Nor did he have his usual playful energy—he seemed to have drifted away. As I listened to the mayor welcome the crowd, Charleston and his football crew arrived. They stood over to the side dressed in black slacks and white robes like angels, but I knew better. Charleston pointed his middle and index fingers toward his eyes as if he'd poke them out and directed them back at us. He mouthed, "I'm watching you."

Vatray mouthed back, "Fuck you," and gave Charleston the finger.

It took two footballers to hold Charleston back but I

wished they'd let him go so he'd get himself kicked out of the store.

Once all the choirs were in position the lights of the Crystal Bridge went dark. The crowd below howled and an announcer's voice told the story of the first Christmas complete with the bells and whistles about the little baby Jesus. From east and west sides, and from the bottom floor of the Crystal Bridge to the top, each school was announced as well as the song they would sing. They sang "Silent Night," "Joy to the World," "Deck the Halls," "O Christmas Tree," "Hark! The Herald Angels Sing," and "It Came Upon a Midnight Clear." The standard Christmas carols.

When it was our turn, I watched Mr. McCree for direction as I sang full bodied and fully present. After the lights dimmed Mr. McCree gave us a thumbs up. I smiled at Lorraine and Vatray in the dark. Singing seemed to bring Vatray back to himself because he pinched my arm and giggled. A few songs later all the lights on the Crystal Bridge lit up simultaneously to show all of the choirs while we all sang "O Holy Night." In the first soprano section Karla's head lifted high as she sang. When she spotted me looking she smiled big. My heart stopped a millisecond. In a way I'd been waiting for some sign from Karla that she knew I still existed and that she once loved me. I nodded my head then looked away toward Mr. McCree. As we sang the last note the lights were turned off again and I wondered if Karla's smile meant she still liked me.

We lined up to go downstairs and thankfully Charleston and his crew didn't get on the elevator with us. On the way down I mentioned Karla's smiling, but Vatray and Lorraine agreed she was messing with my head. The elevator doors opened and Mr. McCree made us move swiftly through the department store. Outside it was still cold, I put my gloves on as we stood and looked for Mama and Mr. Handsom. Vatray's parents didn't make the performance. Tonight they attended an event held at the Governor's Mansion in Buckhead. Vatray said he didn't care because it meant he could hang out as late as he wanted. Still I spotted his lips turned down just as he finished bragging.

The crowd outside the store was so large I didn't know how Lorraine and I would find Mama and Mr. Handsom. My worries dissipated when the tall Mr. Handsom spotted us. Mama waved and I saw she had on gloves and a large wool scarf wrapped around her head and shoulders. I shouldn't have been surprised because Mama was the queen of being prepared for the unknown. I looked back inside the store and saw the same security guard looking and still watching. If I could have found the nerve I'da flashed a hefty "fuck you" high in the night's sky with my finger waving in the frigid air.

I noticed a mystery boy standing nearby examining us. He was regal, slender, and collegiate. He was dressed in a sapphire suit coat and sported a Jackson Five Afro. He smiled like he knew us, or maybe just Vatray. I looked at Vatray who couldn't decide if he should smile or frown. I walked toward Mama but I kept the mystery boy in view. the boy ogled Vatray like he wanted to eat him. I stood next to Mama and Vatray moved swiftly to join us. Mr. McCree moved in our direction, smiling, with Ms. Inez traveling in his footsteps. When he reached us his attention was diverted to the unknown boy, waving first then hugging. Before Mr. McCree could speak the mystery boy bragged we were the best chorus and that we'd hit all our notes at just the right time. We were simply sublime the boy said throwing around big words.

Mr. McCree thanked him with a large painted smile that covered his entire face. A stranger would have thought Mr. Mc Cree was being a fake, yet I knew he was just nervous, though I didn't know why. The mystery boy continued on about our great voices I was wondering what made him an expert when Mr. McCree found his manners and introduced him as Calvin Sims, a friend from his days as choir leader with the boys' chorus of Eleven Light City. I looked at Mr. McCree and then I looked back at Calvin and wondered how they could be friends, Mr. McCree was old enough to be Calvin's father. Calvin nodded in all our directions and said hello.

I was observing Vatray as he kept up the pretense of being disinterested in Calvin when Lorraine signaled it was time to ask permission to hang out in the city. Our plan was to stand as a united front with Lorraine as our spokesperson. Our approach was to say less and get more. Don't over-explain, I said. Experience had taught me to spit it out and wait for Mama's verdict. Now Vatray stood at an angle with his back to me. I could see Calvin looking directly at him, while Mr. McCree jabbered about nothing and Ms. Inez looked on. I was so focused on Vatray and Calvin's connection that at first I didn't see Mama's head nod with permission. Lorraine continued on saying there's a large group of us from the chorus and we'll go to Wendy's after the movie. I poked Lorraine, and shook my head for her to drop it. But all of Lorraine's talk about students hanging out made Mama ask about Karla. "She sang with us tonight," I said not wanting to tell Mama Karla had a boyfriend. Just as we exited the store I had seen Karla holding hands with Hunter again, but this time both sets of parents beamed like bright headlights in a rainstorm.

California Mama had shown up to answer yes to our

request but then the real Mama arose again. "Be careful and your curfew is still 10:30 p.m. In the house at 10:30 p.m." Mama repeated. "Get home before your daddy."

Now Mama looked at Vatray. "What about your folks, they gave you permission to be out tonight?"

I was glad Vatray had enough manners to say, "Yes, ma'am," when he answered Mama. If for no other reason than politeness would halt Mama from asking more questions and make her think of him as civilized.

I watched Mr. Handsom gather Mama's arm like a son might and walk through the waning crowd, headed toward the parking lot. I wondered if Mama would let Mr. Handsom drive her car. Though Mama liked her independence she had no shame being chauffeured around town.

Lorraine and I moved to stand on both sides of Vatray. Calvin and Mr. McCree held Ms. Inez's arms and sandwiched her in between. They looked like a variety pack of cookies—yellow-brown, caramel, and dark chocolate. "Well, get home safely," Mr. McCree said and the three of them waved bye as they walked toward the bus depot, looking fishy if you asked me.

Before I could ask Vatray how he knew Calvin, he poked my arm and pointed toward the glass doors. There stood Charleston and crew, who'd waited until we were alone. Now they ran in our direction. Vatray shouted, "Come on," and Lorraine and I hightailed it behind him. We ran up Peachtree Street and turned of running toward some warehouses—it looked hopeful until the street turned into and alley. Not a good idea, I thought, until a warehouse door slid opened and a cute girl leaned out. She signaled us to hurry. Once inside, she and Vatray slid the large steel door closed with a slam then turned the lever and locked it with a click.

I could hear Charleston shouting and calling us chickens yet he was the one clucking like a bird. Then he said, "You can't hide forever Tray-Tray, I will find you," and he hit the door with a bang. We jumped back as the sound echoed in and around corners of the warehouse. I took some deep breaths and wiped sweat from my forehead. The cute girl seemed unaffected. She smiled and pointed us away from the loud voices and the clamor. We walked down a long dark corridor and landed in a back area. Now I saw where we were, the Rich's department store warehouse. We entered a loft area with dozens of large fabric baskets on casters. All types of clothes: shirts, jeans, dresses, sweaters, and winter coats. The containers were labeled Damaged. Return to Manufacturer.

"Hey y'all this is my cousin, Max," Vatray finally said. Now I could see the cute girl without being in flight. She looked familiar yet I'd never met a girl with a boy's name, and I thought it was cool. Lorraine was so transfixed Max certainly wasn't a boy. Max smiled thinly, raised her hand up, and said, hey. I elbowed Lorraine to close her mouth.

Max walked to one of the bins. "Here," she said and handed me a dark blue pair of Jordache jeans with the Jordache on the butt. "These look like your size."

In a million years Mama would never ever buy them. I stood with my mouth flapped opened but managed a "No, no—I can't."

"It's not stealing," Max insisted. "The store is going to send them back or give them away, they're irregular or torn somewhere."

To my eyes the jeans looked undamaged and Max zeroed in on me as I studied her. She had feline eyes, full lips, and crinkled hair pulled back into an Afro puff. I looked down and saw she had long legs and wore red cowboy boots. Lorraine elbowed me to stop staring though I'm sure Lorraine had just snapped out of her own stare. But I had an astute attention span so I held mine longer. I looked Max directly in the eyes and she didn't blink, I decided she was telling the truth.

Now Max gave Lorraine and Vatray each a pair of Jordaches. She told us to put them on—we'd be more comfortable where we were going. I made Vatray turn his head while I changed out of my stupid skirt. Lorraine was the only girl who'd worn slacks to the performance, but she threw her nice pants down and put on the jeans, which surprised me.

Max walked toward another big bin and when she turned I saw she carried three sweaters in different colors. "Izod Lacoste," Lorraine shouted and looked weak in the knees. I wondered how I'd get this merchandise in the house past Mama but then my mind went back to the hateful security guard. It would be our dumb luck if he smelled us in the warehouse from the store and came snooping around.

"Does the store security come to the warehouse?" I asked.

"Nah, the store isn't connected to the warehouse," Max said. "The store guards are gone now and the warehouse security guard is old. He naps a lot."

I didn't want to be a square but I wanted to know how we'd get the new clothes out the warehouse without being caught or running into Charleston when Max read my mind and explained there was another way out, that we'd leave when the old man security guard was on patrol. I took her understanding what I needed as a good sign. She sounded so self-assured I wondered if she was in college.

Vatray broke out the Mad Dog. He'd secured it in two

drinking flasks that he'd stolen from his daddy's collection. Vatray's daddy wasn't around much because he was always working. And Vatray bragged his daddy won the two flasks but lost a pinky finger, still Vatray was vague about how, and the story moved between a broil in a Vietnam Bar and a knife fight with some badass boys.

I watched Max as she pulled Dixie cups from her book bag. Inside I spied her notebook with the initials PPP. I'd seen those initials in the corner of the graffiti painted in the girls' restroom. My mind lit up, was Max the graffiti culprit? How? She wasn't a student at Douglass. And what was her job at Rich's? Who gave her permission to run around Rich's warehouse like a little Christmas elf handing out gifts?

Max gave each of us a paper cup and Vatray filled them with Mad Dog.

"Here's to my cousin, it's good to be the mayor's daughter." Vatray said and chugged the wine. Max coughed as she drank. Lorraine and I looked at each other forgetting the wine.

"It's bad luck not to down it," Vatray said.

I gulped it and Lorraine followed. Then I piped up. "Are you the mayor's daughter?" I asked.

Max gave Vatray a look then she turned toward me. "Yes, but I don't publicize it," Max said and kept her eyes on me.

I eyed her back for a while then said, "That's cool." I elbowed Lorraine. "We won't tell anybody. Right?"

Lorraine looked at me and then Max. "God—who cares?" Lorraine said and held her cup out for more wine.

It turned out some nights and weekends Max worked as an operator for Rich's Pink Pig ride. She loved working the night shifts. At night she could hide her friends as she took the Pink Pig on practice runs. She didn't need the money like the men and women who also worked the ride. But Max liked odd things and her daddy wanted her to know how people, business, and cities were run.

We drank a few more Dixie cup shots before Max led us up to the rotunda—winded and a bit sweaty we exited out where an amusement ride lived. Back in elementary school I rode it as many times as Mama would allow. It was no ordinary ride and folks came from small towns and far flung suburbs to downtown Eleven Light City to partake. The ride sat on monorail up about eleven feet on the roof of Rich's department store. It circled around the largest Christmas tree in the south—a tree that could be seen for miles outside the city. Then it drove itself down one level to Santa's workshop and Christmas Village. It was filled with fake snow, mountains of colorful gift boxes, faux toys, plastic reindeer, funny looking elves and a jolly robotic Santa. It didn't take much to convince me to ride the Pink Pig, but Vatray added it would be more fun to ride without adult supervision. I looked up at the eighty-foot Georgia Pine and as its Christmas light twinkled I thought of Karla. And even with her new high-sadiddy ways I knew she'd love to be with us.

We contorted our bodies to get inside. I sat on my knees, Vatray sat up front with his legs crossing the aisle, and Lorraine lay back with her elbows between two seats. Max fired up the ride and it started off slowly.

Priscilla the Pink Pig had an oversize head, a frozen cartoon snout, and rosy cheeks. She had a perpetual smile that made her look clownish. In back, her butt coiled into a tail. From the ride I saw a 360-degree view of downtown and the ever-expanding city limits. The buzz I felt lulled me into thoughts of Karla. I knew it was final, she wasn't my girlfriend, even though she smiled at me during the performance. Max had also directed a smile my way when we were standing in the warehouse. But, I still couldn't distinguish what a girl's smile meant—does she like me, like me, or does she only want to be my friend? Lorraine said that's why it was best to get them to kiss you. I'd kissed Karla a lot and in the end she didn't want me.

I distracted myself by watching Vatray doodle on a pad. He drew a nighttime scene of the city using chalk. He placed a lit-up crown floating in the midnight skies above Eleven Light City. Then I saw him doodle the initials PPP.

"Vatray, what does that mean?" I asked.

"Oh, it's Max and my tag name. It stands for Pink Pig People."

"Charleston was right. You graffitied up the girls' restroom," I said.

"Yeah—Max and me," Vatray said. I couldn't believe how matter-of-fact he was about it. "The ELC behind the times, every city got graffiti murals."

"Yeah, on abandoned trains and nasty walls," Lorraine said. "The girls' restroom is nice and clean, fool."

I didn't completely agree with Lorraine. I saw graffiti as art, but the girls' restroom didn't need Vatray's help. "Y'all not gonna tell—are you?" Vatray asked.

"I'm not," I said.

"Nah," Lorraine said. "But, go fuck up the boys' room next time."

After fifteen minutes I'd grown tired of the ride, and that was about the time Max stopped it and called us to come down. I still had a little buzz from the wine but it was time for Lorraine and me to get the bus home. I grabbed bubble gum out of my book bag. As we were gathering our stuff Max looked at her watch and said it was best for us leave the way we came, the old security guard was probably on his rounds.

I saw a clock and couldn't believe it was already 9 o'clock. Still, we had plenty of time to get the bus home before my curfew. Outside in the alley Max slid the warehouse door closed and locked it. We turned onto Peachtree Street and heard a loud whistle, then another. I spotted Charleston and his crew speeding our way. Max ran with us and I wondered why. Vatray led the way, and we ran past folks still out in the city. We ran on through the heart of the city and down a passageway that led us down below the city to an area called Underground. In a matter of seconds we stood in front of a building that looked like it wasn't open.

"Where the hell are we?" Lorraine asked.

"It's a gentlemen's club," Vatray said. "My dad knows the owner."

"They won't let us in," I said.

"Yes they will," Max said.

Before we could finesse our way in, there stood Charleston with his three football fools. We turned around and stood there with our book bags and shopping bags, huddling side by side like football linemen before they squatted to play.

"Where y'all going?" Charleston asked, though he didn't want an answer. Charleston and his boys bum rushed us and held our arms even as we shouted, "Let us go!"

Charleston grabbed Vatray, but got more sleeve than arm as Vatray wiggled to get away. Charleston wrapped the sleeve around Vatray's arm and snatched him close then coldcocked Vatray in the jaw. The punch toppled him onto the sidewalk. Somehow Charleston still held on to the sweater without falling himself. Then Charleston leaned over Vatray, "I know you did it. I saw you running down the hall with paint on your hands." Charleston pulled Vatray up from the ground and I could see a little blood in the corner of his mouth, but that pulling gave Vatray time to reposition himself and he hammered his free fist across the side of Charleston's head. In shock, the football boys gasped, then released us at the sight of their reigning bully down on his knees cradling his big noggin.

Max shouted, "You fight like a sissy!"

Charleston slumped up and mumbled, "You want some of this?" but couldn't stop holding his head to actually fight anyone. Vatray grabbed his overstretched sweater and pulled it back over his head. Max used a ripped piece of a Rich's bag to wipe away the blood from Vatray's mouth.

Someone from inside the club must have reported what was going on. The next thing I knew a few folks came outside the dark doors. I hadn't expected any of those folks to be Mr. McCree and Calvin Sims.

"Why are you students outside this establishment? And why are those boys running away?" Mr. McCree asked and pointed to Charleston's football buddies who'd all run off without him. None of us said anything. "I heard high school students were out here fighting, and imagine my surprise to find members from my own choir and the mayor's daughter fighting," Mr. McCree said.

One of Vatray's flasks fell from his book bag and he snatched it up quickly.

"Oh I see—there's even been some drinking. This is a regular ole party." Just as Mr. McCree finished speechmaking, Ms. Inez came out the club holding Miss Hazel's hand but let go just as they saw us.

"I knew it, I knew it," I said to Lorraine who nodded to agree.

Mr. McCree continued, "Quiet, Armstrong, Inez as you

see we have a situation here. Can you and Hazel take Miss
Armstrong, Miss Handsom, and Mr. Wainwright home?"
The women nodded their heads—yes. "I'll take Mr. Hathaway and Miss Sharp home, I know their folks." Then Mr.
McCree said something that made me mad. "And when you
get home take a good look at yourselves fighting and
drinking in the streets."

I guess we looked rowdy, but why was Mr. McCree in a
gentleman's club with a boy more than half his age? And
why were the two old women leaving the same club holding
hands? Then I saw Calvin give Vatray the eye and Vatray
turned his head. I didn't care what Mr. McCree said. They
were big ole hypocrites.

The Old Folks Mafia drove us home to Dixie Hills in
silence. Charleston held his head while Lorraine and I
ignored him. I looked out at the city from the women's shiny
Buick Skylark. I'd get home before curfew but after Mama
found out what went down I wouldn't need a curfew for a
very long time. Hopefully Daddy wouldn't come home
from work early. I didn't want a butt beating to go with the
house arrest Mama would lay down.

The women drove to Charleston's house first and Miss
Hazel walked him to the door. I didn't hear Charleston's
mama scream out or lose it and I wondered what Miss
Hazel said. When the old women dropped Lorraine and me
off, Miss Hazel walked Lorraine to her door and Ms. Inez
walked me to mine. Mama came to the door looking
perplexed when Ms. Inez did something amazing, something no adult had ever done for me. "Hazel and I saw the
kids downtown heading home and offered them a ride. I
didn't want you to worry," Ms. Inez said.

Mama thanked her and I went to my bedroom. Mama
was so pleased she didn't notice my new jeans and sweater

under my coat. In the dark, from my bedroom window, I watched the two women pull in their driveway across the street. They both got out and walked toward their front door. Miss Hazel went inside and turned on the front porch light. And in the brightness of that light Ms. Inez looked in my direction and waved good night.

On the fairgrounds near Lakewood Stadium a few boys parked then turn off their engines. When the red dust died down the boys jumped from their cars and popped up their jackets collars like Super Fly. They stood near their cars talking loud, and roughhousing between swigs from a shiny flask. When they looked in our direction Lorraine and I pretended to be disinterested. It was the flock of girls who arrived in their vehicles and tight jeans that diverted the racer boys' attention. Now they seemed softer as they stood and chatted with the girls.

Lorraine and I hopped out the car—it felt safer with the girls' arrival. I'd tried to play it like one of the cool kids but I was too excited that Vatray had told us about the fairgrounds. I was more excited that Max was coming. I hadn't seen her since Rich's.

Now I watched Lorraine light a cigarette. She pulled and inhaled the smoke then exhaled it into the autumn night's breeze. Though there was no proof to back it up, these fairgrounds had always felt sacred, hallowed, even sanctified to me. I imagined Native American folks once lived here and had blessed this land southeast of downtown Eleven Light City. Again Lorraine inhaled, deeper this time, and I looked off to the city's lights—they flickered like a hundred cigarette lighters at a rock concert. Minutes later Lorraine took the last drag and threw the butt on the ground. With my boot I put it out, picked up the butt and put it in my jeans pocket. I wasn't superstitious, but I respected Native people.

"Man-oh-man-oh-Manischewitz," Lorraine said. "Why you acting like my mama?"

"Litterbug," I said and refocused my eyes back on the city lights. I wondered if Lorraine really remembered what her mama was like. The last time she saw her she was only five.

But I knew what my Mama was like. Still she'd managed to blow my mind when she found real driving lessons at a proper driving school and signed me up. Mama didn't think Daddy was a good teacher, after all he'd failed miserably when he'd tried to teach her. On their second, and last, lesson Mama had almost hit a mailbox with Daddy's fiery teaching methods exploding in her ear. Frustrated but determined Mama paid a whole other man to teach her to drive. She was in her forties then, just before she and Daddy adopted me.

Mama also allowed me to get my learner's license followed by my official driver's license. She even gave me her old gray Chevy Caprice that had been collecting dust in the backyard, but when I petitioned to have my curfew extended to twelve thirty Mama's mouth grew tight lipped and she insisted nothing good happened after midnight. "You'll get to be out until eleven, then you have thirty minutes to get home."

Still, I guessed Mama wanted her girl child to have the

ability and the skills to be able to take care of herself. To drive a car to safety if need be. Now that I was bona fide, I was also available to drive Mama to the store on Saturdays and to church on Sundays. Maybe this was what folks meant when they said something was a win-win. And maybe the other saying Mama liked applied here, too, you don't get something for nothing.

Vatray and Max still hadn't arrived, but others had come. The racer boys walked with their girlfriends and visited other cars. I could smell reefer in the air. Lorraine moaned, "If you weren't in such a hurry to see that girl we'd have something to drink."

I looked in the other direction as Lorraine lamented. We'd sort of graduated from Mad Dog to drinking Manischewitz, it cost a little more yet it was still cheap enough for me to afford between my allowance and the money I earned running errands for the women in the Old Folks Mafia. Plus, Manischewitz tasted more like wine than Mad Dog's grape Popsicle. It tasted like the grown folks' communion wine Lorraine and I had snuck and drank at church.

Getting wine wasn't always easy. Mama and Daddy didn't keep spirits in the house. Daddy had stopped drinking whiskey and wine because it made him paranoid. In his younger days, on Saturdays after Daddy got good and liquored up, he liked to play cards. If he suspected some guy cheated, he'd fight. He'd even thrown several men off porches in his younger days. Mama warned Daddy if he didn't stop drinking he'd end up in jail. So now every now and again Daddy had a beer while he and Uncle Robert cut hair, but he'd stopped playing cards all together.

Lorraine used to supply us with drinks but had to stop stealing wine from her daddy's liquor cabinet. He was getting suspicious of how much his poker buddies actually drank. Cab Handsom even wondered out loud if his friends were stealing his supply.

In order to get wine we relied on winos or college students outside liquors stores. College students were known for running off with your money, and sometimes the wine. So we choose the winos that looked the most decent. With enlarged bellies and swollen lips they walked like pet zombies to purchase our wine and get themselves a treat. So far Lorraine and I had been lucky. Though we never got change back, we didn't expect to. We gave the winos enough for our purchase and what was left over was theirs. I guess there was some honor among certain drunks. But tonight I'd been too thrilled to stop for wine and now Lorraine poked out her bottom lip as we watched the growing crowd.

From off in the distance a sound came tumbling toward us, it was a cross between a foghorn and a cow in distress. It made me think of the San Francisco Bay and the horns that set off as the fog rolled in. But in landlocked Eleven Light City the only bay was a bay of pine trees you could find looking in most directions.

Charleston came barreling up on two wheels in his old Dodge Charger with a Model T horn he'd found in a junk-yard on the west side of town. These days Charleston was the co-captain and a high school All-American. He had his pick of colleges and universities from around the country, and a gaggle of girls from around the way—all of whom wanted a piece of his success.

Charleston jumped out of his Charger with his new set of football boys—his old crew had graduated. He walked toward us in a leather-sleeved letterman jacket with the number eleven, strutting like he was John Shaft.

"What's happening, dudettes?" Charleston asked and

raised his hands to get a high five, but Lorraine and I ignored him. Once he realized we weren't going to high five him he turned to his boys who were happy to do so. Now Charleston wrapped his arms around me tightly but released me as quickly as he grabbed me before saying, "You know you love Charlie Rockets." Popping the collar of his jacket, he now directed his energy toward Lorraine.

"Raine, don't act all high saditty. That Rich's stuff was last year—its 1978." Charleston went in quick for a hug. Lorraine tried to get away but Charleston held on to show he could. Seconds later he let go, smiled big, elbowed his football buddies, and laughed. "Who told y'all told about the races?" he asked but Lorraine and I acted like we didn't hear him. Charleston studied our faces then he laughed louder this time. "Oh, y'all don't know what's going down!"

Charleston walked toward the gate that locked the race-track of the fairgrounds. He pulled out a tool I'd never seen before and went to work on the padlock. Three deep breaths and a few clicks later, the lock was on the ground. I couldn't hide my shock. "Now you two baby chicks are in for a surprise. This is a Cannonball Affair. Welcome to the circus, girls."

I didn't know Cannonball but I'd heard rumors and conflicting urban tales. Some said he stood six feet eleven inches but didn't know how to play basketball. Others said he'd killed the kingpin who showed him how to racketeer, and that he'd done it with his blazing eyeballs. Others said his mama and daddy raced cars back in the day and that's how he'd learned to sponsor races. What I knew for sure was kids feared Cannonball and if he was coming, then Hiawatha's brother Fig might be on his tail, and Earlee and Felicia after that.

More cars came until I counted twenty-five. Charleston

directed the drivers who wanted to race to park on the other side of his Charger. Lorraine and I wondered out loud when did Charleston get in charge? We both shrugged our shoulders because neither one of us knew the answer. A few more cars came and Lorraine and I eyed up a kitted-out white Chevy Camaro with tinted windows and wire hubcaps. The car drove over to us and as the electric windows zipped down, Vatray's head popped out. I leaned down to talk and discovered Max was behind the wheel. Vatray rolled out the car door shouting, heeeyyy. His body swayed like a drunken dragonfly.

Max parked the car and when she walked over Lorraine stood up a little taller. "Hey Onnie," Max said and my heart sped up. I felt special because she remembered my name. Lorraine cut her eyes my way as she waited for Max to say something to her. When she didn't, Lorraine jumped in Max's path and said, "Oh remember me, from the Pink Pig? The night we sang at the lighting of the Christmas tree. You gave me an Izod shirt and pair of jeans." And just like a kindergartner Lorraine stood even taller as she waited to be acknowledged.

"Oh yes, I remember," Max said. "Hello."

I saw Lorraine's whole chest deflate when that was all Max had to say. Now Vatray elbowed me and I spoke up.

"It's nice to see you again," I said smiling and showing more teeth than was necessary.

"I ask Vatray about you all the time." Max said.

My smile grew bigger, a bit out of control, but somehow I managed to close my mouth. I wanted to ask Vatray if he had some brew left over but my mind got jumbled up on if Max was being polite or if she liked me. I didn't have anything to go on. I'd never experienced a girl flirting. Karla and I knew we liked each other. Plus when we started our kissing game in the backyard we were seven years old and didn't know to flirt.

Charleston instructed the racers to line up in order. He'd laid out on a large chalkboard with who would race and when. A crowd of racer boys looked to find their names and ran off to line up their cars. Now Charleston shouted, "Let's get this show on the road!"

With Charleston heading things up for the drag race Vatray went to get the flags out of Max's car. It appeared that Vatray and Max also worked for Cannonball. I wondered if Vatray had really forgiven Charleston for chasing, grabbing, and hitting him in the mouth. Maybe Cannonball had smoothed the waters.

I walked through the crowd to move my car to the nonracer side when I overheard a boy say, "I guess there won't be no mess if we're all from Douglass High."

Another boy answered, "There won't be no mess period —this here is a Cannonball event. He's got his security boys mixed in the crowd."

I told Lorraine what I'd overheard. "Cannonball ain't gonna show up to this sideshow. And that Fig still ah asshole without a car—how he gonna get here? And nobody's seen Earlee or Felicia. Folks say they both in jail."

"Jail! You never told me that," I said.

"You know the gossip mill up in the Hills. Who knows what's what," Lorraine said.

Maybe Karla was right. Maybe God got Earlee and Felicia for their evil ways. But it was more like they got themselves in trouble. Stupid criminals seem to eventually get caught. Now I released a sigh of relief. I guessed Cannonball recruited some new boys that included Charleston. I hoped Charleston knew what he was getting into.

Moments later, unannounced, the mystery boy from after the chorus performance at Rich's department store showed up. Calvin Sims stepped out of his old '67 Mustang ragtop. He looked like a well-groomed man from the pages of *Ebony* magazine. Though his car was sporty, it needed a paint job. Calvin wore a camel wool jacket with nice dark trousers and Stacy Adams shoes. I wondered if he knew the fairgrounds were dusty, and why was he here? I watched Calvin as he walked in my direction. I felt slightly enchanted, as he seemed to look at me, though I didn't know why. He landed next to Max and gave her a big kiss directly on her lips, which he followed up with a hug. Vatray stood nearby not making eye contact. Next Calvin did a dude-style handshake to greet Vatray. As Calvin turned to walk away he slapped Vatray on the shoulder, which almost toppled Vatray over. Lorraine and I looked at each other with what the hell eyes. It's hard to put a puzzle together with missing pieces. One piece of that puzzle I hadn't foreseen was Max and Calvin were a couple. Why else would he kiss her like that? And now I also knew I couldn't compete. Who could? So Max was only being friendly after all.

Vatray came over like nothing was fishy with two flags in his back jean pockets. He even gave us a big ole fake smile as he wobbled his head to keep it aligned with his body. Before I could ask, Vatray offered that he'd known Calvin Sims forever, from way back when they were in the Eleven Light City boys' choir. It turned out Mr. McCree was their director. And I thought, of course he was, Mr. McCree sure did get around.

"You could've said so at Rich's," I said.

"Too much was happening," Vatray said. "I'm telling you now."

While Lorraine and I stood examining Vatray I over-heard Charleston talking to one of the security boys and he referred to Calvin as Cannonball. I hadn't had a drop to drink, so I knew what I heard. This was crazy talk. How in the world could Calvin be the legendary Cannonball? Now the alleged Cannonball walked across the dusty fairgrounds just like a regular person. Nothing extra. My mind spun and spun around like a dust storm—maybe he was some alien beast dressed in a man's skin. That's it, he was made to look everyday, but a creature lived inside. With the dust kicking up fierce on the fairgrounds I imagined we'd been dropped at the O.K. Corral or into some gun-slinging Western town like Dodge City. Guns should have been blazing because the badass of them all stood nearby, but this legend had fallen short, like every other hullabaloo that blew up in Eleven Light City. Seeing him walking around made it all deflate even faster in front of my eyes. The mystery man Calvin "Cannonball" Sims wasn't a gangster, didn't have flaming eyeballs, and wasn't six feet eleven inches tall. He was a regular dude who wasn't scary and didn't even look crazy.

It clicked for me then, this was the stuff I hated about Eleven Light City, it was this closed-off world where nothing and nobody was new, somehow everybody was recycled from one side of town to the other. Calvin and Max walked our way. I could see that Calvin was some years older than us, maybe a sophomore in college, maybe a junior. Calvin smiled as he walked past Lorraine, Vatray, and me arm in arm with Max. They looked a bit like royalty. The crowd parted like the Red Sea and they walked through as if it were a Soul Train line but without the boogie-down dancing.

Charleston stood listening to Cannonball's instructions though he allowed his eyes to wander over and watch Lorraine, Vatray, and me. Max motioned Vatray over and he gave her the flags and from out of nowhere some of Cannonball's big muscle boys came and stood in front of the lined-up cars. I could see Charleston was third in line. I hoped he'd do well, even if he was a thorn in my side, and a competitive imp.

"Baby girl, let the games began," Cannonball shouted over the crowd. Max dropped the flags down and the two cars at the starting line struck off and kicked up so much dirt I was glad I wasn't up front. With flashlights at the end of the track, one of Cannonball's boys flashed a simple code: one flash if the left car won and two flashes for the right. Charleston won his first round, but he came over to us complaining that the track was too slick. Even Lorraine got in on the act by agreeing with Charleston. This was the first time I could remember them agreeing on anything and it was spooky to watch.

Charleston continued to run his mouth and Lorraine stood by his side as Vatray hung back to listen. I tried to catch Vatray's eyes and motion him to come over, but he ignored me. Cannonball came over and started talking.

"Good round, Charlie Rockets," Cannonball said. "Now get ready for the next one." And off Charleston went to line up his car. Lorraine decided to watch the race closer to the finish line. Vatray's face looked like he needed to release steam from his eyeballs and eardrums, still he and Max helped Cannonball collect money from bets, while a set of muscle boys walked around with them. From the looks of it they would make money.

Charleston rolled his car up for his second round and I watched from the sideline. That was when Cannonball came over to talk.

"Hey, Onnie Armstrong, right?" Cannonball said, revealing a row of perfect teeth. The tone of his voice was smooth, it reminded me of Billy Dee Williams. His half-hearted politeness unsettled me, and the bass in his voice echoed in my ears like Darth Vader's, but mostly Cannonball freaked me out because he just walked up on me like he knew me.

"Hey Calvin, I mean Cannonball," I said and took two steps back.

"Just Cannonball," he said. "Vatray told me you're a great driver, you drive fast around the student parking lot and without fear. And you live near Charlie Rockets, right? Well, we're always looking for good drivers. I'd like a girl to challenge these knuckleheads." I froze and didn't say anything. "Let me know if you're interested," he said and strolled away like he'd offered me bubble gum.

Cheers from the crowd and honks from car horns over-took my senses. The noise even tried to take away all of what Cannonball said. I saw Lorraine high five Charleston. She ran over, shouting that Charleston had won the whole damn thing, and was I really talking to Cannonball?

"Yes," I said. "And he offered me a job—racing cars."

I watched Cannonball drive away with a group of muscle boys. Charleston came over with Max.

"So he asked you, huh?

"Yeah," I said.

"You still don't know what's happening," Charleston said with a devilish smile and walked off. I watched him get in his Charger and he drove off with his boys.

Max put her arms around my shoulders and said, "He's

just a giant crybaby. I bet you'd be a great racer." I couldn't think about racing because I couldn't stop thinking that Max was touching me, how good it felt, and how much I liked it.

As I DROVE up the wooded road that led to the fairgrounds I spotted an old man walking. In his hand he jiggled a large rope of keys that dangled from his pants pocket. Instead of seeing if he needed help I ducked my head down and sped up. In my mind I felt he'd be all right, maybe he was looking for his car. When I arrived at the racetrack, Charleston, Vatray, and Max were already there. They busied themselves arranging props and making hand-drawn signs. Cannonball was nowhere in sight. I wondered if I should tell them about the old man but every time I tried to get their attention they ran off doing Cannonball's bidding with the words "I'll be right back tossed" in the wind.

At school Vatray hounded me several times a day asking, are you going to race? He'd whispered the question in my ear in the cafeteria, on our way to class, even daring to talk in the chorus room whenever Mr. McCree stepped outside for a quick minute. Over and over I told him I didn't know. Truth is I'd decided I'd try but I knew I couldn't drive the car Mama gave me. So even though I wanted to race I didn't have a car to drive.

Charleston walked around school acting like he had a reason to be mad at me. And because the next race wouldn't happen for two weeks I got used to not talking to him. I'd watch him walk off like I wasn't there. I had learned not to get caught up in those hide-and-seek games from practicing with Karla. After we entered the eleventh grade, Karla and Hunter were inseparable, and I couldn't stand him, and not only because he dated Karla though this alone was a good reason.

Hunter was tall, clean-cut, and handsome, but he was also arrogant, snooty, and full of himself. This showed in the way he floated above it all, walking around and not acknowledging anyone else existed. He looked straight ahead and only spoke if he wanted to, as if he were French nobility strolling in some ornamented park or a prized canine parading around a dog show.

Perched in the window of the school building I had a hawk-eye view of the lovebirds. He drove his Mama's black BMW CSi. But when he walked with Karla down the long cement sidewalk that led to the student parking lot, he seemed to always walk a little faster than she. Karla seemed to have to scramble to keep up. Once in the parking lot a flock of girls paraded by waving and speaking to Hunter as he got in the car.

In the school cafeteria I overheard those same girls talking. "Why is he dating her? She's kinda cute and all, but doesn't she live in that ghetto—Dixie Hills? I mean really," a small-mouth, big-head girl said.

"Well—you didn't hear it from me, but I heard Miss Girl puts out big time to keep him happy. Freaaak! If you know what I mean," a gap-toothed girl with a designer bag said.

Mad, I dropped my tray on the table to break up their conversation. Sets of enlarged eyeballs glared at me and I walked off with my lunch tray in hand.

THE DUST that got kicked up made me cough. Out rolled Lorraine and Hiawatha not bothering to wait until the red cloud settled down. They exited Lorraine's daddy's Jeep

Renegade. For the same amount of time Vatray worked on talking me into racing, Lorraine tried to talk me out of it. She even threatened to tell Mama, which she took back the second she'd blurted it out. Still Lorraine had landed on racing wasn't a good idea. Now I looked at Lorraine quizzically.

"It's still a bad idea, but Watha and me thought you might need back up," Lorraine said and smiled. Hiawatha rubbed my arms and smiled too.

I spotted Charleston with a group of muscle boys rolling big cylinders to help outline the end of the dirt track and I wondered why. I'd lost sight of Max and Vatray, but I guessed they were mingling.

While listening to my records in my bedroom I'd daydreamt about Max touching me again. Even giving me a big ole French kiss while we slow dragged to the Chi-Lites. When Lorraine pulled my arm it was as if the needle on my record player scratched. "Hey," I said. Lorraine held onto my arm as she walked me over to the side to talk, away from Hiawatha, she also plopped out a new flask. When I reach to get some brew she snatched it back. "What about me?" I asked.

"What about you? This is Mad Dog and you don't like it anymore. Aren't you about to race some stupid car? You can't do both," Lorraine said.

Lorraine sound like she was Mama, and she was being stingy. I grabbed the flask and took two quick gulps. Lorraine snatched it back, accidentally spilling some on the red dirt, which made it look like modeling clay. Lorraine frowned at the mistake and spat out her commentary, "You drive fast but not that fast. How you know you can even race? You can't race your Mama's car."

"I won't know until I try, and Vatray said Cannonball got a car."

Hiawatha came over and Lorraine stopped talking and tucked the flask back in her jacket pocket. Lorraine still managed to roll her eyes as if to say, you're crazy. We all stood and watched as other kids' arrived. The gulps of wine gave me a small buzz of courage but it didn't stop my knees from knocking.

Cannonball arrived in an old, faded black Chevy, something from the fifties. I imagined he found it a junk-yard, maybe the same place Charleston found his Model T horn. The old Chevy rattled and put-putted when Cannon-ball drove it inside the gate and parked. As Charleston walked past me he gave the evil eye, then mouthed "smart-ass." He jumped inside the black Chevy and drove it closer to the track.

"You ready to do your thing?" Cannonball asked as he approached with a smile, which took me by surprise since I sensed genuine warmth from his energy. Cannonball walked over to the old, broke-down Chevy. The only things cool about the car were the tinted window and shiny new tires. I walked behind the car and noticed the tag read BEN 4211. Cannonball got in, cranked the car, and left it running. He looked at me and said, "It's all yours."

Max arrived back on the scene as I stood outside the car. I guessed she'd finished collecting money and doing Cannonball's bidding. Max nodded her head as if to say it was all right. I hesitated and against my intuition I got in the car, put on my seat belt, and drove down the track. If Mama could see me now she'd wish she hadn't sent me to learn to

drive. I'd gotten my first taste of racing at the driving school
we practiced on a paved track and performed many maneu-
vers, both offensive and defensive techniques, to keep us safe
on the road. The lesson I loved the most was backing back
through the orange traffic cones. I'd swerve through going as
fast as I could. The only problem was I wasn't supposed to
drive fast, and the actual lesson was to drive forward. "Car
number seven," the teacher shouted over the loud speaker on
the track. "Slow down and stop backing that car."

As I sped down the fairgrounds track I could feel the
old girl's power. It jolted me a bit but it didn't scare me.
Sparks of adrenalin produced themselves throughout my
body. It was like the ultimate control. I was at the wheel and
I could make the mechanisms do whatever I wanted. I drove
up and down the track several times before Max flagged
me down.

"How fast did you get?" Cannonball asked.

"Eighty-five," I said. "It's fast but kinda old, I don't know
if it can go faster."

"It's old but it's a classic '57 Chevy. It's got thunder in
the pipes if you press the pedal down hard toward the end
of the straightaway," Cannonball said.

I revved the '57 Chevy at the starting line. Max
snapped the flag down and I jumped the car forward like I'd
been racing my whole life. I went from zero to sixty miles
per hour in eleven seconds. I did that five or six times.
When I brought the car back after the last time, Cannonball
said I was ready.

Before the race I took a moment and looked up at the
stars and over to the city lights. I didn't exactly pray, but I
wanted to win as many races as I could. Cannonball said I
might get prize money at the end of the night. A vision of
Karla popped into my brain and I wondered what that do-

good girl would think about me racing? I was certain she wasn't thinking about me. She was too busy being Hunter's girlfriend. Now Max walked up, "Just do your best and everything will be cool."

Three boys agreed to race me. Five boys refused and one of those was that knucklehead Charleston. I rolled my eyes as I passed him, and he grabbed my arm and forced me to walk with him. Once we were off to the side and before I could say, "Let go!" Charleston began talking. Cannonball was using me but he wasn't using Charleston because most boys with cars raced. Cannonball was using me as a sideshow, a freak-fest. There were safer ways for me to make a little cash. What about Six Flags? My main problem was I didn't know how to be a real girl. Girls weren't supposed to be racing on dusty tracks at night. And why wasn't Max driving, she was Cannonball's girlfriend. Or even Vatray for that matter, he was his boyfriend. And Cannonball would easily make thousands but he'd only give me fifty bucks. I stopped registering any more words because my mind froze on him saying Max was Cannonball's girlfriend.

Charleston loosened his grip and I elbowed him in the ear. His head snapped back and he said, "Damn girl, that hurt." As I walked off I shouted back, "Forget you—asshole."

"Forget you, Onnie Armstrong. If I have to race you, you'll be one of those nappy-head fools to me, you remember that."

Charleston wanted to get in my head and I knew it. I'd already guessed Max was with Cannonball and deep down inside I had guessed he'd had sex with Vatray. The first thing that came to mind was Cannonball was a greedy bastard, but I wanted to race. I wanted to be good at something. And unlike Charleston's small, provincial mind, I never wanted to be like other girls because I wasn't like most girls.

In my first race I was up against a goofy sci-fi geek whose chess club friends pumped him up to race. I won by a car length. After we brought our cars back from the straightway and he exited his friend's truck, I couldn't help but notice he'd peed his pants.

In the second race I was up against a pretty boy from Collier Heights. I didn't know him but he was way too busy brushing back his hair in the rearview mirror to pay attention to the road. I zipped down with him then left him in the dust.

On my third outing I was up against one of Charleston's football buddies. Charleston had planted him in the rotation. He drove up in a Nova SS. Lorraine came over to give me friendly advice. "This idiot looks serious, he won't be playing with himself when you pull off. My Daddy said if you name a car it'll treat you right." One of Cannonball's muscle boys shouted to clear the area.

We revved our cars and as we both zipped off I shouted, "Thunder Ben!" I sped down the runway, but lost by half a car length. Charleston won all his rounds and he laughed off any race with me. "Cannonball will have to sweeten up the pot if he wants me to race you."

I made fifty dollars like Charleston said. But it was fifty more than I had. Mama always stressed the importance of saving but if Mama could see me pocketing my race money she'd say it was nigger-rich money because it was ill-gotten gains that I'd earned too quickly. Still, I plan to hide it away in my closet like I did the money I earned doing odd jobs for the Old Folks Mafia. If I decided to race again I'd make more. The big man Cannonball had invited me back.

I stood off on the sidelines while Charleston, Max, and Vatray worked to clear out any evidence we were there. I watched a parade of red taillights exit the fairgrounds. Lorraine and Hiawatha followed with a wave bye from the Jeep Renegade. Cannonball had already disappeared with his muscle boys. For a long moment I imagined I was the lesbo-king of the raceway, driving down to the cheers of the crowd. In real life I hadn't heard any cheers. Unlike what Charleston thought, it was good to be different, to stand out from the crowd. Plus, being a gay Southern girl, I didn't have any other choice.

Lorraine and I drove up the wooded road without head-lights. At medium speed I looked out into the thicket of trees on watch for the old man with the keys. From a crouched-down position Lorraine let me know it was dangerous to drive without lights. "No shit," I said and we passed the area I'd originally seen the old man. The full moon gave off plenty of light. With the old man nowhere in sight I turned my headlights back on and Lorraine popped back up because that was our signal the coast was clear.

It was Vatray who told me the old man I saw was named Jeb. After my eyes flashed without warning me, Vatray asked if I knew him but I shook my head no. Yet, I did know him, he was Daddy's fishing buddy Old Man Jeb. Cannon-ball paid him a couple hundred bucks to turn his head and keep a look out for the police. I imagined as the groundskeeper for the fairground Old Man Jeb knew the ins and out of the area.

After we parked the car Lorraine informed me that at

times I was so weird. That some old man older than my Daddy couldn't see who the hell was in a car at night. After I mulled it over I knew she was probably right but I decided to keep that to myself.

At school Vatray told me Max said this, that, and the other about my bad-ass driving skills. I didn't care about that. I wanted her to say something like she wanted to go on a date with me. Or she wanted me to come to her house and look at a movie. Vatray talked so much if you kept listening you might get the answer to a question you were to embarrass to ask. Now I knew where Max lived, West Lake, which bordered Dixie Hills to the west. That was where another set of the black elite lived—the blue-blood black with old money going back to slavery and Reconstruction, Mama said. Whenever I talked about Max, Lorraine asked, "Now who's trying to date in the upper classes?"

Lorraine and I stood near the racetrack and watched the usual setup. Hiawatha declined to come saying she didn't like to watch racing. I'd guessed it was a little too rough and tumble for her taste. Charleston passed by with a shit grin on his face and I wondered why until I found out Cannonball had offered him something he couldn't refuse. If Charleston beat me, Cannonball would get his car painted any color he wanted. He'd also get extra money from the night's pool. If he lost Cannonball would get his winnings.

Lorraine insisted the real reason Charleston decided to race me was the crowd had been talking about how much of a pussy he was for not, and he needed to prove them wrong. I'd watched Charleston after Cannonball made his offer and watched him calculate all the odds in his gigantic brain. After a few quick tabulations Charleston shook Cannonball's hand to cement the deal.

Max walked me around the track to remind me of all

my driving points. Don't choke at the finish line. At twenty yards out take a deep breath. Ten yards double pump the gas. And then speed through the finish line.

"How can I tell the yardages?" I asked.

"At twenty yards Vatray put red barrels on both sides, and you have to guess ten yards, but it's gonna be seconds later," Max said. Then she told me her daddy might be the mayor but his daddy, her granddaddy, was a bootlegger and racecar driver from Lukaweski, Georgia.

After the early races were finished I had won four out of five. Charleston again won all of his. From the starting line Charleston sang a song from the Douglass High cheerleaders' songbook. "Elevate your mind, get yourself together. Elevate your mind, get yourself together," Charleston chanted over and over. Then when he was finished he had a warning, "You gonna lose to me. You always have, you always will."

I shouted from the '57 Chevy. "What you talking 'bout. We never raced before."

"Listen up, I can draw better than you, outrun you, beat you at football, even get more girls—or whatever! You're ah tomboy, I'm ah real man," Charleston said and revved his engine.

My blood boiled as I revved the '57 Chevy. I zipped up my jacket, tightened my seat beat, and turned my head away from Charleston. Max came over and through the rolled-down window she held my face between both her hands and gave me a soft kiss on my lips. I wondered why she'd done it as I rolled the window up. Cannonball pulled out a miniature bullhorn, which gave the atmosphere a circus quality. My revving turned into a *VROOM*. Now I kept my eyes on the road, my hands on the wheel like Daddy told me to, like the driving teacher instructed, and like Mama might have said had she taught me to drive. *VROOM, VROOOM* went both cars. Then on his freaky little horn Cannonball shouted "Ready, set, gooooo."

Max cracked the checkered flag like a bullwhip in a cattle drive. I pressed the pedal down hard, and Thunder Ben jumped to the charge. I looked out in front of me, not to the side, in front of me, and I kept my hands pasted on the steering wheel. I pressed down as hard as the pedal would go. Zero to seventy in seconds. I didn't know how many seconds, just that it was fast. And at the red barrel I took a deep breath and milliseconds later I double pumped the gas and got up to a hundred miles per hour across the finish line. I thought I won, there was no car across from me when my eyes glanced across for a quick look-see through the red dust. There was no car next to me when I pulled off to the side. I looked to see where Charleston was and discovered his Charger had hit a red barrel and rolled off into an embankment of dirt. Charleston's car must have spun off and landed in the brushes. I jumped from my car to find Charleston. He laid halfway out the driver's side door. That was when I noticed Charleston didn't have on his seatbelt.

"Did I win?" Charleston mumbled.

"Yes, you won," I said. How else could he have landed in the brushes before I finished?

Blood oozed from his mouth. "Good. I told you I'd beat you." Charleston garbled and slumped over.

A few muscle boys pulled Charleston from the driver's side and placed him in the passenger seat. As they moved him Charleston gave out a loud howl. Both of Charleston's legs were busted up, one at the knee and the other on the side of his shinbone. "Where's Cannonball?" I asked.

"He left," one of the muscle boys said. I turned back and saw a large dust cloud forming from the exodus of the racer crowd fleeing in their cars from the fairgrounds. One of Cannonball's boys jumped into Thunder Ben and drove off. I felt a little sad but I knew it wasn't my car.

Max, Vatray, and Lorraine were by my side as we watched Charleston bleed from his mouth and his leg and moved in and out of consciousness. "Somebody's got to call an ambulance," I said trying to help keep Charleston upright in the car seat.

"Somebody has," Max said. "But we need to go. The EMTs can take care of him."

I looked at Max, Vatray, and Lorraine. They seemed to be waiting for me to say something.

"Lorraine please talk to her," Max said. "If we don't go, we'll have to explain what happened to the cops. Racing is against the law. I can't get caught, I'm the mayor's daughter."

"He'd leave you," Vatray said and shrugged his shoulders. "He tried to mess us up downtown—remember."

"I don't care, I'm not leaving him bleeding out," I said.

"Shit, shit, shit," Lorraine said.

Max looked at me, not knowing me well enough to know what to say. She and Vatray turned and escaped down a back road in her white-on-white Camaro. Off in the distance I could hear police sirens and ambulances coming our way. "Let's take him," I said.

"Where—to a hospital? Lorraine asked.

"At least away from the fairgrounds," I said and jumped into Charleston's driver's seat. I took the same dusty road out that Max had taken. Lorraine drove my car. On the way out I spotted Old Man Jeb near a building that looked like a large outhouse. Maybe it was his caretaker's shack. I hoped he didn't get a good look as we zoomed past.

Grady Memorial Hospital was where I was born. It was where most black folks in recent memory were born in Eleven Light City. It also had the best trauma department in the city. Lorraine parked my car in the hospital parking lot. I drove Charleston's Charger and parked it on the street right outside the emergency room. On the way to hospital I thought out loud on what we could tell the doctors. Charleston continued to go in and out of consciousness. I remembered from *General Hospital* that if there was a car accident they called the cops.

It took both Lorraine and me to hold Charleston up and get him inside. At the front desk I stood lying, while Lorraine watched. I explained that as Charleston played a friendly game of football he stumbled down an embankment and banged up his leg and mouth. The nurses recognized Charleston from the local newspapers with photos of him diving to a touchdown. The nurses began to coo-coo around him, then put him on a rolling hospital bed. They didn't ask about insurance or give me a second glance so I guessed I was in the clear.

While the doctors and nurses worked to patch up Charleston I called his mama to give her the bad news. It was well after midnight, and I woke Mrs. Wainwright. At first she didn't know what I wanted. As I kept talking she eventually screamed out, "I'm on my way!" Lorraine and I needed to get a move on. It was best if Charleston was alone to explain what happened to his mama. I went in and found Charleston resting quietly. I gave him his car keys and Charleston said thank you to me for the first time ever.

Charleston dropped his head as the doctor explained it would take his shin a long time to heal and that he may or may not be ready to play our senior year of high school. I tried to hide the feelings on my face. Charleston began to cry and I rubbed his back. His tears abruptly stopped when Lorraine came in and reminded me Mrs. Wainwright would be there soon and we should get going.

"Thanks Raine," Charleston said. And Lorraine looked like she'd witnessed a miracle. I gave Charleston a kiss on his forehead and we exited.

On the drive home Lorraine asked if I thought Vatray had purposefully placed the red barrel too close on Charleston's side. I didn't know but I wouldn't put it past Vatray either.

The streets of Dixie Hills were quiet in the early morning hours. Not even a stray dog stirred. I'd missed my curfew by two hours. I parked on the street instead of the driveway—it seemed prudent. The street created less opportunity for Mama and Daddy to hear me coming home. I'd contemplated spending the night at Lorraine's house and just dealing with the fall out in the morning. Both Mama and Daddy slept like logs so I decided to take my chances. In the middle of the night when I stumbled to the bathroom all I ever heard from their bedroom door was snoring.

I went up the driveway and walked through the opened gate. This might be how a burglar might do it. I walked through the backyard by the light of the moon. It was funny how big the house looked in the dark. I placed the key in the door very slowly. The door made a long, luscious squeak, akin to a haunted house in a movie. I paused and waited to hear if Mama and Daddy heard it. Nothing! Now I methodically took off my boots and tiptoed out the kitchen, through the dining room, and on into the living room. With my bedroom door in sight my insides relaxed. Then the lamp turned on.

"You know what time it is?" Daddy asked with a can of beer in his hand. Not interested in me answering he continued. "What kinda of cathouse you think we running? Out wid some badass boy, 'cause even bull daggers get home before this." I wondered just how many bull daggers did Daddy know.

Now I could see Daddy was on his third can of Budweiser. Two others lay abandoned on the end table under the lamp. I took a small step back, put my keys in my jeans pocket, and picked up my boots. "I thought you didn't drink," I said and took another step back.

"You don't question grown folks. If I want a beer or two —I do it. Yo' mama can't say nothing while she knocked out sleeping, dead to the world," Daddy said.

"Charleston had an accident and I thought..."

"You thought like lit, you thought you farted but you shit." These were not Daddy's words of how one fucks up and didn't know it, they were Mama's, but every now and again, though illiterate, Daddy would spit out words like a trained theologian. "If you think you can come in here any time you want, you got another thing coming," Daddy said and he careened himself up and lunged at me.

I stumbled down, hitting my knee, but managed to run for the kitchen. I flung the door open and jumped down the steps. Daddy stood in his striped pajamas looking at me through the burglar door screen with the porch light on. Now I could hear Mama calling, "What's going on?"

I stood in the backyard breathing hard and watching Daddy watch me from the door. When Mama arrived on her crutches Daddy and I competed to tell our story.

"That fast-ass heifer came in here after one in the morning!" Daddy shouted.

"Daddy's been drinking beer, he's got cans all in the living room. He drinks while you're asleep," I tattled.

"And she..."

"Enough!" Mama said. "Onnie get in this house."

I looked around the backyard. It still had apple, peach, and plum trees. It still had my old swing set frame without the swings. There was the old water spigot with a few rusty buckets lying around. Mama's clothesline was in place. Daddy's tool shed, though weather beaten contained the same old cement bags, tools, and a lawnmower, but it wasn't my yard anymore. It wasn't ever my house. I never really belonged here. So I answered Mama, "No ma'am." And I ran though the yard, down the driveway. I got in my car and the wheels screeched down the quiet streets of Dixie Hills.

## 10/ BLUE BLOOD BLUES

In the predawn hours I streaked through the empty streets of Eleven Light City. I squared my foot and pressed the gas pedal firm and I imagined my old Chevy Caprice was a sparkling new BMW. I raced myself down Peachtree Street running a red light or two as I jetted all the way through downtown, then midtown, but I slowed when I landed in the eastside neighborhood of Butter Milk Bottom. Down past a few shotgun shacks, busted-up cars, and a cluster of sleeping winos, Max pointed and I rolled into the parking lot of an everyday building. Now parked we waited for the sunlight that later paraded itself over the façade of the ash gray structure. In one window shadow people busied themselves through drawn curtains. Outside the door a sign read "Saturday Hours: 7 a.m. to 3 p.m." We were early. Max pulled out a thermos filled with hot cocoa then gave me a half smile as she poured the dark chocolate into a cup. I wondered how she could muster any smile at a time like this. As I blew my hot cocoa cooler I examined Max as she stared out in space. Where had her mind travelled?

Two weeks ago Max telephoned out the blue. I hadn't seen her since the race night at Lakewood Stadium three months before. That night I'd watched her white Camaro taillights drive out of sight and I didn't know if I'd ever see her again. Lorraine warned me, Max wanted something. Charleston, with his legs still recuperating, couldn't believe I didn't just hang up on her, but Mama thought it was a small miracle I'd been befriended by the mayor's daughter. Maybe there was hope for me yet, a new friend who was a girly girl and the first daughter of the city. Perhaps Max could persuade me into becoming the daughter of Mama's dreams.

Still Daddy had an entirely different take. He couldn't care less who befriended me. Max being the mayor's daughter didn't register as something good or bad, Daddy was indifferent. What he held onto was I'd disrespected his and Mama's authority the night I fled out the house and drove off in the middle of the night. Then returning when I wanted—at daybreak. To Daddy I'd become a wild-ass teenager who if they didn't stamp down on and control right now would freely practice my lesbian witchcraft out in front of the world. Daddy even speculated that I'd probably already done so the night I drifted into the midnight.

In those wee morning hours when I ran into the night I discovered Eleven Light City had a shadowy side with aimless people drinking coffee at all-night joints and purposeful pimps looking to add to their flock. I sat at the Krispy Kreme on Ponce de Leon Avenue in midtown and ate two donuts with milk as I pretended not to eye up the guy with all his belongings in a black trash bag, sitting with a woman who sported a black eye and no front teeth. Another man came to the counter, sat next me, and introduced himself as Black Magic. He wanted to buy me another donut or anything I wanted. He had so much to tell me and show me, he said. A waitress named Vegas called a cook from the back and he came out with a baseball bat and told Mr. Magic to get to stepping. Black Magic hissed back and relocated himself outside with two women then marched off down Ponce to find business.

"Baby girl," Vegas said. "Did you run away from home? Why are you out here in the middle of the night?" I shrugged my shoulders and then she smiled and gave me more milk, this time with two shots of coffee and a grilled cheese sandwich.

When I darted off into the night, away from Mama and Daddy, I hadn't run away only to run away from Mama's policeman questions and Daddy's unpredictable ways—I was, in effect, buying myself some time.

When I was ten, after I learned I was adopted, I decided I'd run away after Daddy yelled then swatted me for the umpteenth time for doing something simple like break a mason jar. That day I decided I'd had enough. After all, they weren't my real parents, I said to myself. I made a peanut butter and jelly sandwich and I grabbed my book bag which I packed with two shirts, one pair of socks, and the thirty-five dollars I'd saved from chores. Mama was in her bedroom, Daddy was off fishing with Old Man Jeb, and on a Saturday afternoon I stole away in broad daylight. On my way to the train station I stopped by Miss Lizzy's candy store, which was one block away from our house. It was located in the back of her house but it had a separate entrance. Over a Mr. Goodbar bribe I spilled the beans to Miss Lizzy about my whole plan to run away to Athens. It was where Karla and her family moved when her mother had breast cancer.

"Why Athens?" Miss Lizzy asked. "And how you gonna get to the train station?"

"It's pretty I heard. And I'll take the bus," I said.

"Where you gonna live once you get there? And you'll need a job, but the problem is what kinda job can a fifth grader get?"

"I don't know, I guess I'll figure it out," I said

Miss Lizzy smiled with gleaming eyes and nodded her head like she understood. Then she asked me to wait and she stepped away from the counter for a few seconds. I continued to eat my candy bar while I eyed up the other candy on her shelves. With an offer to drive me to the train station, Miss Lizzy locked her shop door and drove us toward downtown in her old Cadillac Deville. In front of the train station Miss Lizzy let the car idle and waited for me to get out. "Good luck," she said. My heart beat faster and faster as I looked out at the station's entrance. I turned my head and I faced forward in the car. "Maybe I'll go another day," I said. And Miss Lizzy drove me home. After I shut the front door Mama called me from the kitchen. "So you went downtown with Miss Lizzy?" Mama asked.

"Yes ma'am," I said. And Mama left it at that.


I CONTINUED to watch while all the underground people of Eleven Light City crawled out to make an appearance. Three roughs with gold grills and gold chains practiced a make-shift rap at a booth, a woman with lots of bags sat quiet in the corner, while two men dressed in women clothes refreshed their makeup. "Baby girl," Vegas called again. "It's time for you to go on back home. This isn't a place for you." From a payphone inside I'd called Mama and told her I was on my way. Outside I moved fast to my car, Black Magic watched me and the cook with the bat escorted me.

Back home Daddy stood in the driveway like an itchy-handed triggerman waiting for me to get out the car. Mama called from the front door, "Amos! We keep our business in the house." I darted from the passenger side of the car and ran toward Mama. Daddy moved as fast as his old limbs could and trailed me. In the house Mama laid down the new driving laws: I could drive back and forth to school, to chorus recitals, and chauffeur Mama on her household errands. Daddy interjected that what I needed was a good, old-fashioned ass beating which he was happy to perform. Mama turned and said, "Onnie's half-grown and you're too old to beat anybody." Still Daddy stood with a drool of spit in the left corner off his mouth and when Mama walked toward the kitchen I jumped to walk with her.

But Mama changed her driving tune when Max came over to visit and personally asked if I could take her to an early morning event on the impoverished side of town to help poor kids. Mama smiled so wide I thought her jaw might lock in place. Even Daddy looked on mesmerized, his eye rolled back and forth while he grinned. Max regaled Mama with talk about the big, glossy debutante balls where black girls wore *Gone with the Wind* gowns and long, white gloves. "It better than the prom," Max said while Mama beamed and pretended Max was black royalty.

By all accounts Mama was a good-looking woman but she'd always felt a little less than because she was dark-skinned with one leg. It wasn't something Mama talked about but I'd overheard her and Uncle Duecer talking about why she really married Daddy. "We both had missing parts, so we matched." As for Daddy, maybe he felt the same way about having one eye.

To explain things to me in more detail, Max invited me out for pizza at some gay dive in midtown. It was situated between a drycleaner and a boarded-up storefront and was appropriately named G's Pizza. It sat on the edge of Piedmont Park. At night the park had the reputation of being a gay-boy pick-up spot where anonymous sex could be had down between large clusters of trees, away from any potential sidewalk traffic, or out in the open near the pool or tennis courts.

That night in the dimly lit pizza parlor, which was almost empty, except two sets of single boys eyeing each other up from across the restaurant, Max pressed herself against me in the booth and I felt my skin vibrate under my sweater. The waiter placed the pepperoni pizza on the table, along with two Coca-Colas. Before we took a bite Max took the liberty to give me a peck on my lips and then kiss me some more, but it wasn't like I minded. Then she stopped in the middle of a kiss, took two swallows of Coca-Cola, and revealed her real news—she was pregnant.

INSIDE THE CLINIC the walls were painted dirt beige. Two small plants sat at the edge of the receptionist's desk, which was adjacent to a large bulletin board. The board was covered in white butcher paper but contained no information, no posters or brochures. Max had done her research and felt the nurses and doctors in the ghetto would be the least concerned that she was the mayor's daughter. Most might not recognize her, which made the poor side of town an easy choice.

Now the nurse came out with a clipboard, intake forms, and a pen.

"How many months?" The nurse asked.

Max put two fingers up like she was in kindergarten.

"Who's the father?"

Max looked at me, and I looked away with my hands on my chin. When I asked, Max wouldn't answer. And now she still refused to answer. Instead Max shook her head uncontrollably until she made herself cry. The nurse got up and sat next to her and laced her arms around Max as if to cradle a baby.

"There, there, honey, you'll be alright. You may not know, and that's okay too."

Was it okay? I couldn't imagine Max didn't know. Could she have that many boyfriends? I thought about my birth mother. Mama said my original birth certificate read Father Unknown. Yet, the one that Mama had in her box of official papers listed her and Daddy as my parents. It also listed my race as a Negro. I didn't like either.

The nurse must have known Max didn't want anyone to know who the father was and she continued. "Have you ever had an STD or been pregnant before?"

"No," Max said.

At school I'd listened like a fly on the wall while girls discussed how boys didn't like the feel of condoms. Those same boys said they could pull their penises out before they came. Other said condoms killed the sex mood. Now Max was crying in her hands again. I tried to help by rubbing her back.

We walked back to the waiting room filled with shame-faced boys and angry-eyed mothers. I was neither. I imagined I was the gay girl cavalry that swept in to rescue the damsel in distress. I didn't know what I meant to Max but I was here. We found two chairs together. We sat, not talking, only looking at the variety of girls that came in the clinic. Nobody made eye contact. Though it was a poor community, these girls had come from all over Eleven Light City. Some had come on buses, others in cars, but someone accompanied each girl.

Finally, a nurse came and got Max. Max wanted me to come with her but the nurse had already told us they didn't allow it. I sat back in my chair and stared off into space. It turned out an abortion clinic was a horrible place to daydream—well, not any good thoughts at least. I wondered if Max would be okay, if one day she'd regret the abortion. There were a few girls at Douglass High that got pregnant and they seemed to fall into two categories: the ones who were scuttled off to relatives in another town before their pregnancy showed too much, and the ones who stayed while pregnant, and braved classmates and teachers looking, pointing, and talking about them as they walked down the halls. After delivering their babies they returned to school. Both sets of girls were treated as outsiders, social outcasts. It was interesting to find out that a straight girl who'd decided to have her baby could be shunned more than a suspected lesbian. This discovery also gave me insight into Max's decision. Without a baby Max had a shot at a great future, with a baby she would become a black teen statistic.

I didn't have sex with boys so I couldn't get pregnant. I was lucky that I hadn't started my period when Earlee stuck his nasty penis inside me. I'd figured gay girls didn't have periods because for a long time Lorraine, Hiawatha, and I had been spared the bloody visitor. I didn't know if Karla had started hers but she was only half gay. Lorraine and Hiawatha eventually succumbed to the fate of all girl kind—menstruation. So far I was still free from bleeding.

As for having sex, Mama didn't teach me one thing about it. Only that I should keep my legs closed and that God didn't like girls doing ugly things. Neither was helpful. In health class we got one hour devoted to sex, there I learned I was no longer a virgin, but that rape wasn't sex. Great, I hadn't had sex but I still lost my virginity. Most days I didn't think about being raped or Earlee taking something from me that I could never get back. Other times my mind went to dark places where I wanted to mess Earlee up bad. One day, randomly, Lorraine informed me that a prisoner stabbed Earlee in the leg after he'd raped the guy.

Two hours passed and I began to worry about Max, but the receptionist said everything was fine and on schedule. Though the clinic was air-conditioned I needed to get out of the cramped waiting room. Outside beyond the parking lot I discovered one man and one woman picketing the abortion clinic.

"It's a child, not a choice, it's a child, not a choice, it's a child, not a choice," the man and woman repeated and shouted. Though persistent, their voices sounded frayed and weak as the sun reached for the ten o'clock hour. It was spring, still it was hot. I guessed that by noon their protest would dissipate to nothing, like two abandoned ice cubes on hot Southern concrete. But for now they aimed their sidewalk counseling toward me.

"Don't kill your baby, save a life," they both chanted. Now they raised their sign, which had the same message. As they got closer their faces looked touched, maybe by the Holy Spirit, or the onset of a heat stroke, but these two red-faced, thin white people on the wrong side of town would not win any friends here.

"Young lady, can we talk to you? Have you heard Jesus

came to save your soul and the soul of your baby?" the woman asked.

"Young miss, there is a church nearby. We can take you there. You can get counseling and a hot meal. Would you like to go?" the man asked.

"I'm not pregnant and I never go anywhere with strangers," I said and moved back toward the clinic's door.

"If you aren't pregnant, why are you at an abortion clinic?" the woman asked, moving in closer.

I watched them both with alarm in my eyes. I'd had practice with unsolicited religious folks—on Saturdays the Jehovah's Witnesses scoured the Dixie Hills neighborhood like soldier ants on a mission. Over the years Mama sent me to the door and without being purposefully rude I'd cultivated my response, "We are Baptist, and we won't change our minds." Usually they'd ask if they could leave their literature and I always said yes, but through the latched burglar-bar door.

With my hand on the clinic door I answered the woman, "That's none of your business." I opened the door and walked back inside the clinic. From inside I watched the couple walk slowly back to the sidewalk with their signs hanging low.

Seated back in the waiting room, I was glad Max hadn't heard the crazy couple's ramblings out in the parking lot. I supposed nobody came to abortions lightly, but once they did shouldn't they be left alone? I wondered what Mama would think of Max having an abortion. She had put Max on such a pedestal. But Mama's own miscarriages meant nature had naturally aborted her offspring and they'd been replaced with me. Maybe this was what our science teacher, Mrs. Freeman, meant when she taught us survival of the fittest. Maybe folks with missing parts couldn't have babies.

I wondered if Max had parts missing I didn't know about. Still I guessed Mama might have been alright with Max securing her future. After all Max was going to be a debutante, presented to society, a coming out to the city as a young lady of promise, a pretend virgin, to the audience. Mama would be a front-row eyewitness to the charade because Max invited Mama to come to the ball.

I'd gone to the counter to speak with the receptionist again when Max came out the side doors. She looked frail and weak. I gathered her arm and walked to the car. By now the sun pointed to high noon, somewhere in the high eighties the radio said as I cranked the car. The crazy white couple looked our way and I turned on the air conditioner. We were young, we were free, and we had the whole day ahead of us. Before the thin white man and woman could get to us I peeled out the parking lot and zipped through Butter Milk Bottom and onto Ponce de Leon Avenue to make my way back to our side of town. As we turned down Peachtree Street the coloring in Max's face returned. I looked over at her and smiled, "How you feeling?"

"A little groggy, just happy it's over. I never want to see Cannonball again."

"Cannonball—is he the father?"

"Never mind that, you were so cool today, let's just go to my house," Max said and lifted her index finger to direct me to come closer. Once our faces were almost touching Max kissed me in the center of my cheek then smiled. Now Max laid back in the car seat and closed her eyes.

I hopped onto I-20 headed for Max's house. Down past stone houses with manicured lawns and tennis courts out back my mouth dropped open when Max pointed to her house. I pulled into their long, cobblestone driveway. Two men worked on the property bagging grass and shrubbery from the freshly mowed lawn and clipped hedges. I parked Max's Camaro in its garage space. I walked around to the passenger side and opened the door. I held her arms as she got out. As we walked I watched the gardeners watching us. "Good afternoon, Miss Olivia," one of the gardeners said. "Do you and your nursemaid need help?"

"No—no thank you, Leroy," Max said. "We can manage."

Nursemaid, I whispered to Max, but she said not to listen, that Leroy was old and senile. He thought anybody Max brought home was her personal assistant.

But Leroy had also said the name Olivia, the name Max acted like didn't exist. The one she refused to use out in the world. No one in her family or circle of ritzy friends called her Max except Vatray, and he'd never say it in front of Max's parents. Max was her street name, but I didn't know why she needed one, it wasn't like she was a spy.

As we walked the stone path around to the back of the house, I eyed the grounds filled with greenery, flowers, a pool, and a tennis court. Along the back of the house Max stopped and pulled open the sliding-glass door. I followed her inside to a large sunroom with two over-stuffed sofas and a tray of lemonade on the coffee table. From where we sat I could see a room filled with books from floor to ceiling. Max leaned back on the sofa and I sat next to her. She pointed for me to take a glass. As I drank, a shadow entered from the hallway near the library and when my eyes focused there stood Max's mother, Rowena Simone Maxwell Sharp. She was tall, majestic, and light-skinned. She somehow seemed to float rather than walk. She was dressed in an angel-white summer dress and ruby-red high heels, and I wondered if she ever clicked them like Dorothy in the *Wizard of Oz*. Now she sat on sofa across from us with a glass of something on the rocks.

"Is it complete, dear?" Mrs. Sharp asked.

"Yes, Mummy," Max answered and worked hard to settle herself on the sofa. A maid came in and covered Max with a blanket as Mrs. Sharp continued her questions. "So, you're Onnie Armstrong?" she asked and sipped her unknown drink.

"Yes, ma'am," I said quickly, as I examined her up and down.

"My dear, my eyes are up here," Mrs. Sharp said and waited for me to look at her directly. "Now it's important to keep this secret. Not even the mayor can know. Olivia says you're trustworthy. Is this true?" Mrs. Sharp downed the rest of her drink.

"Yes ma'am," I said as if she were a drill sergeant.

"Young lady, we're not in the armed forces," she said, irritated, then let out a breathy, "Ohh God."

I cleared my throat to calm down. "No ma'am, I mean, yes I can keep it to myself."

"Great. It's settled." Mrs. Sharp stood up and put her glass down. "I see someone took the time to raise you. You girls will be okay, right?"

Max and I both said, "Yes ma'am," but in a regular way.

"Good. I'm off to a Links meeting, a little champagne brunch. And Onnie, you should come over more often. There may be other jobs we can have you do. Okay, cheers, girls!" Mrs. Sharp walked toward the sofa and gave Max a kiss on the forehead. She looked and smiled at me. Up close I saw her better. She may have looked like Dorothy Dandridge, but she was scary like the Wicked Witch.

Mrs. Sharp had been an opera singer of note. She'd performed in the Paris Opera and at the War Memorial in

San Francisco. She'd toured all over Europe but had given up her career to marry Jarvis Sharp, a local boy with promise. Though Mrs. Sharp never garnered the fame of Marian Anderson or the clear voice of Leontyne Price, none of that mattered because she was born a thoroughbred, a blue-blooded black and at the end of the day this was more important than air.

The cook made me a sandwich. Max didn't have an appetite and she was tired so I sat and ate while Max slept. I wondered what it felt like to be Max, to do the things she got to do and have a glamorous life. After two hours Max was still asleep so I tucked the blanket around all her edges and slipped out the sliding-glass door. Outside near the garage, Leroy waved goodbye. "Welcome to the staff," he said as I walked down the cobblestone driveway headed home.

On a ballroom floor at the Peachtree Plaza Hotel fancy black girls pranced around in white gowns and long satin gloves. Nicely positioned princess crowns were bobby pinned in their hair, and like marionettes on strings they bowed to their fathers. Their fathers spun them around in a make-shift waltz that blended classical music with disco, Tchaikovsky with Donna Summer. Dressed in black wingtips, the more swift-footed daddies managed not to step on their daughters' frocks. Now the dads delivered the girls to their escorts. And Max, with her head tipped back, held Cannonball's hands frozen in time as they waited for their musical cue.

Outside, summer was on its way, but inside, the ballroom was made cool with the help of air conditioning. I looked around the room at all the big-time bourgeois black folks in diamonds and formal wear and wondered what Mama would think. Mama had a dualistic mind when it came to rich folks. She disapproved of how they squandered money, while she also dreamt of being invited to such a lush private affair. Mama was a teen living in the poor neighborhood of Fifth Ward when she first heard about girls being presented to society. Debutantes. White Dixie debutantes. It wasn't something she wished she could be, but rather it was something that she thought would be nice to have, like a porcelain figurine of a child sitting under a tree or a nicely beveled vase used for fleshly cut flowers.

It was Max's bragging about the ball—before the abortion, back when she wooed Mama to her side—where black girls got to come out to society that reinvigorated Mama's original notions and got her so excited. Max sat on her throne, really a chair in our tiny dining room, and talked with so much animation about the event with hundreds of white roses, candelabras, and freshly ironed tablecloths, that I thought I'd already been. By the end of the story she promised Mama a ticket. Weeks later, Mama still had an extra spring in her step. In that same dining room where I sat doing homework, I'd spied her dancing a prosthetic farm-girl jig. Mama slung her fake leg around the kitchen from the stovetop, where she was cooking fried chicken, to the washing machine where she put in a load of clothes.

FROM THE BACK of the ballroom I couldn't make out Max and Cannonball's facial expressions but Cannonball held Max close, deliberate with ownership. In his fitted tux, he moved around the dance floor like Fred Astaire with Max, his Ginger Rogers, but they were used to dancing in front of an audience, at least that's what Vatray reported out. He was my date to this swanky affair and he'd appointed me his confidante. He retold the years of his and Cannonball's Saturday morning trysts in empty dance studios, dark coatrooms, and abandoned choirboy chambers where their liaison lived. It wasn't that different for Max and me except

I didn't have an invisible relationship that lasted from grade
school, or sexual rendezvous in the shadows, to recount.
Max had kissed me on three occasions: on my cheek at the
racetrack, at the gay-boy pizzeria before the abortion—with
tongue, and one last kiss after the abortion, no tongue.

Nowadays I didn't get to talk to Max much, which
pissed me off. Mrs. Sharp's reins had gotten tighter and
tighter after the abortion, at least that's what Max claimed.
Over the last seven months Max and I had gone from
talking almost every day to talking a few times a week to
Max not being allowed to return my phone calls. But that
abortion was eleventh grade stuff, last year's mistake, and
now it was second semester of our senior year. Mrs. Sharp
needed to let it go. Although Max and I didn't go to the
same high school, we would still be in the same graduating
class of 1980. And after that we'd be off to college. So I
guess the pressure was on to see what I could make happen
between Max and me.

The only college I'd been accepted to was Spelman.
Mama presented the letter addressed to me, already
opened. Before I could read it she shouted, "You got in, you
got in! Spelman wants my baby." I looked over the accep-
tance letter. "Now you can go to college here and live
at home."

"What! What about California? I haven't heard back
from Mills College, UC Berkeley, or CCAC."

"Well, if you haven't heard by now they must not want
you," Mama said. "And don't be silly. You know you can't
make it on your own." Mama snatched the letter back,
placed it in the envelope, and held it in her hand like it was
made of gold.

I went to my room and called Max. Luckily the house-
keeper picked up and said she'd leave her a message. In my

bedroom I tried to think what it might be like to live with Mama and Daddy for four more long years. I imagined it would be like living in a torturer's chamber on a bed of nails with spit water as my only nutrient. It sounded crazy and it had nothing to do with Spelman but I would rather never go to college than keep living with Mama and Daddy.

In a way, college was Mama's dream. Before Mama lost her leg in the railroad accident she always wanted to be a schoolteacher. In 1934, Booker T. Washington was the closer of the two high schools for colored folks. And though it was only a mile and a half from her house it might as well have been a hundred. She had one leg, two crutches, and little money. Grandmama Cora Mae broke the news to Mama. She couldn't go to high school though she was a straight-A student because they couldn't afford the bus fare. Mama was heartbroken.

I wallowed in my pity, but what good would it be for me to live Mama's dream and not my own? I didn't care if it made sense for me to go school in Eleven Light City. I wanted to go to California. And I knew my college plans weren't specific, I didn't want to study biology like Hiawatha or play drums in a college marching band like Lorraine, or become a professional footballer like Charleston. All I knew was when I was in California I was different. I felt vibrant, I felt like myself. And the more I heard I should stay in Georgia, the more I wanted to go.

VATRAY and I made our way closer to Max and Cannonball on the dance floor. Near the front we spotted empty chairs at a table and slid into them like stowaways sneaking from steerage to first class. Up close I could see Max smile at Cannonball and he smiled back with an icy cool demeanor.

They swirled around the dance floor like Beauty and the Beast under faux stars and a crystal palace chandelier. Around, around, and around they danced. I watched to calculate the closest spot she'd reappear near me. When Max landed in that spot I planned to will her to see me—to discover I'd come. I not only wanted her to be stunned I was there, I wanted her to be surprised by my new appearance, maybe even jealous. Maybe even wishing she had me, that I was her girlfriend. Vatray, my unsolicited love advisor had suggested I come as his date, a sort of beard. Though his mother and father knew he was gay, they'd washed their hands of trying to reform him. They were out of town and they'd left Vatray with the debutante tickets saying, "We can't worry about what you might do."

"You'll pop their eyes out their sockets," Vatray promised with a wicked little smile. Then he continued to say if I came I would not only see Max I'd also flip her out if I allowed him to make me over. I could be my own version of a dyke Cinderella at the straight girls' gathering. It sounded appealing. See Max and freak her out while winning a victory for gay girls everywhere!

With face powder, blush, eyeliner, mascara, and lip gloss, Vatray decorated my face. I wore a white pantsuit borrowed from his sister's closet because I'd refused to wear a dress. At Rich's department store we picked out a pair of low-heeled sparkle shoes that finished off my outfit. Vatray hot combed my hair, gelled back the sides, and feathered up the top in a stylized Mohawk. I looked like an Indian chief in a white lady's pantsuit. When I stepped into the den for Mama to look over Vatray's creation she almost fell out her chair, then she stood to clap. Even Daddy sat up and gave me a nice, manly head nod, which unsettled me. For the first time I felt a surge of pride emitting from both Mama and Daddy. Apparently I'd done something better than singing in an award-winning school chorus, making good grades, or getting accepted to college. For the evening I was straight. A real girl, a girly girl, and in their eyes, that was better than anything I'd ever done.

At the hotel lobby, while Vatray and I waited for the elevator, I spotted two white men smiling in my direction. This was proof I looked feminine, two men smiling. A blanket of fear covered me. I turned away from them and grabbed Vatray's arm as the doors opened.

From the elevator up to the debutante ball I looked out at Eleven Light City. I could remember a time when the Peachtree Plaza didn't exist. The part of downtown where it now sat was once an area Mama and Daddy would only drive past, it wasn't safe enough to walk. Now, after the boarded-up buildings were demolished and the hippies had grown up and gotten jobs, the hobos and winos were pushed out to the latest unsavory parts of downtown. The Peachtree Plaza now sat on prime property. It was the newest and tallest hotel in Eleven Light City. It was modern, circular, and made of mirrored glass. It was seventy-three stories high with an outside elevator.

As we rode up Vatray bragged that his daddy's company had helped finance and build the hotel, and that the view from those rooms gave a sweeping panorama of the city. It reminded him of the time when he and his family stood and looked out at Grand Canyon at dusk. I couldn't figure what one viewing had to do with the other. What I saw now was as spectacular as the sunset over the city. How would it be better from some overpriced hotel room?

BEFORE THE BALL I'd never been in the Peachtree Plaza's

elevators, only the lobby. On weekends Lorraine and I drove around the city and from time to time we made it our business to go downtown. Lorraine would say, "Hey, there's a new hotel downtown, wanna check it out?" And after we found parking on the street we'd push through tall revolving doors, past doormen and bellhops, to enter the lobby of the newest hotel. These lobbies were enormous, snazzy, and plush. We moved forward with purpose as if we had a room upstairs. Just like Mr. Handsom said he did when he was on the road with his jazz band in the fifties, "Act like you belong!"

Sitting on chairs with side tables we'd talk and make up stories about the people that passed by. Somebody was a killer, someone was a jewel thief, another person was hiding from her husband, and we'd giggle. Sometimes security guards eyed us up, but they never said "Get out!" so we stayed and watched. I never knew what we were looking for in those hotel lobbies, but what we got was invisibility—no one cared we were there so we played make-believe like little girls.

Mama wouldn't have approved of what she would describe as our vagrant behavior. We had backyards, and our own bedrooms to hang out in. We didn't need to steal away to a strange hotel lobby where dangerous people lurked and perhaps even snatched young girls into who knew what, with prostitution being worse than death. For Mama it wasn't about money or being girls with social status. For her it was about piety and proper ways of being a good Southern girl. And although we were Southern girls, we were also modern girls and chaperoned parlor visits from would-be suitors was old fashioned. Besides, we were baby-butch lesbians—we were the suitors. Still, Southern decorum dictated we not be in the public square hanging out any-ole-any-place among strangers and foreigners. And in this case foreigners were people who were not born in the South, who were not born in Dixie.

MAX SPUN around three more times before her eyes found mine. I don't know what my face looked like, but Max's face dropped that airy grace she plastered on like makeup. It stopped free flowing along with the music. It sunk in, her mouth dropped, and her lower lip dangled. I took this to mean she was not only shocked to see me but that she also thought I looked good. When Cannonball discovered what had diverted Max's attention his neck snapped back and his smile turned upside down. As they continued to dance Cannonball's eyes flashed on me, then rested on Vatray, and for the first time I saw Cannonball look nervous. He turned his head and pretended Vatray and I had disappeared. Vatray smiled like a fat man at a feast and could barely contain himself knowing that he made the cool and controlled Cannonball crazy. I guessed Vatray got what he came for but I found later the gay games had just begun.

WHILE I WAITED to hear from the California colleges I no longer had to wait for my period to start. It arrived just before winter turned into spring. It arrived quietly, like a mild spring rain but grew to become a ferocious beast spewing blood like the hot days of summer. I wondered how in the world do girls do this.

"Oh well, some folks start late, then flow heavy," Mama said. "Count your blessings you've been free of the cleanup until now." Mama insisted on accompanying me to buy pads at the drug store. This after she made homemade ones from white cloth stitched over filler fabric—Mama didn't have any menstrual product in the house, she'd long since gone through menopause.

On a drive to Douglass High I shared my news with Lorraine. "Welcome to your monthly misery," Lorraine said as we pulled into the student parking lot.

"That's not helpful," I said, parking the car.

"I know, but oozing blood hurts."

I paused and looked at Lorraine. "What about you and Hiawatha—y'all do stuff when you're bleeding?"

"I know you not asking about doing-the-do?"

"Just answer. You wear pads, tampons, or wait until you're not bleeding?" I asked while I looked to see if anyone stood near the car.

"None of yo' beeswax. But I'm a tampon girl," Lorraine said and got out the car. As we walked, Lorraine spoke in a low tone. "What about Max, the schemer playgirl? I hope you're not trying to do it with her?"

"Oh, so Hiawatha's making you wait, huh!" I said as we walked inside the school.

"Yeah, maybe prom," Lorraine confessed and looked around.

"Prom? You said y'all weren't going."

"Yeah, but if I can get some!"

"If—" I said.

"We gotta get to homeroom." Lorraine said and sped up the stairwell. I followed and at the top we peeled off in different directions.

Once in homeroom I thought about what I wanted to tell Lorraine. Max and I had an understanding. She wasn't a playgirl. She was more a girl in hiding, like all of us, to some degree. She had a boyfriend because she needed to throw her mother off her tracks. And Max couldn't be out because her daddy was the mayor. Lorraine couldn't be out and her Daddy was a cool jazz musician. I couldn't be out and mine was an anonymous plumber. Also, Charleston had invited me to the prom and while it might be fun to make the girls crazy that he'd brought me, the lesbo, to the prom instead of one of the cool cute chicks, I still had no interest in pretending to be straight just to go to the prom, just to fit in and be accepted for one night. I'd been to California and had seen gay folks living out in the open and although it wasn't a perfect place, Mama said nothing ever was.

Max and Cannonball danced several more rounds on the ballroom floor before the music crescendoed and slowed toward its natural conclusion. The chandelier's lights beamed brighter and illuminated the entire room in a vast glow. Folks threw white roses at the feet of the debutantes and their escorts, while others at a bar in the back raised their glasses in a toast. Now the couples stood in a large circle that faced out to the crowd. Max and Cannonball were across the room from us. Vatray leapt from his seat and clapped before anyone else. He clapped loudly like someone who wanted to break up a party, because he wanted to break up the party. As the crowd joined him, Vatray stood up in the chair and from his tux pockets he threw out red and black confetti that rained down atop the white roses. Vatray announced, "My man can dance, y'all saw him—give him a hand!" But only the people nearby seemed to hear and they ignored him like an unwanted pimple as the crowd cheered and whistled for the debu- tantes. That was when I spotted Mrs. Sharp coming our way like a bullet from the bar in the back. She arrived as the audience's applause rang out louder. She was dressed in all white down to her peau de soie shoes that poked out from under her gown.

"Come with me!" Mrs. Sharp said more with her hand than her voice.

"Now, Auntie Roe—we have a right to be here," Vatray said, stepping down from the chair.

Mrs. Sharp didn't mince her words and men dressed in black all but picked us up, then directed Vatray and me to follow in Mrs. Sharp's high-heeled footsteps.

From the sideline near the exit doors, Mrs. Sharp clapped along with the room filled with admirers. I saw Max searching the room for us while she and Cannonball lined up behind the other couples and marched off the dance floor. Over the loudspeaker the announcer said the debutantes would be presented now.

Mrs. Sharp motioned the men to keep us in place then she briskly walked back to her table. She and Mayor Sharp walked toward the podium, waving to the audience filled with families, friends, and constituents who performed a standing ovation as if they'd just seen Diana Ross live in concert. The press weren't welcome inside the doors but flashes from the invitees' Kodak cameras went off like do-it-yourself fireworks. It made the affair seem more glamorous. I guessed this was the proof that the Sharps were Eleven Light City's black royalty, some amalgam of Jesse Jackson meets the Jackson Five.

I saw that Max's wayward brothers, who'd both been living abroad, were there standing with the mayor and Mrs. Sharp. The one who lived in London was dressed in a dark blue tux and the other was in a tux with tails similar to the ringmaster at Barnum & Bailey Circus. This was the gay brother, the one Vatray said was sent away to live in Paris. I'd said that didn't seem like much of a punishment but

Vatray explained it was if you actually want your parents to love you and allow you be yourself at home. What I noted was no matter how everybody felt, the Sharp's stood as a family and had gathered themselves as one unit.

The announcer continued, "I present the 1980 Sigma Gamma Rho debutantes, our diamonds of distinction, destiny, and dynasty." That part sounded like a bunch of bull shit, it made them sound like a cheap jewelry collection at Kmart. I watched as each debutante took her turn on stage. The parents and escorts stood nearby while they each girl walked to the front of the stage under a rose-covered trellis. Then the girl's birth name, academic prowess, and parents' names and titles were blasted from the loud-speaker. The girls curtseyed and the audience clapped them into womanhood, young ladies in society. When Max appeared under the spotlit trellis she did a head bobbing bow like Marie Antoinette greeting her court, as though her wig was too heavy. Vatray shouted, "Let them eat cake! I helped her come up with that move." The men in black quieted Vatray by pressing him into a chair. They slid over another one for me and I sat alongside him.

While Vatray stared out into space I watched Cannon-ball as he held Max's hand to help her down from the stage. For a frozen moment our eyes found each other. Max's head tipped to the side. Her eyes closed and when she opened them she smiled small in my direction—for a frozen moment we kept our eyes on each other. I smiled back as if I could read her mind. As if she'd said, I'm tired of these games—I don't want to pretend to be straight anymore, get me out of here! But Max moved down the steps toward Cannonball and they walked to their table.

I GUESS I was a little crazy because even though I didn't completely trust Max I still liked her. I even thought it might be cool to be girlfriends. We'd have a long-distance relationship where she'd fly out to Cali for extended weekends. She had the money and she could study on the plane. Or maybe after I won her over she'd just come live in California with me. Because we no longer saw each other face to face we already sort of had a long-distance connection. Still, she'd lied to Mama's face about giving her a debutante ticket, which made me really mad, especially after I'd snuck around and helped her get the abortion and then kept it secret. Not even telling Vatray after he promised if I'd just confirm Max had one he'd never tell a living soul. And I knew Mama really wanted to go, she'd even picked out one of her better Sunday dresses and had taken her fox mink out of mothballs from the cedar chest. Mama with all her Southern pride still saw Max as the perfect first daughter of Eleven Light City, even after Max never bothered to call, explain, or apologize for reneging on the ticket. "She's busy being the mayor's daughter," Mama announced like she was privy to Max's day planner.

But Max liked the notion of having an image to keep up, and a mother to hide her queerness from—it gave her a sense of power, like moving pawns on a chessboard. When I suggested she apply to Mills College with me, Max held the phone for a very long pause then said she'd think about it. On other phone conversations Max informed me that my problem was I had to let the world know I was different— that I was gay. She suggested I just learn to fit in. Nobody really needed to know my business. If I'd just take a chill pill, I'd be happier and less stressed. I didn't agree and after she said it I held the phone while she repeatedly asked if I was still there. After these talks I could go days without feeling like I missed her.

When the weather cooled and senior year began and our phone calls had become less frequent, I could find traces of Max in the Eleven Light City newspaper, smiling broad for the cameras, usually next to her daddy. One time she was at the opening football game at Southwest High cheering on her school, West Paces Ferry Prep. Another time she'd accompanied her mother and father to the Annual Winter Carnival to raise money and give Christmas gifts to poor kids. When spring hit, there she was helping to hide Easter eggs at an African Methodist Episcopal church. In those same newspapers they wrote Max was the third-generation debutante after her mother and grandmother, hers a grand tradition of blue-blood blacks. Yet, in all the photos of her I noted sadness behind her eyes, they were filled with an uncontrolled wildness that even pulp paper couldn't hide.

A month before the ball, Mama hadn't received tickets from Max and I hadn't breathed one word to Mama that Max had recently stopped returning my phone calls, or that I'd continued to call and would hang up if Mrs. Sharp answered. Yet, Mama managed to know stuff with little to no information. One day she knocked on my bedroom door, but didn't wait for me to answer and opened it. "You're not on the begging list. Now put that in your pipe and smoke it." And as fast as Mama opened the door she snapped it shut.

Shortly after Mama's warning I stopped calling Max, but I couldn't forget her. On sunny spring mornings I'd dart inside the school building and on my way to homeroom I'd kill time thinking about the moment I'd see Max again. What would I say? Do you still like me? Do you think about kissing me? Did you apply to Mills? You want to be girl-friends?

Some days when I walked the halls on my way to class, buried in my thoughts, there was Karla trolling around with her entourage, Glory Bug and May-May, leering at me yet ignoring me at the same time. Other times Karla would be with her Slick Rick boyfriend, Hunter, giggling and pretending to be truest love bugs. The rumor was they fought like cats and dogs. But folks also said they had a lot of sex. I wondered, as Karla smirked by, if she'd also had to have an abortion. If Lorraine walked with me she'd pinch the sweet meat inside my arm and reprimand me for even looking at Karla. These days Karla was a fleeting image, an asterisk on the edges of my mind mostly popping up when she actually came into view, but Max remained fully present in my head.

With Daddy still working the night shift, Mama alone examined my mood at the dinner table. Like an amateur psychotherapist she watched my every move and the words I uttered, taking mental notes. Mama didn't say much but she'd look on with discerning eyes. After I'd moved enough green peas around my plate and ate a drumstick I was allowed to help clean up and be dismissed to go to my room and do homework. Sometimes on the phone I'd talk in low tones to Lorraine who advised me again and again to snap out of it, and to just forget about Max.

Lying in bed just as I fell asleep I felt my happiest because in my dreams was where I could be gay. I told myself this is my real life. I could walk around Piedmont Park holding Max's hand. I could kiss her on a park bench like I saw straight people do. Though truthfully I'd only seen straight white couples kissing out in broad daylight. In my dreams I was safe to make out with Max or even some random cute girls from school. When I woke up after kissing these barely known girls I'd have the feeling I cheated on Max.

AT MAX and Cannonball's table congratulations were plentiful. Max received her constituents with a smile and a head nod, as they showered compliments on her about how pretty her gown was, the lovely detail of her makeup, and the importance of becoming a society woman. While folks conversed and walked around the ballroom, Mrs. Sharp returned. With the men in black standing nearby she walked us to the exit door, but not before Vatray had his say.

"Auntie Roe, you can't just throw us out, we *have* tickets!"

Mrs. Sharp grabbed both our arms and dug her red fingernails in deep. As the men held the doors she pulled us outside into the hallway, which was deserted save for a hotel maid or two. Once the doors were shut she said, "Boy, you know who I am. Don't act crazy. Be glad you stayed as long as you did." Mrs. Sharp took a deep breath, released our arms then zeroed in on me.

"I thought your mother taught you to stay in your place. I expect this from him, stealing from his parents, having sex with old white men in Buckhead. The list goes on! But what gave *YOU* the temerity to come where you weren't invited —in a pantsuit of all things?"

"Vatray invited me," I said. "He has tickets."

"Yes, but *YOU* were supposed to know how to stay in your place with your mother in Dixie Hills. Why do you think she didn't get an invite? She knew this wasn't her place and Olivia knew it when she was running her mouth.

Anyway child, most people wouldn't tell you the truth, but there it is."

And with those words Mrs. Sharp clicked her high heels and walked back inside the ballroom.

I could feel the fumes coming up through the pores of my scalp. They released themselves in the form of sweat that slowly rolled down my face. Now even my Mohawk limped down.

Vatray and I stood with our mouths agape. We walked toward the elevators. I hopped on, but Vatray stepped back. "What you doing?" I asked.

"Going back," he said. "I need to talk to Cannonball."

"Why?"

"Why you asking? You wouldn't understand. You already gave up," he said.

Then the elevator doors closed and I descended.

I went down ten floors and decided I needed to go back up. Without copying Vatray, I wanted to know, tonight, how Max felt about me. I stepped off the elevator and stood in the hallway. I didn't see Vatray and decided to dart into the women's restroom.

From the stall I could hear different women come in talking about the ball. It turned out Max was crowned queen of queens. So she was now the top debutante, which seemed redundant.

"But that's what money will get you. A crown and an expensive gown made in France," one woman said and didn't bother to tip the old lady attendant.

After the bathroom cleared I exited the stall, washed my hands, and tipped the bathroom attendant five dollars. "Do you know another way into the ballroom?"

The old lady directed me through the kitchen and said to tell them I was Miss Essie's granddaughter and they'd let me though. Just as I stepped out, I saw Mrs. Sharp coming my way. I ran back inside, waved at Miss Essie and put my finger to my lips before hiding in a stall. Standing on a toilet, I listened as Mrs. Sharp came in, spoke, and peed. I couldn't believe she was this normal, common even. But Mama always said, "Nobody is better than you, even rich folks have to pee and shit."

Something moved inside me and I stepped out the stall. Mrs. Sharp turned. She eyed me but didn't say anything. Miss Essie watched on. Mrs. Sharp placed a lone Kennedy fifty-cent piece on the tip tray then grabbed a peppermint, unwrapped it, placed it in her mouth, and rattled it around.

Mama had always said I should respect my elders, and if I didn't have something nice to say don't say anything. Yet, Daddy had taught me that I'd have to fight my own battles and win.

I studied Mrs. Sharp's face as she glared, almost in a trance. Like most bullies, she produced furrowed brows, squinted eyes, and a one-sided lip sneer. I remembered Shirlene in elementary school when she double-dog dared me to fight her in the girls' restroom with only the stance of her body. And Daddy when he'd hovered over me like a vulture vying for a false move in order to pounce. And Earlee's smug, satisfied smile when he informed me to relax, I'd like his pencil stick dick. Now I gave Mrs. Sharp the once over and she repositioned herself as if to say, what you gonna do, blue-collar girl—what, what? And although Mama warned, don't let your mouth move faster than your ass, I couldn't stop myself.

"You like sitting on yo' high horse looking down on me and my Mama. But I wasn't ah poor stupid girl from Dixie Hills when you needed me to run your daughter on her secret errand," I said and waited for Mrs. Sharp to say something so I could blurt out Max's business.

But Mrs. Sharp leapt toward me, undignified, like a deranged chimpanzee.

"Shut your mouth," she said and slapped me across the side of my head. Hitting my head instead of my face made me think she had poor aim. Now my ears rang. Still I managed to hear the "Ohh!" sound that came from Miss Essie. And the, "Mummy! What are you doing?" that came from Max as she slammed the restroom door open.

Mrs. Sharp snapped out of bully mode. "Oh, Livee—it was an accident," Mrs. Sharp said, but when Max looked at Miss Essie she shook her head, "No, it wasn't."

Max grabbed my hand and we hurried out the restroom with Mrs. Sharp asking the wind, "Where are you going?"

OUTSIDE A SUITE on an upper floor of the Peachtree Plaza, Max popped out a key from her padded bra. Inside the room, the city unveiled itself, and I discovered Vatray was right, this was a grander view than you get from the elevators. The city's lights were so close it looked as if I could reach out and touch them.

Max looked me over, smiled, and said I looked nice—classy. She liked my hair feathered up though it had fallen some. "More girly is nice on you," she said. She walked us into one of the bedrooms and stood behind a silk screen to disrobe. As she took off her gown and pantyhose, I could see her silhouette, the outline and general shape of her body, her legs, her breasts—but not the real thing. She walked back around the screen in a white halter-top and crisp white slacks, she'd kept her silver heels on. In a large, ornate mirror she repositioned the larger crown she'd won from being named Queen Debutante. Max walked toward me with pouted lips.

"Let me see your face," she said. She examined each side and decided her mother hadn't hit me that hard.

Max sat on the bed and held her face in her hands. I couldn't decide if she had a headache from all the excitement or if she was pretending in order to get sympathy. With Max you never knew. "Mummy's been scared since the abortion. And all she thinks about is, if the word got out I'd be ruined with a big scarlet letter on my chest," Max said and moved her hand over her chest and bare shoulder, as if the letter had already been placed there. She continued, "Mummy said it was best to keep my distance from anyone who knew. I kept telling her you would never tell a soul, especially that Vatray. Right?"

I guess I was the lucky one who knew. And now I kept silent again. I refused to tell her anything, or make her feel better. Plus, Max and her mother must have known I didn't tell Vatray because Max's secret nickname for him was Telephone, Television, Tele-Vatray.

I looked around the suite wondering what was Max up to? Before I could process it, I blurted out, "Why'd you bring me here? Do you even like me?" The frailty in my voice made me sound like a girl in grade school.

Max looked more worried after I'd dropped the questions. She worked hard to keep her face even. Yet before she answered, cloudiness covered it. "Well, are you going to try to get Mummy in trouble?" Max asked, but didn't wait for an answer, as her face contorted more. "I do like you, a lot. But not like you want."

I stood still and waited for Max to lift up her face then I found her eyes. "Why did you tell me you did and kiss me all those times?"

Max looked away as if to find something interesting out in the night's sky, but the clutter of city lights didn't allow her mind to rest and she found me still watching, and waiting. Max turned her head, perhaps she was now waiting for just the right words to come. "I wanted to make Cannonball jealous," she said and paused. "And I needed you to take me to the clinic."

And here it was, the main thing Mama said about people, even said it about Daddy. That plenty of folks were selfish and they'd trample over you to get where they wanted to go. I didn't want to believe it about Max but here was the proof.

"Well, you're a stupid liar," I said and I walked toward the door.

Max rushed to continue, "Mummy said you'd be the perfect person to take me because you weren't like us. You'd keep our secret safe and somebody like Vatray wouldn't. When you and he got close it worried her."

This must have been Max's attempt to smooth things over with a raggedy backhanded compliment that she either expected me to eat up or lie down and take.

Now it wasn't hard to mistake Max's selfishness, her privileged-girl bullshit. I turned away from Max and as I turned my heart felt like it might sink into the ground. Maybe shrink into nothingness, and in one poof, evaporate. Then it, and I, would expire into the deep cavernous cracks of red Georgia clay. Perhaps never to be seen again. This sounds dramatic, but it felt dramatic. Then something shifted inside me and the image of Mama popped in my head like my own personal home movie. And in my mind's movie, Mama was at the kitchen sink with her back to me tossing out unwanted advice: *Hold your head high, even when you receive a blow. Nobody can bring you low without*

*your permission, and I don't care don't have no home, but
sometimes it's best not to care.*

I decided right then and there, I didn't have to care
about Max, that I had a home and it was time to go back. I
placed my hand on the doorknob, but turned back, I looked
at Max and said, "Okay, I'll see you."

"Wha? You're really leaving?"

"I'm going home."

"Just like that, you don't care what happens to me?"

"Nope."

"No?"

"Bye."

I opened the suite door, shaken, but somehow my footsteps were lighter—almost effortless. As I walked down the
hallway I imagined each step I took helped me to release
myself from Max. I spotted Vatray and Cannonball coming
up the hallway, holding hands.

Vatray shouted, "Girl you missed it—the shit hit the fan
while you were hiding!"

It turned out Vatray found his way back inside the ball.
And he'd hidden until he found Cannonball alone and then
he ran up on him and grabbed his arm and professed his
undying love. Cannonball received the news and gave
Vatray a nice punch in the face and then Vatray got a slap
in. Next thing you know they knocked over a few tables and
rolled around on the floor, while Vatray told everyone
within earshot all about their love escapades. Security
guards eighty-sixed them both, with Cannonball's parents
more embarrassed than angry. On the elevator ride down,
Cannonball gave Vatray a look of, are you all right? And
after they were escorted to the front door they made their
way up back upstairs to tell Max they wanted to be together
—to be a couple.

"You want to stick around?" Vatray asked. "Max is gonna need a friend."

I looked at both of them with bruises on their faces and their fumbled-up tuxes and I actually felt happy for them, but I could not play their rich kids' game anymore. I wasn't built for it. "Well, she better go find one," I said and walked toward the elevator.

The streets outside the Peachtree Plaza smelled like cotton candy. I spotted a vendor on the corner, but this was no time for sweets. A few folks meandered down the sidewalk smiling and talking with each other. I looked in both directions and then behind me and once I saw my way was clear I let go a sigh of relief. The sky had set itself jet black except for the sliver of the crescent moon and a few brightly positioned stars. I buttoned my jacket all the way up, even popped up my collar because the warm spring air had turned itself cool.

As I walked down the sidewalk my entire body vibrated in a low hum. When I got into my Chevy Caprice I relaxed a bit and leaned into the seat's cushion. I sat for a while and watched cars move hurriedly to what I imagined were important destinations. I turned the car on, pulled out the parking lot, and joined them. And like some of them I arrived to the place I called home.

I pulled the car in the driveway and discovered Mama's car was gone. I parked on the street and made the trek up the driveway and through the back gate. From the back window I saw the lights were on but when I entered the back door I found Mama and Daddy weren't home. I placed my hand on Daddy's chair, it was still warm and Mama's eyeglasses were lying on the arm of the sofa next to her favorite chair. I checked the kitchen table—no note.

I changed into my house clothes and poured myself

some juice. I'd made my curfew by two hours. Maybe Mama and Daddy had decided to go for a drive. I walked around the house thinking. When they got back maybe I should tell Mama that Mrs. Sharp slapped me, but I decided to keep it to myself because somehow Mama would turn Mrs. Sharp's actions into another reason I should live at home and go to college. Then I remembered not even the college campus would offer me a reprieve, now I would also have to see Max on Spelman's campus and live at home with Mama and Daddy.

I walked the house in circles and at some point landed in Mama and Daddy's room. I didn't go into their room that often Mama didn't like folks stirring around in her private space. Plus, they kept it too dark for my taste. Their bed was made with large Gothic posts like something from a horror movie where captives were tortured. The dressers and bureau were too large for the room. And the woolen curtain only made it seem scarier.

When I was in elementary school I snuck in and found the large jar of Bicentennial quarters Daddy tucked away in his bureau. I also found cigars, tie clips, and an old pocketknife. I began taking the quarters to buy candy. The one cigar I stole Lorraine and I smoked in the corner of her backyard until we got nauseous and threw it away. I continued to steal Daddy's prized coins until he realized they were dwindling. After he beat my butt, he banned me from their room.

Now I looked through their dresser drawers and I only found socks, stockings, underwear, and bras—not a thing that was fun or exciting. In Daddy's bureau he still had his collection of quarters and few new tie clips but the knife must have been in his pocket. I also saw something I didn't see before, a small locked metal box where I guessed Daddy kept money, like I did under a wooden board in my closet. I left Daddy's box alone. All together I found Mama kept her drawers neater than Daddy, which didn't surprise me.

I went to Mama's closet and pulled out her back-up fake leg, the one she used if something went wrong with the primary. When I was a kid, Mama let me touch her prosthetic leg when I wanted. Now I could hold it up move it around like I was a mechanic or engineer. I held it in one hand and bent it back and forth with the other hand. It didn't move smoothly as I had expected. I kept moving it around and the corner of an envelope poked out. I had to pull hard but finally I got the whole envelope out. I opened it and found letters from Mills College, UC Berkeley, and CCAC. I read them and quickly stuffed the envelope back but kept the letters. Just as I exited their room I heard Mama and Daddy come in and shut the back door. I walked to the den and watched Mama as her eyes tried to remain small.

"Why were you in our room? What are doing with my leg?" Mama asked.

"Your leg?" I held it up like I'd won a trophy. "I found my letters," I said and tucked them under my arm.

"And?" Mama asked.

"I'm going to California, I got accepted to Mills College," I said and put her fake leg in her chair.

"Oh yeah? How you gonna get there?" Mama said.

"I don't know yet, but I'm going," I said looking at Mama and Daddy. And for the first time Mama looked but said nothing.

"Susie, Susie, what's she talking about?" Daddy asked and then directed himself toward me. "You don't have enough money to go nowhere," Daddy said. "Coming in here telling us—we tell you."

"I got enough to get a train ticket and travel money. I'll live on campus," I said.

"Susie, we not letting her go nowhere. She might as well say it out loud, she leaving to be a bull dagger."

"I'm leaving to get an education, I'm already a lesbian."

Now Daddy jumped toward me and Mama stood in his path. I darted down low and ran past them. I grabbed the cast-iron skillet left on the stove. It didn't want to hit Daddy, but I wasn't going to allow him to hit me anymore.

"Don't touch my child!" Mama said, her voice rising up as she spat out each word. Still Daddy bucked and Mama shoved him down in a chair like she was a man and he was a child. "Don't—stay," Mama said as she pointed at Daddy. And he sat in place like an obedient hound dog.

Now Mama directed herself toward me. "Put that down," Mama said and I placed the skillet back on the stove. "Now is this about Mrs. Sharp and that Olivia girl?"

My mind raced to understand exactly what Mama was asking.

"You don't have to leave because that crazy woman hit you upside the head. I'm guessing she doesn't have good aim," Mama said.

"How'd you know?"

"I've known Essie Mae Gates since we were girls in Fifth Ward. She's a nice woman and she told me Mrs. Sharp and her daughter are both a complete mess. But I put an end to it. They won't bother you again," Mama said. Daddy didn't seem to know exactly what was happening.

"Well, I'm still going to California because you taught me to have self-respect and do the right thing and Daddy said I had to fight my own battles. I'm going to see if I can make it on my own," I said looking directly at Mama and Daddy.

BETWEEN GRADUATION and planning for college, the next month went by both fast and slow. Mama and Daddy barely talked to me. Meals were eaten in silence and after I washed dishes I'd go to my bedroom without Mama acknowledging I had been there. Daddy moped around not even acknowledging when I passed by. Then again, this was more the norm for him. Still, how was I in the wrong? Mama had hidden my letters. I was supposed to be mad at her, and I was mad at her, not the other way around. But because she wouldn't talk to me, the only ones that listened were Lorraine and Mr. Handsom. "Didn't Mama want the best for me?" I wondered out loud. But Mr. Handsom said it wasn't hate or the lack of goodness, it was the fear of losing me. Somehow that made sense, but even as I understood I still felt wronged.

From Lorraine's house I called Mills College and discovered I was not only accepted I had grant money and a small scholarship. And if I could get myself to California there was a summer program I could attend and they might even have a dorm room for me. I told the counselor I'd get there and just like that my life changed.

Lorraine was happy for me but gloomy that I was leaving. She even tried to bribe me to stay, saying her daddy said I could live with them until she, Hiawatha, and I could save enough money to get our own place. I turned Lorraine down. I knew I needed to leave Eleven Light City.

ON GRADUATION DAY, Mama was in better spirits and she made my favorite breakfast—pancakes and scrambled eggs with cheese and grits. At graduation, in a Polaroid picture

Mr. Handsom took, Mama and Daddy both looked solemn but I beamed like a car light on a dark road.

Packing my clothes and belongings into a trunk and two pieces of luggage took a lot of thought and planning. At times I wished Mama would help me, but Mr. Handsom said I might as well start learning how to figure things out on my own.

On the evening I was leaving, Mr. Handsom stood at the screened-in burglar door and called out to Mama. She barely answered. He explained he didn't want to be in the middle but he also didn't want a runaway situation. I don't know if Mama agreed or not. I couldn't hear her response from my bedroom. Mr. Handsom called for me to bring my bags and I snapped to attention. I brought my two suitcases to the kitchen.

"Is this all?" Mr. Handsom asked. I told him I had a trunk as well and he went to get it. I tried to make eye contact with Mama as she sat at the kitchen table but she refused to look at me and wouldn't speak. No pearls of wisdom spewed from her mouth.

Mr. Handsom returned with the trunk and we went with my bags to his Jeep.

I looked back to see where Daddy was, to at least say goodbye, but he'd disappeared like Lorraine's mama.

In the car Lorraine, Hiawatha and I sat so close in the backseat that we mirrored a can of Vienna sausages. I looked at both of them and was happy they were my friends. In the end, they'd decided not to go to the prom, but on the night of the prom they got dressed up and Mr. Handsom and Mrs. Lightfoot took their daughters out to dinner. After, they were Mr. Handsom's guests at a jazz club where he and his band played and Lorraine and Hiawatha danced arm in arm.

After I turned Charleston down, he found a nice girl from Southwest High to take to the prom. He'd met her at a house party and had called to tell me he really liked her.

As Mr. Handsom started up the car, Daddy appeared at the front passenger seat.

"Get in, Mr. Amos," Mr. Handsom said. "We men have to make sure our daughters get where they're going safely." And Daddy got in the Jeep.

From the backseat I watched Daddy and remembered when he first took me to kindergarten, and later when he taught me to drive. Maybe this was his way to help me get where I was going.

At the train station everyone got out the car. "Miss Onnie Armstrong, this is as far as I go, but I wish you the best out in California. And call us sometime," Mr. Handsom said. He hugged me goodbye and got back in the car.

Now Hiawatha hugged me, too. "Onnie, you're a good egg. Don't get too hot to trot for those Cali girls," she whispered in my ear.

Daddy stepped forward. "You got mo' spine than I gave you credit," he said and moved in closer. I froze a little. And when he reached in his pocket, I stepped back. "Here," Daddy said. "This ah little somethin' to help you out," and he handed me some folded bills in an envelope and his pocketknife. "Call us from the road, yo' Mama done already called Duecer."

A bagman checked my trunk and bags. Lorraine and I walked toward the tracks. I looked to see if Mama had come in the last few minutes to see me off, but she was nowhere in sight. Lorraine and I stood on the train platform while the others waited in the car.

Lorraine told me I didn't have to go, I could just change my mind.

"Why don't you and Hiawatha come to California and live?"

"I can't leave daddy, and Watha and me already registered at Clark. And you know their drumming section needs me."

"And you know I can't stay, but I'll love you forever."

FROM THE TRAIN window I waved goodbye to Lorraine. I spotted Mama and some of the Old Folks Mafia. Miss Dorothy, Miss Lucendy, Miss Hazel and Ms. Inez all smiled big and waved frantic like children at a parade. Ms. Inez even clapped her hands big in the air. I waved back with less enthusiasm, but holding back my real feelings, of being happy they came, didn't stop the tears from falling steadily. And it didn't stop the fear inside my body from racing around fluttering my stomach. I was leaving the only home I'd known. When they were out of sight I slid back in my seat and wiped my eyes. The train rolled outside the borders of Eleven Light City and I could feel the energy that hovered over me my entire life release as I breathe in and out.

As the sun set I remembered the story Mama told me about the time she arrived in Eleven Light City. It was a warm summer's night in 1926. Mama was six years old and like so many black families at that time, she, Uncle George, Uncle Duecer, and Grandmama Cora Mae had stolen away in the darkness, running away from white folks, white cotton, and red soil. They fled from Mr. Sumter, who owned the land they lived on, and who'd shot Granddaddy

Lincoln dead. And without a conviction, Cora Mae feared her sons were next.

From the train's window leaving Monroe, the little girl Susie Mae looked out and saw darkness across the landscape. And it remained dark except for the lanterns outside of the train stations or a lonely kerosene lamp in a far-off window. But, as the train approached the city, Mama saw multiple lights. And she either counted eleven or only saw eleven—maybe she could only count up to eleven. Mama, who liked her stories, her sayings, and a bit mystery surrounding her, wouldn't confirm any origin story. I like to think she only saw eleven lights. Either way, the name stuck, even spread from her generations of friends and family to mine. And she, me, and we, settled on Eleven Light City and we never called this city by its name, Atlanta. As the train continued the landscape of trees increased and the city lights faded away. I looked and I hoped I would find a different life in California, something I couldn't imagine now, something better than Eleven Light City, something better than home.

A year after I left Flax art & design I walked up Market Street on my way home. It was 1990 and I'd lived in the Bay Area for ten years. I boarded a BART train headed home to Oakland. Once on the other side I looked back at the city lights across the San Francisco Bay. They sparkled brighter as the sun set. I'd finally secured a job as a junior designer in a small interior design firm but the apartments across the bay had more space and cost less so I moved, though now I had a commute. The walk from the Ashby BART station took fifteen minutes and although I walked through a quiet neighborhood I stayed alert. Quiet didn't mean safe. Still on early evenings, especially if it was foggy, the troublemakers stayed put until night and the fog melted into one.

At a corner grocery I picked up flowers and made my way home. Inside, candles were burning and I was surprised she'd made it to the apartment before me. Usually she stayed at work late. The smell of homemade chicken pot pie filled the air and I put the flowers in a vase. She handed me a glass of white wine, but before I drank any I kissed Karla on the lips, then we clinked our glasses and sat down to eat.

## ACKNOWLEDGMENTS

The writer's journey is informed by valuable teachers. I claim Abigail Thomas. She taught me how to formulate simple stories that blossom into elegant, graceful prose. Dani Shapiro exposed me to powerful memoir writing and how to illuminate the truth and heart of a story. ZZ Packer illustrated the power of the first line that grabs the reader's attention. And Victor LaValle who insisted that my stories are important, and at every turn reached out to help. I am eternally appreciative for his support, kindness, and friendship.

And sometimes the teaching is informal. Karen Pittelman is the doula who helped birth this baby. I am forever grateful for her insight, her gentle nudges to keep me moving forward, and her ability to show me all of what I'd accomplished throughout the writing process. Alana Devich's flawless editing and nurturing approach helped me bring this novel over the finish line. I want to thank Sulay Hernandez for her generosity of spirit and for her time. Béalleka Makau offered honesty, clear-eyed edits and thoughtfulness. I appreciate Brad Silk for taking the time to read the final draft. Cheryl Boyce-Taylor offered a roadmap for how one can live and be a writer with longevity. Her inclusive nature has given me an artistic haven that I appreciate being a part of. Jewelle Gomez has been a generous friend and responded to every email I sent asking for advice or assistance. And over the course of the years this novel has been in progress, Anton Nimblett has offered insightful thought and input, and I appreciate his friendship.

And as they say, it takes a village, and mine is populated by dear friends and family. I want to thank Sharon Stitt for her friendship, sisterhood, and belief in me. Debra Jones for designing my cover from Sydney, Australia and for understanding no child actually goes to bed when they are told. Alex Sosnov, thanks for reading my book over a long weekend and saying you'd like to attend an awards show with me. Pat Clemons for support with our son and by proxy giving me time to write. To Flora & Pete Beasley for fostering in me the love of books and story telling. To my dearly departed mama, Susie Mae Bell Beasley. Without provocation you believed I could be what I wanted to be, and I'll love you eternally for telling me black folks live all over the world. Those words helped me to step out to live my life.

And to my magnificent, lovely cutie pie wife Kathy, who has been with me throughout this writing process, and has beautifully offered encouraging words in the times I've felt lost. I love you, I love you, I love you!

CPSIA information can be obtained
at www.ICGtesting.com
Printed in the USA
LVHW081559080319
609995LV00016B/644/P

## ABOUT THE AUTHOR

Leona Beasley was born and raised in Atlanta, Geor
is a graduate of the University of Georgia, in Athen
gia; Mills College in Oakland, California; and th
School University in New York City. Among th
things, she has taught art to the very young and to
wrote arts columns, been an educational consultai
worked in children's television.

Leona Beasley writes about the eccentric, often que
funny characters from her Southern youth despite l
escaped to the North to get away from them. She
resides with her wife, small son, and mom-in-law in
City, New Jersey. But she prefers you to keep her lo
on the down-low.

*For more information*
www.leonabeasley.com